George Jean Nathan
and the Making
of Modern American
Drama Criticism

# George Jean Nathan and the Making of Modern American Drama Criticism

Thomas F. Connolly

Madison • Teaneck
Fairleigh Dickinson University Press
London: Associated University Presses

Associated University Presses
440 Forsgate Drive
Cranbury, NJ 08512

Associated University Presses
16 Barter Street
London WC1A 2AH, England

Associated University Presses
P.O. Box 338, Port Credit
Mississauga, Ontario
Canada L5G 4L8

The paper used in this publication meets the requirements
of the American National Standard for Permanence of Paper
for Printed Library Materials Z39.48-1984.

Library of Congress Cataloging-in-Publication Data

Connolly, Thomas F., 1960–
    George Jean Nathan and the making of modern American drama
criticism / Thomas F. Connolly.
        p.   cm.
    Includes bibliographical references and index.
    ISBN 0-8386-3780-9 (alk. paper)
    1. Nathan, George Jean, 1882–1958—Criticism and interpretation.
2. Dramatic criticism—United States—History—20th century.
3. Theater—United States—History—20th century.   4. Drama—History
and criticism—Theory, etc.   I. Title.
PS3527.A72Z59   2000
812.009—dc21                                                              99-10529
                                                                                      CIP

PRINTED IN THE UNITED STATES OF AMERICA

# Contents

# Acknowledgments

I WISH TO ACKNOWLEDGE THE ASSISTANCE GIVEN TO ME BY JAMES Tyler of the Cornell University library. Mr. Tyler and his staff members, Lucy Burgess, Tonya Ippolito, and Julie Lonnberg were extraordinarily helpful to me while I was going through the materials in the George Jean Nathan Collection. They patiently guided me through many hours of research as I sifted through the entire Nathan Collection.

I was also given much assistance by the research staff at the New York Public Library. They alerted me to the Nathan letters in the Isaac Goldberg papers. The Isaac Goldberg Papers are part of the Manuscripts and Archives Division of the New York Public Library, Astor, Lenox, and Tilden Foundations. I thank the Library for permission to quote from an undated letter from George Jean Nathan to Isaac Goldberg. I acknowledge the use of the New York Public Library's extensive H. L. Mencken materials, as well. The Billy Rose Theatre Collection at Lincoln Center provided me with a great deal of information from its scrapbook files on Nathan. I thank the office of Congressman Barney Frank for expediting several requests for information from the National Archives and the Congressional Record.

The Rare Book Room of the Fine Arts Collection of the Boston Public Library provided me with many scarce and fragile periodicals. The Widener Library of Harvard University also provided me with access to very old and delicate periodicals and I thank them for that privilege. The Special Collections Department at the Boston University Library also helped by granting me assess to the Charles Angoff Papers and to the Helen Deutsch Papers.

I thank Fairleigh Dickinson University Press for granting permission to quote from Nathan's works. I thank Farrar, Straus and Giroux for permission to quote Edmund Wilson's letter to Walter Lippmann. I thank the New York Public Library Manuscript and Archives Division, Astor, Lenox and Tilden Foundations for permission to quote from the Isaac Goldberg papers. I acknowledge the use of photographs from Eugene O'Neill Papers and Carl Van Vechten Papers from the Beinecke Rare Books and Manuscript

Library of Yale University, the Cornell University Library Division
of Rare Books and Manuscript Collections, and the Connecticut
College Library. Miriam Spectre of Yale, Laura Linke of Cornell,
and Brian Rogers of Connecticut College and were most helpful
in securing the photographs. I thank Julien Yoseloff, director of
Associated University Presses for his editorial advice and intellectual support.

Laurence Senelick overcame his own antipathy to Nathan and
carefully read an earlier version of this study. I thank him for
many years of counsel and guidance. The noted theatre historian
Gerald Bordman read this book's manuscript and offered many
helpful suggestions. I thank him for his advice and encouragement. The eminent scholar Carl Dolmetsch also provided me with
significant advice. Sherwood Collins, Peter Davis, and Don Wil-
meth also gave me sage editorial suggestions when they read an
earlier version of this book.

The following individuals merit acknowledgment. Michael R.
Ronayne, Dean of the College of Arts and Sciences at Suffolk
University has encouraged the highest level of scholarship from
his faculty, and provided much necessary support for the comple-
tion of this study. The late Julie Haydon Nathan offered me great
encouragement as I began this study. She gave her life to George
Jean Nathan; I wish that she were alive to see the recent renewal
of interest in him. I thank Gwendolyn Waltz, the late Mrs. Haydon's niece, for establishing contact with her aunt on my behalf.
I acknowledge the eager assistance given to me by Patricia
Angelin, the Literary Executrix of the George Jean Nathan Es-
tate. Ms. Angelin was particularly helpful in explaining Nathan's
intentions in establishing the George Jean Nathan Collection. Arthur Gelb, president of the *New York Times* Foundation devoted
many hours to discussing Nathan with me. His personal knowledge of the Broadway milieu has been of inestimable value to this
book. I am also grateful for his personal encouragement. Peter
Kriendler of the "21" Club generously allowed me to interview
him and also offered me the hospitality of "21." Elliot Norton,
the dean of American drama critics, kindly shared many personal
and professional insights about Nathan with me. Thomas Yoseloff
offered his own close knowledge of Nathan and of Alfred Knopf.
He also gave me great encouragement about publishing this book.
Robert Anderson, the distinguished playwright, was most gra-
cious in providing me with direct information about the Broadway
theatre of the late 1940s and early 1950s. Peter Lysy, the archivist
of Notre Dame University, devoted much time to searching for

evidence of matriculation of Nathan's relatives. Sister M. Rosaleen Dunleavy, C. S. C., the College Archivist of St. Mary's College, was extraordinarily generous with her time, proving conclusively that Nathan's mother did not attend St. Mary's with Eugene O'Neill's mother. Michael Hall, artistic director of the Caldwell Theatre Company, Boca Raton, Florida, offered information about Julie Haydon's latter-day acting career. Robert Young Jr. of Sacramento, the great-grandson of William Winter, gave me several books and offered insights into the historical study of drama critics. Susanne Robb directed me to the superb resources of the Allen County Historical Genealogy Center. Mark Rogers's marvelous archival research enabled me finally to ascertain Nathan's Jewishness.

Finally, I must express my profound debt of gratitude to Dr. Frederick C. Wilkins, the editor of the *Eugene O'Neill Review*. Dr. Wilkins originally inspired me to investigate Nathan. This study would not have been possible without his advice and editorial guidance. I am most thankful for his wisdom and friendship.

# George Jean Nathan
## and the Making
## of Modern American
## Drama Criticism

# Introduction: Broadway and Its Brilliance

GEORGE JEAN NATHAN WAS THE FIRST MODERN AMERICAN DRAMA
critic. By this I mean that he was the first professional writer of
the twentieth century who deliberately embarked on a career
whose focus was criticism of the American theater. Neither by
training nor by experience was he a man of the theater; he was
a professional writer. Nathan's acquaintance with the theater came
to him strictly through attending plays. He wrote about the theater because he wanted to and for no other reason—criticism was
what he lived for. He had no particular aesthetic creed and he
made no claims about the possibility of reforming the theater or
its literature and throughout his career he scoffed at both of these
notions. Nonetheless, he *did* believe that criticism could improve,
and through his efforts, it did.

George Jean Nathan's career reveals the conditions of
twentieth-century drama criticism in the United States. He also
shows us some of the more troubling aspects of finding a personal
identity in American society. Considering the beginnings of Nathan's career, his work as a journalist and later as an editor and,
most important, that he was a writer who undertook drama criticism with a vocational devotion, provides us with an excellent
grasp of the historical relevance of drama criticism to the American theatre and to American culture. Nathan's problematic personal identity helps us to place him within the larger context of
American society.

Nathan was more than a recorder of Broadway's brilliance; he
was himself one of its baubles. Nathan came to personify the
Broadway drama critic: elegantly dressed, escorting a fetching
ingenue toward two-on-the-aisle, row E seats; midnight suppers
at the Stork Club; playwrights and directors breathlessly watching
his every sneer or smile; gossip columnists eagerly retailing his
latest bon mots and evening escapades. Nathan flourished during
Broadway's most glamorous era. Unlike the critic of today who is
isolated from the theatre community and would not dream of
making contact with a producer, director, or performer, Nathan
was constantly in the thick of production. He routinely read

scripts and passed them on to producers, and by so doing helped Eugene O'Neill, Sean O'Casey, and William Saroyan secure their first Broadway productions. He suggested the casting of particular performers, most notably Laurette Taylor in what would be the greatest comeback performance of the century—Amanda Wingfield in *The Glass Menagerie.*

He was a favorite of the Main Stem's outstanding press agent, Richard Maney, who called him "our theatre's most stimulating critic and its most feared one." Nathan reciprocated, identifying Maney as "the Cy Young of theatrical publicity pitchers," praise indeed from Nathan, who was a great baseball fan. Or more precisely, a Yankees fan, for he frequently went to their afternoon games with Peter Kriendler of the "21" Club. Another press agent, Bernard Sobel, grew up in Nathan's home state of Indiana and got his primary education in drama by reading Nathan's reviews. When Sobel came to New York to make his way in the theatre, he found Nathan a supportive guide. Columnists such as Louis Sobol and Earl Wilson were in awe of him. Even Walter Winchell, the biggest of them all, made a point of fawning over him. In fact, Nathan was one of the only journalists Winchell never feuded with; he consistently stayed on good terms with him. This was not an easy thing to do. Nathan was notoriously thin-skinned, as the mild-mannered columnist Louis Sobol found out to his dismay one evening at "21" in the late 1940s. Sobol had casually mentioned in his column that, "to George Jean Nathan, every bad play is another Hiss trial." When he walked over to Nathan's table at "21" a few nights later, Sobol received a frigid stare. Peter Kriendler, who witnessed the altercation, still remembers the iciness of Nathan's glare: "Nathan flattened him—reduced him to nothing. Nathan could do that with one look." Sobol tried to apologize, but Nathan felt that somehow his integrity as a critic had been "impugned" by Sobol's punning. He never spoke to Sobol again.

Nathan was no doubt sensitized to any references made about his politics—he was the Left's favorite Broadway whipping boy. *The Daily Worker* pilloried him for decades, taunting him as "the Bilbo of Broadway" (in reference to the notoriously corrupt, racist senator from Mississippi) or blithely branding him a fascist. Nathan never responded to such attacks directly, telling Walter Winchell, "When you are in the brick-throwing business you must expect to get hit by a brick now and then." Nonetheless, he gave as good as he got, labeling John Howard Lawson and company "the little red writing hoods."

Nathan's critical hauteur was often at odds with the cap-and-bells style in which he wrote, and yet his style is the key to assessing the nature of his authority. Moreover, stylistically assessing what might be considered particularly American—in terms of his own self-fashioning and his place in the history of the theater—about Nathan's critical stance reveals that he is at once an iconoclast and part of a tradition. He is an iconoclast because he fought against prevailing theatrical conditions; he is part of a tradition in American dramatic criticism because he waged his battles from the pages of literary magazines. He follows in the wake of Washington Irving, Edgar Allan Poe, and Walt Whitman, all of whom devoted part of their careers to dramatic criticism and editing and fought against the tide of contemporary theatrical trends. But each of these three gave up the fight and turned to other literary endeavors, whereas Nathan put aside all of his other interests and concentrated solely on the theatre.

This concentration of his energy caused Eric Bentley to single him out as "the leading example [in the United States] of a whole lifetime principally and profitably dedicated to dramatic criticism."[1] Nathan's career encompasses the first half of the twentieth century. He began writing professionally in 1905 and did not cease until 1958; he published thirty-four books on the theatre from 1915 through 1953. Nathan's was an especially "critical" presence during the emergence of the modern American theatre and he envisaged the present state of American theatre.

Nathan served as coeditor of *The Smart Set* (1914–23) and cofounder and coeditor of *The American Mercury* (1924–25). These positions enabled him to make his pronouncements from the two most widely circulated journals of and for the American intelligentsia. *The Smart Set* reigned as the "magazine of cleverness" from 1900 until 1923, when Nathan and Mencken left it, and offered up a lambasting of American provincialism and anti–intellectualism. The magazine declined rapidly after Nathan's and Mencken's departure and lost its sophisticated readership. Nathan first articulated his critical credos in the pages of *The Smart Set*. He demanded a new and more serious American drama and a theater that responded to artistic exigencies rather than box office appeal. He deplored the realistic buncombe of David Belasco and the All-American banality of Augustus Thomas. Nathan was no bluenose though. He reveled in the Ziegfeld *Follies*, traced the history of the "modern" leg show (reprinted in *The Theatre, the Drama, the Girls*)[2], and expressed his gratitude to George Lederer for developing this phenomenon.

Nathan and Mencken left *The Smart Set* in 1924 to start *The American Mercury.* This periodical was to be more than the "journal of cleverness" that *The Smart Set* had been. The founders wanted it to be a conduit for all that was the best in American social and artistic commentary; "it was not for the tender-minded." Unashamedly elitist and dedicated to bedeviling what his partner H. L. Mencken termed the "booboisie," *The American Mercury* was Mencken's magazine from the start. He forced Nathan out of his coeditorship after one year, and although Nathan continued with his theatre criticism and his writing of "Clinical Notes," a compendium of random reflections, his position at the *Mercury* became more precarious by the month. Nathan stayed on at the *Mercury*, enduring slights and direct insults. He was forbidden the use of his old office. His desk was moved out to the secretaries' room. He was prohibited from using the telephone. With such heavy-handed gambits, Mencken succeeded in forcing Nathan out. Nathan continued to write for the *Mercury* until 1930, when Alfred Knopf refused to renew his contract and insisted on buying up his shares in the magazine. Even so, by 1924 he had become the most famous and highly paid theatre critic in the world, and he would be hailed by George Bernard Shaw as "intelligent play-goer number one."[3]

Nathan is a misunderstood figure. He was by no means the dilettante boulevardier depicted by writers then and now. Nathan is often linked with others—most notably H. L. Mencken and Eugene O'Neill—and most of the critical attention devoted to him has been in conjunction with other writers. This has resulted in an obscuring of Nathan's singularity. Other writers also distort Nathan's career and place in American theater history because their focus is not primarily on Nathan as a critical force and theatrical figure. For in the limited aspect of his aesthetic focus, the theatre, he was the most influential critic of his time—which is not to say he has had no impact on more recent criticism. Kenneth Tynan's definition of a drama critic noted that "a good drama critic is one who perceives what is happening in the theatre of his time—a great drama critic also perceives what is not happening"[4]; that certainly describes Nathan's attitude and method. Moreover, I have no doubt that most actors and producers would agree that Nathan's "destructive" method is still widely practiced. Moreover, Nathan always wrote with a consciousness of what had come before in the theater—he wrote with a historical perspective. He was never merely a reporter and recorder. Because of his status he came into contact with almost all of the notable theatrical figures of the time. He also followed current European theatrical trends and had studied the traditions of Continental dramaturgy and stagecraft. Thus he was able to provide a context for his criticism to a degree none of his contemporaries could match. When he takes some of the more self-indulgent aspects of "the new stagecraft" to task, for example, he does so from an informed perspective.

> The so-called New Scenery requires, for its complete practicability and effectiveness, the great and telling tact of a first-rate producer like Reinhardt. Without this tact, it becomes a mere affectation.[5]

It is this level of confidence that gave Nathan his authority. The *fact* that he actually knew more about the theater than any of his rivals made him seem omniscient. Later critics would deem Nathan's erudition unsatisfactory because he used the arsenal of his knowledge only as a tactic. Nathan is thus found wanting today because he lacked an overall critical strategy. What is more, Nathan's status as the most learned Broadway drama critic is regarded as oxymoronic by today's critics and historians.

Nonetheless, George Jean Nathan's career reveals some of the continuities of American dramatic criticism. I have mentioned his affinities with Irving, Poe, and Whitman, but as much as Nathan shared with his predecessors, he also differed from them in that he called for American playwrights to profit from European examples and not limit themselves slavishly to following American models. Nathan has exerted an influence on critics who came after him, but his legacy is not as important as his contemporary success. Nonetheless, both his legacy and his success are related to his writing style. Nathan's writing style is an issue that must be addressed for it is wholly representative of the problems of assessing journalistic versus "serious" writing. Moreover, the question of Nathan's style brings up the matter of the conflict between Nathan's elitism and his ambition to be widely influential, a problem shared by all "mass-market" critics.

Understanding George Jean Nathan's relationship to the theatre of his time in terms of the social and aesthetic milieu from which he came and in terms of the identity he fashioned for himself reveals some of the qualities that make him a particularly important American drama critic. His book-length discussion of this identity, *The Autobiography of an Attitude* (1925), explains his belief that the individual persona of the critic is an integral part of criticism itself. Moreover, in explicating his personal critical methods in the *Autobiography*, Nathan also details the history of his own aesthetic—an aesthetic that was honed in the theater. He reveals that he chose the theater as his sphere because it was a place for the "intelligent" exercise of the emotions. Concerned as Nathan was with beauty and the emotional base of the perception of beauty, it is significant that in this book as well as in *The World in Falseface* (1923) and in *The Intimate Notebooks of George Jean Nathan* (1932), he elaborates on his creed of personal criticism and thereby reveals the basis for his critical precepts. Nathan does not expound upon a particular methodology or theory so much as he reveals his own criteria for theatrical excellence. In another of his books, *The Critic and the Drama* (1922), he discusses his own critical method and describes the "intelligent emotionalism" that informs his judgments. Thus, Nathan is essentially an impressionist critic.

What was the basis of Nathan's critical temper? The fundamentals of his creed are found in *The Critic and the Drama, The World in Falseface, Materia Critica,* and *The Autobiography of an Attitude.* Nathan credits Croce and Santayana with influencing him, but he does so in a facetious and consciously contradictory fashion. In fact, the critic who exerted the most direct and personal influence on him was James Gibbons Huneker. Huneker was an eclectic commentator who served as the ambassador from the bohemians to the Americans at the turn of the century. He sought to integrate European and American culture, and Nathan was his acolyte. For despite his cultivation of an attitude that looked down upon his fellow Americans, Nathan was thoroughly a cultural patriot in that he most earnestly desired an American theatre that could stand in comparison to those of other countries.

The nature of Nathan's own social milieu, his odd placement vis-à-vis the bohemianism of the turn of the century and the Roaring Twenties, and his rarefied yet eclectic approach to the performing arts allow his attitude toward the theater to be summed up thus: it is essentially an emotional experience and there is no hierarchy of theatricality. The second point has the greater resonance for our day. Nathan's critical career repeatedly demonstrates that he saw theater merely for what it was rather than for what it could or might be. To Nathan the theatre was a glittering gewgaw resting in sawdust. He had no illusions about it, but he demanded that it always be arresting and "interesting to an intelligently emotional group of persons assembled together in an illuminated hall." Even when he champions playwrights, he praises them for their work as it is. He is never so ingenuous as to hail the dawning of new eras. He is dismissed for such sentiments, and this is an erroneous dismissal because it is not the function of a journalist critic to transcend timeliness. Even the fact that Nathan was able to recognize the greatness of O'Casey and O'Neill is at best grudgingly accorded him by his detractors.

Nathan achieved a position from which he was able to promote O'Neill and the charms of Billy Watson's "Beef Trust" and mock relentlessly the drama of David Belasco and Augustus Thomas. Nathan overturned the genteel tradition of drama criticism, exemplified by William Winter and J. Ranken Towse, which focused on acting, and relocated the center of its attention to the playwright. While Nathan wrote of the theater as he found it, he was never content with the state of the theater, and to the very end of his career he was a zealously "destructive" critic. Nathan's impact on Broadway helps us understand how the theater arrived where it is now, and he is especially useful as a bellwether for the playwrights who emerged during the 1920s.

Looking at the journals for which Nathan wrote reveals that after establishing himself in *The Smart Set* and in *The American Mercury*, Nathan maintained his status and was able to project his own image irrespective of his particular venue. For example, he was not identified as a "Hearst" writer (as was critic Alan Dale) even though during the last part of his career (1943–1957) his weekly column originated in the Hearst-owned *Journal-American* and was distributed by the Hearst-owned King Features Syndicate. (*The Daily Worker*, though, routinely lumped him together with Westbrook Pegler, the rabidly reactionary Hearst scribe.) Both *The Smart Set* and *The American Mercury* had particular readerships and peculiar critical stances. Nathan appealed to those readers and expounded upon those stances. Nathan's success as a critic was as important as his success as a personality on the American scene. The image or cachet these journals projected was a reflection of Nathan's public persona, but the "smart" aura of these magazines also reflected on Nathan as much as they were reflections of his own attitude. It is possible to present a composite of Nathan's readership in the 1910s and 1920s by examining the popular reception of *The Smart Set* and *The American Mercury* and looking at their layout and copy styles.

*The Smart Set*'s tawdry appearance was belied by the seriousness of its literary mission, but it was augmented by Nathan and Mencken's katzenjammer approach to *kultur*. On the other hand, paradoxically, *The American Mercury* was an august-looking journal that was as essential a collegiate accouterment as a hip flask.

In addition to looking at the specifics of Nathan's readership, it is important to note the use Nathan made of his connections in the theater, in publishing, and in journalism; they were instrumental in his own self-creation and he would exploit these links for his favorites as his career progressed. Nathan's uncle, Charles Frederic Nirdlinger, who was a playwright and drama critic, got him his first writing job, and his closeness to another uncle, Samuel Nixon, was probably an influence that kept him from attacking the Syndicate and one that led him to disparage Actors' Equity. For the rest of his life, Nathan would trade on the personal connections he had forged. He was instrumental in securing the first Broadway productions of the plays of Eugene O'Neill, William Saroyan, and Sean O'Casey. Nathan is not to be praised solely for these acts or because he published over forty books or because he happened to have been active during a great period in American theater history or because he became the most famous and highly paid theater critic in the world. The simple fact of his longevity partially accounts for his imputed perspicacity.

Nathan was able to wield his influence by explaining the differences between the theater that he saw and the theater he wanted to see. The fact that Nathan's writing usually appeared in magazines (in particular, *The Smart Set, The American Mercury* and *The American Spectator*) rather than in daily metropolitan newspapers is significant because it raises questions about the role of the critic in the theater and because it gave him a broader perspective. Nathan was able to comment on trends or developments in the theater; he frequently traveled to Europe and was fond of retailing his knowledge of English and Continental stage figures. He was also satirized for bruiting his erudition:

> If there was necessity of mentioning one Montenegrin playwright, he mentioned five hundred Montenegrin playwrights and dropped the opinion that anybody failing to know the complete works of Peter Karageorgevitch of Citenje had no right inside a theater.[6]

Although even an admirer of Nathan, the playwright Robert Anderson, believes that Nathan's technique of "denigrating contemporary plays by citing earlier examples in world theater from which they might be derived . . . got to be laughable."[7] Nevertheless, Nathan was, in the main, a cultural patriot. He wanted the American theater to find its own way, not merely retread European paths.

Nathan wrote about the theater from 1908 to 1958, so he was present practically at the illumination of the Great White Way and lived long enough to see its paling. A notebook preserved among Nathan's papers at Cornell is a sort of theatrical diary. It dates from the 1928–29 season and reveals that Nathan attended 208 shows, 161 of which he singled out. There were at least 225 productions that season; thus, Nathan saw almost every show that was put on in 1928–1929. He must have gone to the theater at least four times a week. The notebook is in the collection specifically to indicate a *typical* year of theater-going for Nathan.

As the century draws to its close and a *crowded* Broadway season has maybe a few dozen opening nights, Nathan's options seem astounding. By frequenting the theatre as he did, however, Nathan has left himself open to the charge that constant theater-going is harmful to one's critical acuity. Even in Nathan's own time it was assumed that continual theater attendance was detrimental to a critic's faculties, and this belief persists today. When he was writing for *The New Republic* in the 1950s, Eric Bentley argued seriously that critics should attend the theater as infrequently as possible; and it has always been taken for granted that critics somehow burn out after too many years of toiling up and down the aisles writing to deadline. Nonetheless, Nathan went several times a week until nearly the end of his life. And he addressed the issue of the allegedly detrimental effect of constant theater attendance as an occupational hazard of drama critics. He wondered why people never assumed book critics would lose their wits from reading hundreds of trashy novels for every decent piece of fiction they reviewed. He argued that surgeons are no less skillful when they perform their thousandth appendectomy or that a trial lawyer defending his tenth client of the week is neither exhausted by the endeavor nor rendered incompetent thereby. One fears that such qualms about the effect of "too much" theater say a great deal more about dread of the theater than they inform us about the ways and means of drama criticism.

George Jean Nathan's Broadway would seem to have vanished. Traces of it exist; theater buildings and a few restaurants that he frequented are still extant. The Royalton Hotel where he lived for nearly his whole life was renovated by a discoteque entrepreneur in the early 1990s and turned into a bizarre proving ground for the latest trends of the hostelry trade. Of the more than thirty magazines and newspapers he wrote for only two, *Newsweek* and *Esquire,* remain in business. His name was retained, as founder, on the masthead of the initial issues of the revived *American Specta-*

*tor*, but the current journal has nothing to do with the periodical Nathan created.

What, then, is left of Nathan's brilliance? No drama critic who devoted himself or herself exclusively to the theater has ever achieved lasting fame. What is more, the sort of criticism he wrote for magazines has almost vanished. So Nathan's is almost an invisible presence in the American theatre. In recent years even the award for drama criticism that he established has become obscure. In spite of Nathan's instructions, it has been presented without any attendant fanfare.[8] Nonetheless, Nathan is still an influence. It is the aim of this study to show how and where his influence is felt.

# 1

## The Critic and His World

A COMPLETE BIOGRAPHY OF NATHAN IS NOT NECESSARY TO UNDER-
stand his place as a critic, but there are some things about his life
that must be emphasized in order to understand Nathan's identity.
And "identity" is particularly important here because in many
ways Nathan's public persona was an integral part of his criticism.
He frequently cited the "personal" nature of criticism—indeed,
it is one of the few consistent tenets of his criticism.

Nathan was born a Midwesterner in Fort Wayne, Indiana. He
grew up in Cleveland, Ohio. There could hardly be anything farther from the caviar-crunching aristocrat who inhabited a suite
of rooms in Manhattan's Royalton Hotel than the little boy who
lived on West Berry Street in Fort Wayne. Nathan's origins are
mysterious only because he successfully hid certain aspects of his
life, creating an effective smokescreen that hid his Jewish origins
and the fact that his father was a wholesale liquor dealer.

For years, doubts have been raised about Nathan's Jewishness.
Nathan himself is the source of these doubts. There need be no
uncertainty about his parents, however; both were practicing Jews
at the time of his birth. Nathan's mother, Ella, was the daughter
of Frederick Nirdlinger, a prominent Fort Wayne businessman
and public official who was deeply religious. Nirdlinger helped
found Fort Wayne's first synagogue, the Achdut Veshalom Congregation. Before a permanent temple could be built, Nirdlinger
even allowed the congregation the use of his house for services.
Nathan's father, Charles, was a member of this congregation and
of the Emeek Lodge of the Order of B'nai B'rith, at one time
serving as its vice-president.[1] So it is clear that Nathan was born
into a Jewish family.

On his mother's side, the German Nirdlingers, there were rug-
ged pioneers who literally crossed the country in a covered wagon
from Chambersburg, Pennsylvania, to settle Fort Wayne. Nathan's
maternal grandfather was one of the founders of what was then

a frontier trading post. And in the next generation of Nirdlingers, two of Nathan's maternal uncles influenced him theatrically. Charles Frederic Nirdlinger was a Harvard-educated playwright and drama critic who encouraged Nathan's journalism career. Samuel Nixon-Nirdlinger (he later dropped the "Nirdlinger" and was known professionally as "Nixon") was an important theater manager who secured free tickets for Nathan's family. Nixon's base of operations was Philadelphia. (Nathan's mother and brother moved there after he went off to college.) Nixon controlled theaters throughout the Midwest and was an original partner in the infamous Theatrical Syndicate, a group of theater managers who totally controlled the American commercial theater from 1896 to 1916. Nixon may have influenced Nathan's rather benevolent attitude toward the Theatrical Syndicate. Even when Nathan describes how Abe Erlanger (a major Syndicate partner) personally barred him from his theaters for years, he does so without a trace of rancor.

On his father's side, Nathan was French. (Nathan claimed that his father was French, but his birth records indicate that Charles Nathan was German.) He probably arrived in the United States in 1874.[2] According to Nathan, his father, Charles Narét Nathan, was one of the owners of the Eugène Perét vineyard in France and of a coffee plantation in Brazil. This is how Nathan wanted his father's business affairs described. In plainer terms, "Charley" Nathan ran a wholesale liquor business in Fort Wayne, Indiana, first with his brother Julius and later on his own.[3]

Nathan claimed that his father spoke eight languages fluently and took frequent business trips to Europe and that the family had spent alternate summers in Europe all through his childhood. Although it appears that Mr. Nathan preferred that his son be trained by tutors for the first part of his education, after the family moved to Cleveland in 1885, he had no objection to having young George enrolled in the public high school there (if he even knew about it, since by that time he had left the family and was providing only financial support). Nathan earned his diploma from Cleveland High School and, strangely, for Nathan always made a point of bringing up his years at Cornell, it is the only diploma of Nathan's that has been preserved.

Ascertaining "genuine" biographical details about Nathan is difficult. He was fond of larding his autobiography with patent untruths. For instance, he claimed to have been born at midnight, February 14th; actually, he was born on the 15th. (Nathan's birth record also reveals that his head was exceedingly large and forceps were required at his delivery.) The outstanding example of Nathan's inventiveness is his tongue-in-cheek claim to a master's degree from the University of Bologna, an obvious joke—"Baloney U."—that far too many people have taken seriously. Thus, there is little one can know about Nathan's early years. He left no personal biographical records, nor is there extensive correspondence available to shed light on his life. Nonetheless, as Nathan repeated this information about his parents, his youth, and his education without contradiction several times during his life, it indicates to us how he wanted to be perceived and is instructive in that regard. He also did much to assist Isaac Goldberg when Goldberg began a book about Nathan as a follow-up to his study of H. L. Mencken. Only when Goldberg wished to bring up Nathan's Jewishness did Nathan cavil. The Goldberg collection at the New York Public Library includes several letters from Nathan that encourage Goldberg while he is writing the book. Nathan not only helped engineer its publication by Simon and Schuster, he also promised to contact friends such as Franklin P. Adams and St. John Ervine about reviewing it.

Not surprisingly, the image that one receives from Goldberg is entirely in accord with the one that Nathan projected of himself in his own writings. Nathan would no doubt be pleased with the frequency with which the biographical details he provided to Goldberg have been reprinted. In his book, Goldberg sums up Nathan's genealogical heritage:

> We may discover at once, even from so cursory a glance at Nathan's ancestry, that he has been markedly influenced by the temperament and the activities of his forbears. In him those temperaments clash rather than harmonize, yet the strains are important and their effect clearly discernible. There is the element of the pioneer, which in Nathan has become metaphorical, aesthetic, perhaps due to the soft charms of his mother. There is his father's spirit of restless roving, which, though attenuated in the son, is sufficiently emphasized.[4]

This is exactly the way Nathan wished to be perceived. Goldberg implies that Nathan is distinctly American, yet also uniquely his own creature. Thus he would find Manhattan to be the perfect hatchery for his critical persona.

Nathan was quite the Broadway figure. His name turns up in contemporary song lyrics and he is referred to in several plays about the theater. Of course, the most famous characterization of Nathan is in the film *All About Eve,* in which he is represented as the acid-tongued critic Addison De Witt (played by George

Sanders in an Oscar-winning performance). Yet there is another famous film character who resembles Nathan, the brutal columnist J. J. Hunsecker in *Sweet Smell of Success* (played by Burt Lancaster). Even though Hunsecker is usually identified with Walter Winchell, there are many correspondences between Nathan and the film figure.[5] The name "Hunsecker" is similar to "Huneker," the surname of James Gibbons Huneker, the idol of Nathan's youth, his critical model and mentor.

What is more, Clifford Odets, who cowrote the screenplay of *Sweet Smell of Success* with Ernest Lehman, regarded Nathan with a vendetta-like loathing and had been trying for years to get at him. Lehman, who wrote the original story, asserts that Nathan was not a source for the character, but he did know Nathan and once spent an evening with him (and Mencken) at the Stork Club in the 1940s. He had also followed Nathan's career during his years as a press agent.

There is another connection. Irving Hoffman, the press agent usually identified with the Sidney Falco character (played by Tony Curtis), was a friend of Nathan's and they frequently went out on the town together. Lehman worked for Hoffman and devised the Hunsecker and Falco characters in a creative frenzy after having written miles of column inches for Hoffman to place in the *Hollywood Reporter*.

The details of the story and film script clearly identify Winchell as the major inspiration for Hunsecker, but like Nathan, Hunsecker is notoriously reactionary, a connoisseur of fine wines, particular about his cocktails, and fussy about his food. It is also worth noting that Hunsecker is from the Midwest, as was Nathan, and that he uses "21" as his headquarters; Nathan went to "21" almost every evening. Winchell was a native New Yorker and was, for all practical purposes, barred from that establishment. Peter Kriendler, a surviving member of "21's" founding family, recalls Winchell's having been there only once. During the early days of World War II, Winchell entered "21" in his naval uniform and went directly to a private dining room for a meeting. This was during Winchell's short-lived career as a lieutenant commander.

The Addison De Witt figure is so obviously modeled on Nathan that elaboration is hardly necessary. All of the character's appurtenances in the film—the cigarette holder, walking stick, stylish dress, and so on—were immediately recognizable Nathanisms. Even actor George Sanders's own aristocratic, Mid-Atlantic drawl was reminiscent of Nathan's affectation of speaking through his teeth. According to his widow, Nathan saw the film and "enjoyed it," which is saying a lot, as he detested most pictures.

Each of these characterizations presents us with the Nathan figure as the quintessential urban sophisticate. Each lives up to Nathan's own motto for public behavior: "Be indifferent." Even though he was the object of attacks ranging from *The Daily Worker* to the Ku Klux Klan, Nathan's hauteur remained unruffled— unless someone brought up his Jewish origins. He lived in dread of "exposure." Other than the details already mentioned, he obfuscated his family background, as if the facts of his real wealth and privilege were inadequate. He repeatedly refused to discuss his Jewishness. He even threatened his unabashedly laudatory biographer, Isaac Goldberg, with withdrawal of his support for the book if Goldberg so much as alluded to the issue.

Nathan's famous romance with Lillian Gish was affected by his attitude about his Jewishness. According to Harold Clurman, she broke off her engagement with Nathan when she found out he was hiding the fact he was Jewish. There is evidence, however, in some of Miss Gish's letters that she broke it off when she *learned* he was Jewish. And Nathan's editorial and publishing partner, H. L. Mencken, the man with whom he was inextricably associated in the public mind for a quarter of a century, sneered at Nathan's background, and anti-Semitically slurred him without hesitation in his posthumously published memoirs.

Writing in the middle 1940s of their pseudobiography, *Pistols for Two*, Mencken said of Nathan's comments about the proofs: "He made suggestions . . . but I recall him insisting upon only one change and that was the deletion of a sentence reading, 'one of us is a baptized man.'"[6] Further on in his memoirs, Mencken speaks of the latter-day Nathan's choice in female companionship: ". . . for though he has denied, in recent years, that he is a Jew himself, a typically Jewish inferiority complex is in him, and it gives him great satisfaction to have some eminent (or even notorious) fair one under his arm." Mencken's definition of an "eminent or notorious fair one" is a woman "who is known by sight to all the Jews and whores who hang about the theatres and nightclubs."[7] Mencken also comments that Nathan was obsessed with "the early stars of café society" and that he was "a social pusher." In a letter to Theodore Dreiser dated 7 October 1933, Mencken complains that, "all Nathan could comprehend was the frothy intellectual and social interests of the Four Hundred, the Bohemian and mentally dilettante worlds."[8]

If Nathan's closest colleague could harbor such feelings and thoughts about him, it is not difficult to understand the extremes of personal cultivation Nathan went to. We might wish that he had fought for himself as an individual rather than as a persona, but beyond the post hoc futility of such a desire, there is also the significant point that Nathan put his energies into his criticism, not his life. For Nathan himself, the critic *was* the man.

In the entire Nathan collection there is almost no personal correspondence. In the scant nontheatrical material, two letters stand out because of this. They are from a society friend of Nathan's who explains in great detail his family's tenuous links to the Habsburg court. Such letters support Mencken's accusation of "social pushing." One of the reasons Alfred Knopf found Nathan objectionable was his willingness to tolerate the company of rich bores who fawned over him and treated him to golf matches near their Long Island preserves. Another personal item in the Cornell Collection along this line bears it out: Nathan's record of his membership in the Penguin Island Country Club.

Clearly Nathan did not want anyone really to know him. He was obviously quite concerned about being Jewish or, rather, of being thought Jewish, surely not a unique situation, but one that provoked reactions from those in the know. In his memoirs Harold Clurman reports:

> At Cornell Nathan had been a flashy undergraduate, a foppish playboy with pretensions to continental sophistication, which he never quite abandoned. . . . All of this was an evasion, a mask to hide something in his background that might cast doubt on the validity of his snobbishness and his aristocratic stance. One day acting on a hunch, I asked Sinclair Lewis whether Nathan was Jewish. "Only a hundred per cent," Lewis answered. Nathan, he went on to explain, had broken with Lillian Gish, his intimate friend, because she went ahead and visited his mother in Indiana after he had asked her never to do so and thus discovered that Nathan was Jewish.[9]

The erroneous Indiana reference in Lewis's account aside, Lillian Gish makes no references to this incident in her memoirs; rather, she makes it clear that it was she who turned Nathan down.

In the Mencken collection in the New York Public Library, however, there are letters that indicate that she did indeed harbor some ill feelings toward Nathan and that Miss Gish herself may not have had a wholly benevolent attitude toward all creeds. Lillian Gish's reactionary politics and prickly nature were no secret in the theatrical community. In a letter to Alfred Knopf dated 26 October 1938 Mencken details the following:

Lillian told me a lot of interesting stuff about Nathan, who was formerly her slavish admirer. . . . He gave her his word that he had no Jewish blood. He wanted to move from the Royalton to a Park Avenue apartment. He asked Gish to make the rental arrangements for him. [Mencken assumed it was because it was a restricted apartment house.] The agent would not rent to Gish when he found out it was for Nathan. The agent refused to believe that Nathan wasn't Jewish, even on Gish's word that G. J. N. had so sworn. Since the breakup of their affair Lillian shows a considerable animosity to Nathan. She told me she believed he was going downhill professionally and that Brooks Atkinson and John Mason Brown were doing much better work. This seemed to me to be unlikely, but she insisted that it was true. . . . Gish told me that the influence of the Jews in the theatre is fast becoming intolerable.[10]

In a letter from Lillian Gish to Mencken dated 20 May 1939 she reveals some of her "animosity to Nathan" and her politics: "I saw George a few weeks ago. His girls get younger and younger. No doubt he is the father of the Peruvian boy born to the five-year-old mother." She finishes this letter by urging Mencken to read Douglas Reed's *Disgrace Abounding* and *Insanity Fair*.[11] Reed was a notoriously anti-Semitic British journalist who ended his days in South Africa penning venomous tomes such as *The Conspiracy of Zion*.

From these snippets of correspondence a slightly more complex image of Nathan (not to mention Lillian Gish) emerges. Perhaps Nathan was intent on keeping Lillian Gish in the dark about his background because he feared her prejudice would end their relationship. But this is not the only time Nathan was concerned about the issue of being Jewish. In letters to his biographer, Isaac Goldberg, he is emphatic about ignoring it altogether. These statements are all the more important as they are the only evidence we have that comes straight from Nathan himself; indeed, they are among the few letters *from* Nathan available anywhere.

In the Goldberg collection at the New York Public Library, there is a series of letters concerning "Jewishness" in the Nathan file. Some of the letters are not dated by year, but it is safe to surmise that the letters are from 1925 or 1926 because they refer to the book Goldberg was working on about Nathan. Unfortunately, Goldberg's letters to Nathan have not survived. The first selection is from a letter dated "Saturday." It was handwritten by Nathan, indicating perhaps that he regarded the issues it discusses as being of an especially personal and private nature, the other letters in the file were all dictated. The letter reveals contemporary attitudes about ethnicity and religion as well as Nathan's own feelings about these matters, and it is important to note that this is as close to making an unguarded profession as Nathan ever gets:

> I indicated the deletion of the Jewish allusion for a simple reason. The common practice of arbitrarily discerning biological and psychological influences in the Jew because he is a Jew seems absurd and objectionable to me. Huneker you will recall regarded the habit as so ridiculous that he never failed to reduce it to burlesque. Whenever I read this or that about a man because of a Jewish strain in his blood, it makes me sick. Heine was no more Heine because he was Jew— though the thing has been emphasized *ad nauseam*—than Swinburne was because he was a Christian. The same with Carrel and Loeb— and even Brandeis, Nathan Straus or Al Jolson. Temperamentally and professionally these men are not in the slightest sense or degree actually different from Christians of the same position. Carnegie, a Scotchman and hence theoretically a close-fist, was as generous as Straus. Brandeis I cannot differentiate from White or Holmes. Carrel, the Jew, and Pasteur the Christian, are not what they are were and are because of race. If Al Jolson is the [illegible word] music-hall singer because his father was a cantor, than what of the [illegible word]— Irish Tommy Lyman? If the great stage impersonators of Jews are great because they are Jews, then what of the Irish Jimmy Hussey, the best of the lot? It is always the Jew himself who insists upon such things, the more observing goys have in the main given up the practice. Even Zangwill's nonsense is now dismissed not on the grounds that he is a Jew, but simply and fairly, on the grounds that he is a horse's ass, like Belloc. You are not the man you are because you are a Jew anymore than Mencken, say, is because he is a Lutheran. As a matter of fact, Mencken is more of a Jew—following the conventional Jewish reasoning—than you are, or than I am. He has three so called Jewish traits—in the rubber stamp sense—to one of either of us.
>
> Let us have done with such business. It makes the Jew a self-conscious and silly figure, and he should not be one. The next time I read in your writings of Spinoza, say, that he was a Jew, I shall take the first train to Boston and kick you in the pantaloons.[12]

Here Nathan admits to being Jewish, but in the most dismissive manner. He mentions his Jewish background only to mock the notion that it is of any importance. In what would seem to be a follow-up letter dated 22 September, Nathan is evidently responding to Goldberg's insisting that some reference be made to Nathan's Jewishness:

> I have no more to say about the Jewish matter, save to protest strongly against it on the ground I have already indicated. Why all the race consciousness? The sooner all Jews forget it, the better it will be.[13]

In light of the ongoing controversy over Mencken's anti-Semitism, Nathan's remarks about him are intriguing. Finally, in a letter dated 3 June 1926, Nathan tells Goldberg. "Please see my point of view and leave out the Jewish matter."[14] Goldberg did.

There may be something else behind Nathan's alleged denial of his heritage. Much has been made of Nathan's being taken into the Catholic Church shortly before his death in a ceremony in which Walter and Jean Kerr served as his sponsors. It has always been assumed that Nathan's mother and Eugene O'Neill's mother attended the same convent school, St. Mary's, in South Bend, Indiana, when they were girls and that they were friends there. This school was popular with Protestant and Jewish families as well as with Catholic ones because it offered a college-level academic program for young women. This frequently reported information about Ella O'Neill and Ella Nathan is now in doubt. There is no record that anyone named Nirdlinger (Nathan's mother's maiden name) or even anyone from Fort Wayne, attended St. Mary's. In 1938 Nathan told Jim Tully that his mother "had been educated at a Notre Dame convent."[15] He made no mention of St. Mary's or Eugene O'Neill's mother. Nathan's uncles, however, did attend a Catholic school, Notre Dame, in South Bend, Indiana. In the university's archives, there are records of five Nirdlingers who attended the school at various times from 1859 through 1888, two of whom are listed as "Israelites." Although Samuel Lambert Nirdlinger, who matriculated in 1887, was a Catholic.[16]

Nathan's mother was herself a convert to Catholicism and may have made efforts to ensure that her children grew up to be practicing Catholics. That Nathan did not do so tells us something about his own character, but his nearly lifelong agnosticism was always tempered with a sympathy for the Church. Julie Haydon reported that Nathan had received childhood instruction in Catholicism, but this may or may not be true, as her source was Nathan himself.[17] Nathan's widow also identified Nathan's brother, Fritz, as a devout Catholic. Mencken's memoirs reveal that Fritz Nathan was engaged to a wealthy Catholic woman, Marguerite Egan, who insisted he be baptized. Mencken claims that he imparted the entire Baltimore Catechism to Fritz in one night.

He also implies that Nathan's brother converted strictly for the sake of his bride's money.[18] Nathan himself, though, always had sympathy for the Church. In November 1933, Theodore Dreiser upbraided Nathan for refusing to publish his article mocking the Catholic Church in *The American Spectator.* Dreiser was rather severe with Nathan for allowing satirical material about every Protestant denomination to run, but not articles chastising the Church. He even made references to Nathan's pro-Catholic bias when he coedited *The Smart Set* and *The American Mercury.*[19]

Although Freudians would no doubt look to his father's abandoning the family as a source of Nathan's complicated personal religious equation, it could be that he sincerely felt that he was not Jewish, although he never explains any such feelings to Goldberg. Even the admission of Jewishness that he makes to Goldberg is at best a backhanded one. It is more likely that Nathan's own insecurity and desperate desire to be a "genuine" aristocrat caused him to go to such lengths to disguise his true background. This aspect of Nathan's identity is a fascinating reflection of some of the inherent contradictions of American life. It would no doubt cause him no small amount of chagrin that in the "definitive" *Literary History of the United States* edited by Robert Spiller et alia, he is mentioned only twice: as the coeditor of the *American Mercury* and as an "American Jew writing in English."[20]

Although the public persona Nathan labored with such effort to create is superficially pathetic, we must recall that Nathan spent his entire life in a society that cheerfully excluded Jews from hotels, apartment houses, clubs, and neighborhoods. Nathan himself was a victim of such prejudice; he was kept out of an apartment building on Manhattan's Upper East Side because he was Jewish. Nathan's determination to blend into the cosmopolitan backdrop of Manhattan via the Stork Club and his own table at "21" is indicative of the struggle to define precisely what an American identity is. That a cultural commentator of Nathan's status had such difficulty with his own identity remains as troubling as it is instructive.

The facts of Nathan's upbringing were actually much more cosmopolitan and aristocratic than would be considered normal for an American child. He grew up in a wealthy and privileged atmosphere. He felt at home in the capitals of Europe, yet he was constrained by the cultural realities of American life that precluded someone of Jewish background from attaining complete social acceptance. Nathan's creation of a coldly elitist public persona, one that sneered at all things parochial or conventionally considered to be American, was perhaps a response to a culture that rejected the cosmopolitanism that he was brought up with as a child and cherished as an adult. Nathan was a deeply conflicted man, one who strove to present himself as a citizen of the world who happened to live on the island of Manhattan. Yet while scraping away at this cosmopolitan veneer, one must recall that Nathan successfully projected his self-created image throughout his career. Indeed, the 1945 edition of *Current Biography* describes Nathan thus: "His favorite restaurants are the '21' Club, the Colony, and Fourteenth Street Lüchow's." Elsa Maxwell, the high-society social director and columnist, is quoted in the same article describing him as:

> one of a strange, ill-assorted, but charming group of people who dine with "Dumpa" (the Fifth Avenue and Newport Mrs. Hermann Oelrichs) every Christmas. Nathan under a Christmas tree, giving and receiving presents, his eyes swimming with sentimental and true affection for his friends, is not the man his public confessions would lead you to expect.[21]

Being a renowned man about town was an important facet of Nathan's latter-day persona. Nathan associated with almost all the columnists of his time. He had seen the emergence of the newspaper gossip column, and to the likes of Walter Winchell, Louis Sobol, Ed Sullivan, Sidney Skolsky, Leonard Lyons, Dorothy Kilgallen, Earl Wilson, and Robert Sylvester, he was a formidable figure. His reputation as a legendary participant in The Roaring Twenties, someone who had frolicked with Zelda Fitzgerald, made up the famous trio with Mencken and God, *and* had discovered Eugene O'Neill gave him special status among the Broadway scribes. Even the fabulously effete Lucius Beebe doffed his opera hat to Nathan. But the foremost reason for Nathan's popularity among the columnists was that he provided excellent copy. He was always good for a line or two. Like Nathan, the big-time columnists were responsible not only to a Manhattan readership but also to a whole nation of readers. They reported on the entire stage of Manhattan, leaving the actual theaters to Nathan and his colleagues, but it was incumbent upon the columnists to detail the comings and goings of the Manhattan elite in order to show the suburbs and hinterlands what "real New Yorkers" were up to. Thus were fueled the dreams of glamour-besotted bobby-soxers and hep cats.

Another reason he was good copy was the fact that he was unmarried. As Nathan himself details in his book *The Bachelor Life*, he was one of the most famous and sought-after single men in New York. His romances with actresses and dancers were notorious. In addition to his celebrated, lengthy romances with Lillian Gish and Julie Haydon, Nathan also conducted numerous other liaisons. One of the more touching mementos among Nathan's papers is a series of signed photographs of the diminutive dancer Ann Pennington, she of the fabled "dimpled knees," who starred in several editions of *The Ziegfeld Follies* and in George White's *Scandals*. Throughout his life, Nathan always singled out this *Follies* star as a paradigm of pulchritude. Which is not to say that he was never serious about relationships. His decade-long and, by most accounts, tortuous love affair with Lillian Gish was a prelude to his fourteen-year liaison with Julie Haydon. Nathan gave in to her importuning and finally married her in 1955. Haydon was totally devoted to Nathan; after his death she spent the remainder of her own long life in service to his memory.

Nathan was absolutely at home in restaurants and commanded respect bordering on reverence wherever he dined. Nonetheless, there is the odd assortment of spurious stories in circulation (courtesy of Orson Welles and other tall-tale tellers) alleging that he was a skinflint. Welles dined out on the canard that the service people at the Royalton routinely urinated in Nathan's tea and committed worse atrocities in fulfilling his room-service requests. Such anecdotes fly in the face of common sense as much as in the face of the evidence. Nathan was welcome everywhere he went; indeed, he was a sought-after customer. He respected service people. In his articles he frequently pays tribute to his favorite waiters and chefs. He even wrote a pamphlet on the eating and drinking establishments of New York.

What is more, we have the living testimony of Mr. Peter Kriendler of "21." Mr. Kriendler recalls that Nathan visited "21" almost every evening, arriving precisely at 5:00. He ordered two iced teas and left at 6:00. He also dined at "21," but not as frequently. In a small notebook, he recorded all the money he spent. Mr. Kriendler describes him as "careful" with his money, but a fair tipper.[22]

No stranger to nightclubs either, he was a regular at the Stork Club's "Cub Room," its enclave for celebrities only. There he frequently joined Walter Winchell at Table 50 (the most important table in Manhattan, if not the world) and his assessment of Winchell's nightly monologues became proverbial: "He tells me in several thousand words how wonderful it is to be Walter Winchell." When Winchell's daughter developed theatrical ambitions, he asked Nathan to ascertain whether she had any talent, and Nathan was sufficiently impressed by her ability to offer her encouragement.

Thus, the legend of Nathan as a coldly arrogant person does not necessarily bear close scrutiny. It is simply that he chose his friends very carefully. His colleagues in the New York Drama Critics' Circle elected him their president (1937–39), and it was well known that he was the most influential member of the circle. In the late 1940s and into the 1950s, Nathan called on Brooks Atkinson at the *New York Times* almost every afternoon. Arthur Gelb, then assigned to the drama desk, remembers his entering the office and disdaining anyone who dared to cross his path, but once with Atkinson, Nathan immediately began chatting and bantering warmly with his long-time colleague. According to Gelb, Atkinson was amused by Nathan and found him almost "freakish." He adds that Atkinson had "tremendous compassion for Nathan during his years of failing health."[23] Certainly the two were diametric opposites in attitude and demeanor. Atkinson's polite and friendly approach to the theater and to life made them an odd pair.

Nathan and Atkinson also had a significant professional difference. Atkinson refused to mix in any way with any members of the theatrical profession.[24] This is his lasting legacy to American drama criticism. Since his time, critics have functioned on what is presumably aloof plane, removed from the hurly-burly of theatrical production. The closest most critics get to the production process nowadays is a preopening interview and, unfortunately, most of those interviews are little more than puff pieces inflated by "human interest." True critics have no business writing feature stories, but editors think otherwise. It is curious that no conflict of interest is perceived in these printed tête-à-têtes between critic and performer, director, or playwright. Recently, though, the *New Yorker* drama critic John Lahr has been the subject of controversy because of his technique of mixing interview, feature article, and criticism. Lahr's attempts to defend his technique on the basis of being involved in the theatrical process are not satisfactory, as he never seems to have anything negative to say about the performers, directors, or playwrights he interviews. Nathan never hesitated to involve himself, but he also never hesitated to write negatively about plays or performers. Nevertheless, throughout his career, in spite of his formidable reputation, theater people sought him out.

Admission to Nathan's sphere was not limited to critics. Bernard Sobel and Richard Maney, two press agents, remember Nathan with affection and admiration in their respective memoirs. Sobel had been inspired by Nathan when he was a student in Indiana. Later, after moving to New York, Sobel became an acquaintance of Nathan's. He recalls being with Nathan at "21" when the critic said to him:

> "Bernard, can you get me an introduction to the little dancer in that musical at the Imperial?" That he should want to meet a chorus girl was surprising. [Sobel is perhaps a bit ingenuous here.] . . . I arranged the introduction, and five minutes later he said to her, "I watched you through the second number in the show. I noticed the way you moved your hands, your facial expressions, your sincerity. I think you should play Alice. I'm going to suggest that you do the part for the next Wonderland revival. I can see you . . . [Sobel's ellipsis]. "You are startling," the girl interrupted. "I've always wanted to play Alice. . . . Mr. Nathan, you're psychic." George Jean Nathan was right. He's almost always right. His early books steered a whole generation of theatre lovers to the right road and to a knowledge of the wider aspects of the theatre which the continental dramatists opened.[25]

Sobel's comments are representative. Nathan must have been adept at choosing his friends, as it is far more common than not to encounter positive recollections of him. Unpleasant comments about him are almost always made by individuals with a personal grudge against him. This is worth noting only in light of Nathan's professed indifference to the world at large.

Another of Nathan's colleagues who thought highly of him was Richard Maney. He was the most important theatrical press agent of the century and was the inspiration for the sozzled but steadfast press agent, Owen O'Malley, in Hecht and MacArthur's play, *Twentieth Century*. Maney and Nathan had a lot of respect for each other; in his memoirs he recalls Nathan with great warmth.

> In the forty years that he has scoffed at its frauds and its flapdoodle, George Jean Nathan has been our theatre's most stimulating critic and its most feared one. A gay iconoclast, skilled with the stiletto, Nathan has debunked most of the theatre's great. His ridicule has loosed the homicidal urge in hundreds of victims. Nathan's influence on drama criticism was as marked as that of his long-time associate, H. L. Mencken, on American letters.[26]

Maney was writing at the close of his career and had no need to curry favor with the critic.

Nathan may have made few friends, but when he chose to be a friend, he was full of fun and camaraderie. After the two became friendly in the early 1940s, William Saroyan planned to write a play about Nathan. Saroyan told the famously soft-spoken columnist Louis Sobol that he would call it 'The Youngest Man in America' and that "it was to be a play with music, of course." Sobol, Saroyan, and the playwright's fiancée Carol Marcus, once spent an evening touring various Lower East Side boîtes. Their night on the town culminated in a visit to The Old Roumanian a place where:

> a crew of four musicians wore jackets and ties and where a girl named Roxanne, with a fine voice sang . . . chants requested by Messrs. Saroyan and Nathan. . . . Nathan insisted that he wanted to play "Egern on the Tegern See" on the piano. He started for the tiny platform, but before he could settle on the piano, Saroyan started singing a Japanese lullaby in Armenian-Chinese double-talk, which inspired Nathan to dance a Viennese waltz with Carol Marcus.[27]

Such anecdotes reveal how much Nathan enjoyed Manhattan nightlife and how he rolled through half a century of frivolity.

Of course, Nathan's most famous, if most fractious, friendship was with H. L. Mencken. They first met when both were youthful reviewers for *The Smart Set*. Together, they would forge the most influential literary partnership of their time. In the second and third decades of the twentieth century, during the years when he wrote for and coedited *The Smart Set*, Nathan reached his zenith as a critic. These were also the years of Mencken's greatest achievement. Nathan started at this magazine in 1908 and became editor with H. L. Mencken in 1914. In that year, the publisher Eltinge Warner offered him sole editorship, but Nathan insisted that Mencken share the helm with him. At *The Smart Set*, though, Nathan was very much the senior partner, and it was he who was responsible for setting much of the magazine's tone. Nathan attended to the day-to-day tasks of running the magazine, whose offices were in New York. Mencken stayed in Baltimore and came to the city only twice a month to go over the issue and confer with Nathan just before it went to press.

After he and Nathan left *The Smart Set*, Mencken would attempt to continue this working arrangement at *The American Mercury*. At this magazine, Nathan was coeditor in name only. The publisher, Alfred Knopf, favored Mencken, and the new operating arrangement included a pay scale that was most unfavorable to Nathan. At *The Smart Set*, their salaries had been equal. At the *Mercury*, Nathan was paid only two-thirds of what Mencken made. The obvious tilt in scale was one of the causes of Nathan's departure, especially as Mencken expected him to continue to do the same amount of work for the greatly reduced salary.

The professional parting between Nathan and Mencken that the *Mercury* precipitated has been touched upon—and either magnified or minimized—for partisan reasons by everyone who has ever dealt with these writers. Let it suffice to say that of the historical players Nathan, Mencken, and Knopf, the only *sustained* rancor that existed among them was the ill feeling Knopf seems to have had for Nathan, and it must be stressed that it was entirely one-sided. There is no existing written evidence that Nathan had any particular feelings, positive or negative, for Knopf,. The only surviving exchange between them is strictly business correspondence and it is always cordial. Knopf, on the other hand, went to considerable lengths to alienate Mencken from Nathan. He really did not want Nathan to have anything to do with the *Mercury*. Mencken, to his credit, reciprocated Nathan's loyalty and demanded that Nathan share the editorship, even though this initial loyalty was to prove short-lived. Mencken did not, however, agree to share his authority. Late in his life, Knopf published a vituperative personal attack, "H. L. Mencken, George Jean Nathan and *The American Mercury* Venture," in which he accuses Nathan of backstairs intrigue and spiritual cowardice. Knopf insists that Mencken wanted a "complete divorce" from Nathan and concludes his article with a quotation from a letter in which Mencken calls Nathan "a rat." He makes no mention of the series of reunions the two had through the 1940s, even though they were widely publicized, and he generally characterizes Nathan as a rather pathetic soul who was utterly cast adrift when Mencken rejected him.[28] Publisher Thomas Yoseloff describes Knopf's treatment of Nathan during the critic's last years as "shameful." He states that Knopf was "very cool to Nathan by 1952, and it [their relationship] had reached almost the stage of open warfare." He adds that by this time Nathan regarded Knopf with bitterness. Nathan had good reason. Knopf had not only refused to publish an anthology of Nathan's writings that Charles Angoff planned, but had also indicated he would cease publishing Nathan's work altogether.[29] Nonetheless, Knopf changed his mind about publishing the anthology, *The World of George Jean Nathan,* when he learned that Mr. Yoseloff's company would do so. Knopf also apparently backed down on his threat to stop publishing Nathan's writings as his company issued Nathan's final book, *The Theatre in the Fifties,* in 1953. We must recall, though, that Nathan continued to publish reviews and essays until shortly before he died in 1958. Although it is possible that Nathan's failing health kept him from compiling his articles into books after 1953, it may have been that he knew he no longer had a publisher. Unfortunately, the Knopf corporate records of this era have not survived to provide a definitive answer.

Of course, Mencken corroborates this negative view of Nathan. He cites declining sales as the cause for Knopf's desire to dump the critic and reports (in the manuscript of *My Life as an Author and Editor*) that Nathan's books never sold more than 2,000 copies and that sales virtually disappeared after the first year.[30] This is belied by the fact that some of Nathan's books went into second, third, and fourth editions. *The Popular Theatre*, first published in 1918, was reissued in one of Knopf's Borzoi Pocket Editions (duodecimo progenitors of mass-market paperbacks) in 1923 and reprinted three times thereafter. If Knopf actually did sever his long-standing ties with Nathan in 1953, why then did he publish Thomas Quinn Curtiss's Nathan anthology *The Magic Mirror* in 1960, two years after Nathan's death?

The Nathan, Mencken, and Knopf tangle has another twist. In spite of Knopf's allegations, from a legal perspective there is evidence that the only intrigue going on among the three was engineered by Knopf. A 20 November 1929 letter from Nathan's attorney, James Banks of the Central Hanover Bank and Trust, instructs Nathan not to sell his stock in *The American Mercury* to the Knopfs (Alfred Knopf's father and wife were also his business partners). Banks tells Nathan that

in the agreements from 8 November 1924 and 20 May 1929, the Knopfs misrepresented the stock's value. They deceived you in inducing you to release Mencken and to cancel the other provisions of the 8 November 1924 contract and to insist that your articles be carried until 1 February 1932.[31]

The legal advice in this letter is especially interesting given the sanctimonious tone of Knopf's account and its not so subtle implication that Nathan somehow got the better of Knopf in their financial dealings.

As for Mencken, it is clear that he took great offense to a chapter Nathan wrote about him in an abortive book of memoirs called *Friends of Mine*. This volume was to be published in 1931, and a dummy of the book is preserved at Cornell. Nathan sent the chapter to Mencken and solicited his comments. Mencken was outraged by it and Nathan responded by excising all the offensive material from it. It seems that Mencken was incredibly sensitive about his marriage and could not accept the ribbing Nathan gave him about his church wedding. Nathan's joking is understandable, given Mencken's lifelong crusade against religion and the decidedly antimatrimonial stance he had taken over the years. Be that as it may, the allegedly offensive material is now available among the H. L. Mencken papers in the New York Public Library, and how or why it managed to incense Mencken is nothing less than a *bizarrie*. What is more, Nathan apologized to Mencken and cut out all the bothersome passages, but Mencken would not be assuaged. Also in the library's collection are several letters dated throughout 1930 from Nathan to Mencken (as well as angry letters from Mencken to Knopf) about this matter. Nathan is clearly surprised at Mencken's distress but is equally willing to make things up. Ultimately, Knopf refused to publish the book, and Nathan reworked the material from *Friends of Mine* into *The Intimate Notebooks of George Jean Nathan* in 1932.

Strangely, though, other than letting Nathan know that he was offended by *Friends of Mine*, Mencken never communicated his anger directly to Nathan, and as correspondents they remained close friends. Nonetheless, they never worked together again. Ultimately, the dissolution of their editorial partnership was harmful to both Nathan and Mencken individually and to the *Mercury* as a whole. Mencken helped Nathan recognize that journalism could be used as a means of raising critical standards. Nathan's rapier wit tempered Mencken's meat-ax approach. Mencken's influence gave Nathan a touch of the crusader's zeal (witness the critic's labors on behalf of O'Neill), and Nathan's nonchalance helped to cool Mencken's overheated boob-baiting. While Nathan worked as an editor he was able to define the role of the drama critic and discuss in a significant way what the function of the twentieth-century drama critic should be. In the long run though, it is not Nathan's personal relationship with Mencken that is most significant; the question of whether they had a falling out scarcely matters now.

The most important theatrical relationship Nathan had was, of course, his friendship with Eugene O'Neill. He is most closely and frequently associated with the playwright. Nathan is generally credited with "discovering" the playwright and supporting his career. Nathan's influence was important in securing a Broadway theater for *Beyond the Horizon* and for persuading audiences to accept O'Neill as the outstanding American playwright of his time. Nathan worked ceaselessly on O'Neill's behalf throughout his career. He boosted the plays and the playwright—always with discrimination, though.

The two were also fast friends. Nathan was one of the few allowed to make visits to O'Neill's homes, and the two socialized whenever the playwright visited New York. Alone among the people O'Neill had known before his final marriage, Nathan passed muster even before the imperious Carlotta, O'Neill's third wife. Indeed, O'Neill had intimated to Nathan that he had wanted him to serve as best man at his wedding to Carlotta. He visited the couple in France and later when they moved to Georgia. Lillian Gish accompanied him to O'Neill's château, Le Plessis, near Tours in France. O'Neill had even suggested a double wedding for them all. After the couple had been married for nine years, Nathan told Jim Tully in a January 1938 *Esquire* interview that Carlotta "is my idea of the perfect wife."[32] Carlotta reciprocated this warm feeling in several letters to the critic. To the end of his life, Nathan knew that his greatest accomplishment had been to champion our greatest playwright. Nathan and O'Neill's friendship is a singular bond in American theater history.

Nathan was an aloof and remote figure who had few friends. His icy hauteur was legendary. O'Neill was a painfully shy and detached figure. Both men lived for the theater. Indeed, each gave up the quotidian rewards of small talk and family pothering for an essentially monastic approach to life. Granted, neither was an ascetic. Le Plessis, Tao House, and Casa Genotta were certainly not shrines to anchorism, nor was Nathan's dingy den at the Royalton Hotel a cell fit for St. Benedict; but nevertheless, they wholly devoted their lives to their careers. Once O'Neill had decided to become a playwright, his life gradually settled into a routine, especially after he married Carlotta in 1929. Nathan remained a bachelor until nearly the end of his life. It would seem that his half-century as a drama critic reduces his life to a chronicle of plays attended. As Nathan himself asserted, "Why do I need to write my memoirs, my life is in my criticism."

Most of Nathan's critical judgments concerning O'Neill are, of course, sound, but one can question what he writes about O'Neill the man. Nathan created his own autobiography nearly out of whole cloth and sometimes strove, too, to create a public image of O'Neill that contrasted not only with the glowering visage made famous by photographer Edward Steichen in the fashionable pages of *Vanity Fair* but also with reality. In a bizarre work of fiction, *Monks are Monks*, Nathan presents O'Neill as Eustace O'Hara, "the only American playwright worth a God-damn." O'Hara is sketched thus:

The only son of a stevedore, he had worked his way through two years at Harvard, being then expelled for making a rude noise with his mouth during an open lecture by the eminent Professor George Pierce Baker, and subsequently and in rapid succession serving the world and his own belly as a freight-car conductor, banana-peddler on a Staten Island ferry, bathroom steward on the Albany night boat, Nantucket lifesaver, Greenwich Village speakeasy waiter and shillaber with the Sells-Floto circus.[33]

Even when Nathan wrote about O'Neill in the nonfiction vein, he labored mightily to counter the prevailing popular image of O'Neill as a "champion sourball." He retails anecdotes of O'Neill spending his happiest hours singing along with Rosie the player piano. Not that Nathan was averse to showing his readers O'Neill's somber side. But Nathan wanted the public to know of O'Neill's allegedly playful side, too.

In *The Intimate Notebooks of George Jean Nathan*, he retails two canards about O'Neill: the infamous beer-bottle-toss-through-Woodrow-Wilson's-window-that-got-him-expelled-from-Princeton tale and a slightly off-color recollection of O'Neill's 1926 visit to Yale to receive an honorary degree. According to Nathan, the only time he ever heard O'Neill laugh out loud was when the playwright told Nathan about the climax of his New Haven sojourn. Near dawn, O'Neill observed three members of the class of 1880, a bank president, a railroad tycoon and a U. S. senator, playing a game of leap frog. Nathan has O'Neill recount that

> one of them fell down and rolled half-way into a sewer, the three singing barber-shop at the top of their lungs, wobbled across the street ... to where there was a mailbox. With a lot of grunts and after much steaming and puffing, the bank president and the vice-president of the big railroad got down on their knees and hoisted their old class-mate, the Senator, up on their shoulders in line with the slit in the mail-box. Whereupon the Senator proceeded to use the mail-box for a purpose generally reserved for telegraph poles and the sides of barns.[34]

Dubious doings indeed. The reality of O'Neill's life was certainly fantastic enough in its own way. Son of an alcoholic matinee-idol father and a morphine-dependent mother, he was a prep-school graduate, a gold prospector, a suicide-attempt survivor, and an able-bodied seaman. Nathan, however, felt compelled to give his own twist to O'Neill's life, almost as though he were *the* conduit to the reading public for information about O'Neill. Perhaps spiking the details as he did was his way of maintaining control over O'Neill's public image, something O'Neill cared very little about.

By so doing Nathan projected his own personality onto the playwright's, giving O'Neill an image he had created that contrasted with the one O'Neill had only inadvertently created for himself.

Even so, Nathan's name is inextricably linked with O'Neill's. He did not blindly praise all of O'Neill's work, nor did O'Neill deem Nathan the sole critic worthy to judge his work. Nonetheless, O'Neill did share the manuscript of Long Day's Journey with Nathan, and this demonstrates irrefutably that he trusted Nathan as much more than a drama critic. Commentators have long been mystified by this friendship. Nathan was drawn to O'Neill because of the playwright's supreme independence and confidence in himself as an artist. Why then does he fabricate a friendship between their mothers—to forge a personal link between himself and O'Neill? Perhaps if he reached for bonds between himself and O'Neill that were beyond truth's grasp, he did so because he saw them as an opportunity for immortality. And for this, as the old song has it, he is more to be pitied than censured.

Nathan's close involvement with Mencken and O'Neill obscures him as a critic and as a personality. Mencken's papers are now available, making speculation about any sort of long-lasting feud between him and Nathan problematic. As we have seen, they grew professionally distant but remained friends throughout their lives as is evident in surviving correspondence. Conversely, certain of O'Neill's letters indicate that the two were not as close professionally as has generally been assumed. In 1932, O'Neill was anxious about Nathan's writing the introduction to a planned one-volume edition of his plays. He did not want himself to be associated with only one drama critic. He also did not wish Nathan to select the ten plays that were to be included; he reserved that right for himself.

Mencken's attitude toward Nathan is similar to his attitude toward almost every other literary person he ever worked with or became close to. There are similarities here with his friendships with Theodore Dreiser, James Branch Cabell, and Sinclair Lewis. Mencken forged a close bond with each of these men, but later chose to close each one out of his life. Mencken's relationship with Nathan, however, was not so clearly broken off. At the same time he was penning vitriolic comments about Nathan for his memoirs, he was enjoying a boisterous and widely reported reunion with his old friend during the 1940s. The two corresponded until Mencken's death.

O'Neill's failing health through the 1940s and 1950s prevented him from seeing anyone with regularity, but the playwright and the critic stayed in touch through letters, a painful parallel, as neither O'Neill nor Mencken was able to write his own letters in his final years.

Arteriosclerosis took its toll on his vitality, and Nathan's health failed rapidly through the 1950s. He intermittently lost the use of his hands as a series of strokes befell him. Although he continued writing for several periodicals, his last book was published in 1953. Nathan became increasingly frail, relying almost completely on Julie Haydon. Brooks Atkinson worried about Nathan's financial condition, as he was incurring large medical bills and presumably taking in little money. He even planned to solicit funds from Nathan's wealthier friends should the necessity arise. When Atkinson learned that Nathan's checking account was overdrawn by $6,000, he had to step in. A bank officer asked Atkinson to obtain power of attorney in order to get Nathan's safe deposit box opened. The officer believed that a cache of stock certificates and bonds might lay therein. Atkinson tried to get Nathan's permission, but the old critic played out his final scenes with splendid melodrama. Day after day, he rebuffed Atkinson's attempt. Day after day, Atkinson tried to reassure Nathan and persuade him to put aside his fears and suspicions. Finally, when Atkinson enlisted a cohort of other friends, Nathan relented.

Armed with the power of attorney, Atkinson and a few others proceeded to the bank. In his words, "It was a Dickensian experience." Nathan's box was several floors beneath the ground. Descending through various vaults, heavily barred doors clanging behind them as they went, Atkinson and company finally reached the chamber. The safe deposit box was so large it had to be moved by truck into a counting room. The inventory began: shares of stock, unclipped coupons, bonds, savings account statements, passbooks, years of compounded interest. "They counted ten thousand, twenty thousand, forty thousand—and when it got to over four hundred thousand Atkinson stopped feeling so sorry for Nathan."[35]

Nathan's marriage to Julie Haydon in 1955 put his name in the headlines because he had been the most famous bachelor in the country. Two years later he again made headlines when he entered the Roman Catholic church, after having been one of the nation's most notorious agnostics for over half a century, taking the Holy Eucharist at St. Patrick's Cathedral on 9 October 1957. In spite of these flickers of limelight, Nathan's was a ghostly presence on Broadway as the 1950s drew to a close and, sadly, by the time of his death, many were shocked to read his obituary. They had thought he was already dead.

# 2

# Turn-of-the-Century Critical Trends and the Making of a Drama Critic

SIX YEARS BEFORE NATHAN BEGAN HIS CAREER, T. S. MORAN, WRITing in the January 1899 issue of *Metropolitan* magazine, describes New York's dramatic critics as being the object of a large and devoted following.[1] Moran comments briefly on fourteen critics (including William Winter and Alan Dale), recounting their personalities and writing styles. The picture that emerges from his article is one of a mild-mannered group of journalists who are kind-hearted enough to record their opinions so that "nice" people might have something theatrical to discuss between the soup and fish courses at dinner. Winter is "looked up to by the conservative portion of the public"; Dale "has made enemies of a few actors and managers, but he has entertained the readers." Moran judges these critics first and foremost as writers. He is not interested in their attitudes toward the theatre. So, it seems gratuitous for him even to mention the theatrical experience of Edward Fales Coward (of the New York *World*), a former actor, and Franklin Fyles (of the New York *Sun*), the coauthor with David Belasco of *The Girl I Left Behind Me,* among other popular plays. A generalinterest magazine such as the *Metropolitan* is not the place to look for a detailed examination of drama criticism, but an article like this one does tell us something about the critical milieu at the turn of the century. It was polite, restrained, and widely read.

The situation had not changed much twelve years later. An anonymous article from the May 1911 *Green Book,* a magazine published specifically for theater enthusiasts, presented even less serious commentary than *Metropolitan* offered. Entitled "A First Nighter Says . . . ," it purports to be the anonymous confessions of a Broadway insider. Therein we learn about the physical appearance of the various critics, whether they smoke, and what sort of haberdashery they favor. It describes Alan Dale (of the *American*) as "the best-known critic in New York." Dale is the only

newspaper critic mentioned in Moran's article who was still working as a drama critic in 1911. Nothing at all is said about the
critical proclivities of the others—Acton Davies (*Evening Sun*),
Louis V. De Foe (*Morning World*), Arthur Warren (*Tribune*),
Adolph Klauber (*Times*), George Fry (*Globe*), W. T. Bliss (*Mail*), or
Robert Gilbert Welsh (*Telegram*). As with the *Metropolitan* piece,
no mention is made in the article of the dramatic aesthetics of
the critics. Its author, however, shares with T. S. Moran a concern
for what a given critic's journalistic experience has been. He informs us that Welsh was also a "newspaper poet" and that Bliss
had been the city editor of the *New York Mail* before he became
its drama critic, a career move totally inconceivable today.[2]

It would not be until Nathan's time that drama critics would be
scrutinized *critically*. Even Nathan's own uncle, Charles Frederic
Nirdlinger, a playwright as well as a critic, offers little explanation
regarding what it is that he is trying to do as a critic of drama.
In an 1899 collection of his reviews, *Masques and Mummers*, the
chapter entitled "Of a New Philosophy of Dramatic Criticism"
contains theory that could just as easily be applied to painting,
music, or any of the other arts. In a concluding paragraph he says:

> And that brings me to the consideration of what constitutes the real
> purpose, the final utility of criticism. With the performer in his per-
> sonality, with the individual effort or achievement, it has no direct
> business. It is only with the general taste, with its direction and correc-
> tion, that it must concern itself. It is not the province of criticism to
> occupy itself with the encouragement or the discouragement of those
> who provide the common entertainment or of those engaged in any
> of the departments of fine crafts and letters. Let criticism but discover
> the truth to the general and strive its utmost to bring them to realiza-
> tion of what is sincere and what is fictitious, what is ugly and what is
> beautiful, what honest in art and what meretricious, and it will have
> done its whole duty. With the effect on the individual of such a course,
> criticism, I repeat, has no concern.[3]

Nirdlinger's nephew would no doubt disagree both with the tone
of this statement and with the point it tries to make. Nirdlinger
wrote for magazines such as the *Criterion*, a high-toned literary
monthly, and a prestigious weekly, *The Illustrated American*, but he
has no more concern with what is peculiar to dramatic criticism
than Moran in *Metropolitan* or the anonymous first-nighter of *The
Green Book*.

In the 1905–1906 theatrical season in which George Jean Nathan began his career as a drama critic, there were 111 Broadway

productions. It was at this time that the Times Square area of New York was consolidated by theatrical managers as the center of the city's theater district. The years just before World War I constitute the seed-time of the modern American theater, the years of Clyde Fitch, William Vaughan Moody, Edward Sheldon, David Belasco, Charles Frohman, the last years of Klaw and Erlanger, the first of the Shuberts. Mrs. Fiske, George M. Cohan, Ethel Barrymore, Maude Adams, and Julian Eltinge saw their names in lights. Robert Edmond Jones was studying in Europe. Nathan made a trip to Europe in the late spring of 1914 with his colleagues from *The Smart Set,* H. L. Mencken and Willard Huntington Wright. (This trip would be the impetus for their collaborative travel book, *Europe After 8:15.*)

Three weeks before the outbreak of The Great War, on 16 July 1914, the playwright with whom Nathan was to have the most important relationship of his career, Eugene O'Neill, wrote to George Pierce Baker that he had decided to become "an artist or nothing." In these years, as the theater became a fully capitalized endeavor so too did journalism. Journalism relating to the theatre was little different in form from the stuff that was printed in other daily departments—a situation that has changed much less than most theatergoers realize. The daily reviews were not always credited with by-lines, and theatrical reviewers were also expected to solicit advertising from theatrical managers, a practice that continued until 1915. And up until 1915 there were two sorts of drama critics: anonymous puffsters and scholarly, genteel types exemplified by William Winter and J. Ranken Towse.[4] There was one exception among all these writers, though, a critic who stood out from his colleagues and who had quite an influence on Nathan.

James Gibbons Huneker is the critic with whom Nathan most closely identified himself, and both he and H. L. Mencken were protégés of the "steeplejack of the arts," as Huneker called himself. Both men were unabashedly loyal to the critic. Mencken felt that were it not for Huneker's efforts, "Americans would still be shipping union suits to the heathen, reading Emerson, sweating at Chautauquas, and applauding the plays of Bronson Howard."[5] Huneker wrote on the theater, music, painting, whatever caught his eye or suited his fancy. Huneker is a key figure in the development of American appreciation of Continental culture. Although a marginal figure today, he was the only American critic of his time who was treated as an equal by European critics such as Georg Brandes and Remy de Gourmont. Huneker also popularized the arcane aestheticism of the American philosopher and novelist Edgar Saltus. Saltus, a turn-of-the-century contributor to *The Smart Set*, was the raffish author of such works as *The Pace That Kills* (see O'Neill's dedication to Nathan of *Ah, Wilderness!*), and he even figures as a minor character in Huneker's "decadent" novel, *Painted Veils*. Saltus' once famous 1891 manifesto on style almost anticipates Nathan's methods.

> In literature only three things count: style, style polished, style repolished. Style may be defined as the harmony of syllables, the fall of sentences, the infrequency of adjectives, the absence of metaphor. . . . Grammar is an adjunct. It is not an obligation. No grammarian ever wrote a thing that was fit to read.[6]

Saltus and Huneker were iconoclasts long before the Roaring Twenties. It is their example that Nathan and Mencken followed.

In 1915 Huneker conducted a column in *Puck* entitled "The Seven Arts." Nathan served as drama critic for *Puck* that year and worked directly with Huneker. Huneker was in some ways a throwback to the "bohemian" school of criticism of the 1850s identified by Tice Miller.[7] And in their way Huneker, Nathan, and Mencken sought to establish for themselves a neo-Pfaffian attitude toward the arts and their own writing. They ate and drank prodigiously and set themselves apart from anything that was genteel. Huneker was the champion of Ibsen and Shaw. He particularly venerated the Norwegian playwright, calling him an essentially moral dramatist, almost as if to bait William Winter.[8] Huneker's writing was urbane and distinctly modernist in tone. Even though he was born in 1860 and was old enough to be Nathan's father, Huneker and the aspiring drama critic caroused as colleagues and were close friends. They met through Nathan's uncle, Charles Frederic Nirdlinger, in 1906.

Nathan was living with his uncle at the time, and Huneker, who had worked with Nirdlinger on the *Criterion* and *Town Topics*, encouraged Nathan to join his circle of beer-drinking companions at Scheffel Hall.[9] There Huneker held court and demonstrated his talent for identifying any brand of beer simply by dipping his finger in a tankard and touching it to his lips.[10] He also regaled his acolytes with his stunning erudition and backslapping bonhomie. It was in this coterie that Nathan probably first heard of H. L. Mencken. The exact details of their meeting are unknown, as both men have left several contradictory accounts, but the year is certain at least—1908, when they both went to work for *The Smart Set.*

Years afterwards, in 1922, Mencken recalled the thrill he and Nathan had felt just being in Huneker's presence by describing the finale of a typical session with him:

> he brought to a close *prestissimo* the most amazing monologue that these ears . . . had ever funneled into this consciousness. What a stew indeed! [it ranged among such topics as] . . . the precise topography of the warts of Liszt, George Bernard Shaw's heroic but vain struggles to throw off Presbyterianism, . . . the early days of David Belasco, the varying talents and idiosyncrasies of Lillian Russell's earlier husbands, . . . the true inwardness of the affair between D'Annunzio and Duse, . . . Ibsen's loathing of Norwegians, . . . the best remedy for Rhine wine *Katzenjammer*, . . . the genuine last words of Whitman.
>
> I must try to give you . . . some notion of the talk of the man, but I must fail inevitably. It was in brief, chaos, and chaos cannot be described. But it was chaos made to gleam and coruscate with every device of the seven arts—chaos drenched in all the colors imaginable. Chaos scored for an orchestra which made the great band of Berlioz seem like a fife and drum corps.[11]

The most important aspect of Huneker's relationship with Nathan was his twofold encouragement of the younger critic's interest in contemporary European drama and of his disgust with the current state of American drama. Huneker commented on his colleague in his "Seven Arts" column after Nathan's first book of drama criticism, *Another Book on the Theatre,* was published in 1915, calling him "witty, wise and cruel, . . . the Bad Boy of New York drama criticism."[12] Huneker's assessment still stands as an accurate summation of Nathan's image. He was more forthright about Nathan in a letter to their mutual friend Mencken, dated 24 November 1915:

> I read Nathan's last book . . . and enjoy him better between covers than in *Puck.* A writer more malicious, more brilliant, and better informed unless on *our* beautiful drama would be hard to find. Paris is where that young man ought to be. There he would be appreciated. Here he only bruises his brain against the eternal box-office.[13]

In terms of aesthetic temperament, Huneker was Nathan's most important critical precursor. It must be stressed, though, that that is the limit of their historical connection. The title of Huneker's *Puck* column, "The Seven Arts," attests to this critic's aesthetic eclecticism.

Huneker's twenty-two books include volumes of art, music, and literary criticism; general essays about life and culture; music history and theory; autobiography and fiction. Only one of his books, *Iconoclasts*, is devoted solely to drama. Nathan would emulate Huneker's worldliness, but he would limit himself to drama criticism. In this way he established a particular critical niche for himself that contrasts with Huneker's aesthetic escarpment. At Huneker's death, Nathan warmly acknowledged his debt to him:

> The greatest of American critics. . . . [But] a man of no country and no people save that of beautiful things and those who loved them. Huneker made possible civilized criticism in this great prosperous prairie. He taught us many things, but first he taught us cosmopolitanism, and love of life, and the crimson courage of youth. . . . Huneker's books are our foremost university. The man himself was our foremost cultural figure.[14]

Nathan was delighted to be associated with Huneker. He closely identified himself with him personally and was proud to work with him professionally. When he coedited *The Smart Set* with Mencken, he solicited several short stories from his mentor.

There is another critic, however, whom Nathan would have been loath to associate with and with whom he has been erroneously linked: Alan Dale. Huneker's biographer, Arnold Schwab, retails the critical canard that Alan Dale was "the literary progenitor of George Jean Nathan." Schwab states that Dale founded an entire "school of dramatic criticism based upon the flippant remark" and indicates that Nathan was a member of that school.[15] He bases this assertion on comments made by Channing Pollock in his autobiography, *Harvest of My Years*.[16] Pollock was a writer born out of his time; much of his book is musty with nostalgia for the grand old days of the theatre.

Pollock's memoir, while of little intrinsic value, is of some historic interest. He was a press agent for the Shuberts and for Ziegfeld and was also a drama critic and a playwright. Of his 1931 drama, Dorothy Parker said, "*The House Beautiful* is the play lousy." Mrs. Parker's was the majority opinion, and Pollock retired from the stage thereafter. Throughout his playwriting career, Pollock wrote reviews, and among the magazines for which he wrote was *The Green Book*, where he preceded Nathan; he also preceded him at *The Smart Set*. Pollock's discussion of the evolution of drama criticism from the turn of the century to the 1940s reveals an implied antipathy to Nathan:

> In rebellion against William Winter and his apostles there came into being a new school, headed by Alan Dale. This new school was primar-

ily personal; as someone said, "The capital *I*'s flashed by like telegraph poles from a rapidly moving railway train." Dale, whose real name was Cohen, made no pretense of erudition; he was far more concerned with himself than with the plays he reviewed, and with amusing his readers than with instructing them. As readers were beginning to prefer amusement to instruction, this school became the established one. Later the two schools merged; modern criticism is informative *and* amusing; the writer tells you a good deal about the play, while never permitting you to forget his individual bias, wisdom or importance.

Among other results this stress gave increased circulation to Roget's *Thesaurus;* words known to most of us came to be considered trite; anybody could call an actor "an actor"—the clever thing was to call him a clown or, better still, a scaramouch or a zany.[17]

This diatribe against the development of drama criticism in the first part of the twentieth century is of a piece with Pollock's other lamentations about the theatre of his time. Throughout one chapter, "The Glory That Was Greasepaint," he bewails virtually every change that took place in the theatre during his lifetime, from the advent of unions to the absence of musicians in the orchestra pit during nonmusical dramas. Even though Pollock calls William Winter's style "solid, scholarly and very dull," he shares something of "Weeping Willie's" sensibility. Commenting on Pollock's career in 1925, Montrose Moses said that Pollock had been "old fashioned" as far back as 1903.[18] For Pollock, the theater was in one long decline through the 1910s, 1920s, and 1930s. The difference between Pollock's and Nathan's outlooks is all the more interesting when one considers that Pollock was only two years older than Nathan.

Tice Miller also avers that in the earliest phase of his career, Nathan's writing was "self-consciously cute and clever—much like Alan Dale's writing. . . ."[19] He goes on to assert that Nathan's "taste" did not "give evidence of maturity until the 1912–1913 season."[20] But Miller limits his discussion of Nathan's development as a critic to the articles he wrote for *The Smart Set.* The work Nathan was doing at the same time for the *Burr MacIntosh Monthly,* however, indicates that the glibness imputed to Nathan's first *Smart Set* articles is due more to the editorial style of the magazine than to Nathan. From his first appearance in the August 1909 issue of the *Burr MacIntosh Monthly* until the May 1910 issue, Nathan's articles are restrained almost to the point of dullness, and only in the May issue does the tone of his writing take on any liveliness.

The articles Nathan was doing that time for *The Green Book* and *The Bookman* also lack any obvious cleverness or forced humor.

Describing Nathan's earliest *Smart Set* articles in the manuscript of *My Life as Author and Editor,* Mencken comments, "at the start his articles rather repelled me, for they were written in an extremely labored and even tortured style. But in a little while, under the admonitions of Splint [then the magazine's editor] he began to write more simply."[21] In his early writing in *The Smart Set* and other magazines, he favored figurative language for its own sake, for instance making forced comparisons between the oyster and theatrical seasons in the November 1909 *Smart Set.* But what is entirely uncharacteristic of the mature Nathan is his theatrical boosterism: . . . for in the New Theatre rests our hope for a National Theatre," in the December 1909 *Burr MacIntosh Monthly.* At that stage in his career Nathan even gave high praise to the likes of Edward Sheldon and Clyde Fitch. Nevertheless, Nathan himself scorned his own early work. He never reprinted his earliest criticism and always disparaged it.

As for Alan Dale himself and his "school of the flippant remark," the critic is described by T. S. Moran in his *Metropolitan* article as being

> unique among writers on theatrical subjects. . . . He has made a style of criticism all his own, in which the element of humor is prominent. . . . His criticisms are more like interesting newspaper articles than essays, and the biting sarcasm of some of them is not always appreciated by the playwright or actor who receives the scoring . . . but he has entertained the readers of the newspapers that have engaged his services.[22]

Dale was an energetic and attention-getting writer—his colleague at the *American,* Gene Fowler, remembered him as "our frenzied drama critic"—and he was very much a "Hearst" writer.[23] He wrote copy that would sell newspapers. From 1895 until his death in 1928, first for Hearst's *Journal* and then for his *American,* Dale did for theater reviews what Hearst's use of thirty-two-point type had done for front-page news stories. In 1924, it was the *American* that led the crusade to have Eugene O'Neill's *All God's Chillun Got Wings* banned. For his part, Dale had been leading his own campaign against O'Neill since the playwright's New York debut at the Provincetown Playhouse in Greenwich Village. Brooks Atkinson recalls that Dale was "hated and feared" by the theatrical community,[24] and although Nathan would certainly not have disrelished such unpopularity, Dale's antipathy to O'Neill is reason enough to separate the two critics. Dale's and Nathan's reviews do share a predilection for barbed commentary, but Dale's sallies lack the authority of Nathan's because Dale's disposition is acidic for its own sake; he bludgeons away for the sake of bludgeoning. Dale has no aesthetic vision, and he is happily blind. Dale's comments on O'Neill's plays are interesting as they reveal his wit and also demonstrate that even though he was not always off the mark, he was clearly more interested in getting a rise out of his readers than in raising their dramatic consciousness. O'Neill's biographer Louis Sheaffer, clearly biased, dismisses Dale's sense of humor as mere "malice."[25] Of *Anna Christie* Dale has this to say: "Nothing comes through the oleaginous, permeating fog, and there's nothing worth coming through anyway. Better to have presented the fog without either O'Neill or Anna Christie."[26] Dale's assault on *Desire Under the Elms* is reminiscent of William Winter's notorious diatribe against Ibsen: "The theatrical miasma arising from . . . *Desire Under the Elms* made even the subway station directly beneath the cantankerous, cancerous proceedings of the play seem delicious."[27]

Up to the end of his career Dale railed against O'Neill. He called *Strange Interlude* "a sordid mess;" It was an "hysterical analysis of a psychopathic woman" and nothing more than a "six-hour bore."[28] A week later, attacking the play's dinner break, he concluded that "the unification of drammer with dinner is no more possible than that of oil and water."[29] Nathan's well-known enthusiasm for O'Neill makes a comparison of his criticism of that particular playwright unnecessary, but one can contrast their assessments of Eugene Walter's titillatingly "realistic" drama of 1909, *The Easiest Way.* (The play was infamous for its "shocking" penultimate line: "I'm going to Rector's to make a hit, and to hell with the rest.")

The opening of Dale's review reveals his fundamental concern with the play's schematics but is nonetheless arresting:

A weak little drab of a vacuous, aimless woman, too puerile to be moral, and almost too cowardly to be brazenly immoral, pitted against two lovers—one a type of the bestial Broadway booze-feeder, representing immorality, the other a figure of a vigorous Lothario, suggesting non-morality—made out a sensational case at the Stuyvesant Theatre last night. . . . It purported to sketch the now familiar picture of the theatre-woman, struggling for her virtue amid the alleged temptations of Broadway—temptations that are popularly supposed to begin at the lobster-palace and end at the devil, but which last night began at the devil and ended at the lobster-palace.[30]

Dale spends most of his review summarizing the plot. He seems most pleased by the "gripping" nature of the play. He is enthralled by David Belasco's staging and scenery and by the performance of Frances Starr. The thrust of Dale's review indicates his admiration for Walter's ability to put *The Easiest Way* across in a fast-moving and riveting style.

Nathan virtually ignores Walter in his discussion of the play. He is not writing a morning-after review, but discussing the play in an essay on the manner in which directors change plays to make them more commercially viable. He sees *The Easiest Way* as simply a vehicle for Belasco's brand of theatrical realism:

> The character of Laura Murdock . . . was a kept woman with small sympathetic appeal for a popular audience, and if presented as the author conceived it would undoubtedly have had a hard time holding an audience's interests. By visiting upon the character all kinds of such hocus pocus as placing dolls on her dressing-table to suggest her innate childlike innocence, cutting out a number of her retorts to her broker protector and substituting for them a wide-eyed silence to indicate her weakness, etc., Belasco converted her into the materials for matinee slobbers—and the play harvested the sentimental public's dollars.[31]

As to Walter's ability to make his play grab the audience's attention, the quality that Dale found so enthralling, Nathan found little in Walter's dramatic carpentering compelling:

> The technic [*sic*] of Mr. Eugene Walter in the achievement of stage melodrama would appear to be as follows: first, to take a story intrinsically devoid of melodrama; second, to write that story on the smallest possible number of Western Union Telegraph blanks; third, to throw away half the blanks; and, fourth, by way of making the remaining blanks pass for tense melodrama, to cause what is written on them to be recited by a company of actors in a rapid, nervous and confused whisper.[32]

Nathan's view of Walter is that he is nothing more than a contriver of show-shop merchandise and an incompetent one, to boot. He concludes that without Belasco's flourishes, *The Easiest Way* would not have proved such a popular play. Dale reports in his critique how the play went over with the audience and how it managed to be so moving.

Finally, there are Nathan's own comments on Dale. In his book *The Popular Theatre*, he reviews Dale's thirty-year career in the chapter entitled "Its Criticism." He lambastes his colleague in no uncertain terms, impugning every aspect of his criticism:

> For thirty years, this gentleman, . . . has addressed himself assiduously and with infrequent failure to the cultivation of the public's cheapest and most doggerel theatrical predilections. He has rarely sidestepped, rarely swerved, rarely faltered. No play might be so good that his slapstick was not zealously poised to explode a torpedo of low comedy against its trouser seat; no play so bad that his syringe was not perched betimes to spray it with muscadine adjectives and cologned scaremarks. With the fine fervour of the believer in some holy cause, he has often stood far into the night before his mirror to compose his thumb at just the proper angle to his nose that his public in the morning might learn how to deprecate such a writer as Hauptmann or Shaw or Galsworthy. And with a fervour not less ardent, he has synchronously sweated, with the sweat of a Mozart transcribing allegri, over a dressing-room interview with some Casino houri that his public might appreciate exactly how much she loved her Spitz dog.[33]

The reference to Dale's *Familiar Chats With Queens of the Stage* notwithstanding, this is not merely an ad hominem blast. The occasion that called forth this attack on Dale was a positive review of Dale's play *The Madonna of the Future* (Nathan describes it as "intelligent, well-written, and dignified"). For in spite of their vociferousness, Nathan's remarks are not directed so much against Dale himself as against the "school" of criticism that he represents:

> apparent insensibility to the finer things of the American theatre, in view of the manner in which Mr. Dale has over this long period conducted himself, in view of his shave-parlour jocosity and yokel affectations of arbitership and considerable portion of even the humble West Forty-second Street audience at which his writings, and writings of a piece with his, are aimed, has been prone to regard him as one of the usual mirthless Andrews who, slightly to adapt Dr. Johnson, have taken up reviewing plays as a profession by which they may grow important and formidable at very small expense.[34]

The goal of Nathan's argument is to distance himself as much as possible from Dale. Nathan's major grievance against Dale is the older writer's attitude toward drama criticism. Dale seems to take himself seriously, not his criticism. This is the opposite of what Nathan felt critics ought to do.[35] In contrast to his latter-day antics, in the earlier part of his career Nathan strove to develop a position from which drama critics could comment seriously on the state of the American theater. He argued that as there was no decent American drama, there ought to be at least a viable American drama criticism. He made this pronouncement in the "Introduction and Apology" to *Another Book on the Theatre*. Nathan consciously placed himself on a different level from that of his predecessors. It was easy to detach himself from such scholarly-genteel Victorians such as William Winter and J. Ranken Towse, but his brashly confrontational and highly personal style made him superficially appear to be following Dale's lead. Ultimately, though as Dale had no consistent critical aims and put nothing of himself into his work, comparisons between the work of the two men are not really valid.

Accusations of frivolity dogged Nathan from the beginning of his career and have lingered since his death. Writing in *Puck* in October 1914, Nathan addressed the charges levied against him in an article entitled "On the Duty of a Critic."

> Managers, playwrights, and actors detonate with objection to what they designate the "clever school of dramatic criticism." . . . They want a school of dramatic criticism which by its own dullness, will, in comparison, celebrate *their* mediocrity. As a matter of fact, dramatic criticism, certainly here in New York, must be divertingly humorous, merry and witty. *Somebody's* got to supply the amusement for the theatre-going public.[36]

Thus, from the start of his career, we see the hackles raised by Nathan's attitude are of consistent elevation.

Nathan has never been accused of being genteel or of being any sort of puffer. He has been accused of being pedantic and pseudoscholarly (by Joshua Logan, Lehman Engel, and Robert Forsythe, among many others), but Nathan was most determinedly antiacademic throughout his career. He wrote with a long view of the theater and bruited his erudition whenever the opportunity arose, but he was by no means learned in his style. The eclectic nature of his approach was honed early and in a great variety of publications. Not only did Nathan's writing career coincide with a period of intense theatrical activity, it also began during a time when there were many opportunities available in magazine journalism. In the first decade of his career Nathan wrote for the New York *Herald* (1905–07), *The Bohemian* (1906–08), *The Century* (1907), *Munsey's Magazine* (1907–08), *Outing* (1908–10), *Harper's Weekly, The Burr MacIntosh Monthly* (1909–10), *McLure's* (1909–13), *The Smart Set* (1909–23), *Green Book Magazine, The Bookman,* the Associated Sunday Magazine Syndicate (1909–

14), *The Theatre* (1911–17), the National Newspaper Syndicate (1912–29), *Vanity Fair* (1914), and *Puck* (1914–16).

Except for the *Herald*, which was a daily newspaper, and the two newspaper syndicates, all of these were magazines. Each had its own style and particular audience. Nathan had to adapt his style to suit each periodical's individual editorial requisites. Reading through these journals reveals that this was no mean feat; the great differences among them clearly demonstrate that Nathan must have had to do some hard work to have his writing accepted by such a variety of publications. To take two examples: *Harper's Weekly* was a mass-market metropolitan magazine that highlighted news and feature stories, a precursor of *Time* and *Newsweek*, whereas *The Burr MacIntosh Monthly* was an exquisitely produced journal of extremely limited circulation. (There are at present no strictly analogous periodicals, although perhaps an amalgam of *Town and Country* and *Antiques* might come close.) It is characteristic of Nathan that he made light of the struggles involved in adapting his style to these varied publications.

To say that Nathan's glossing over of his struggles to achieve eminence as a critic is typical of his calculated insouciance is not to imply that Nathan had to endure a painful apprenticeship as a Grub Street drudge, even though, as indicated above, he did have to work hard to establish himself as a professional writer. Be that as it may, he was recognized as an important critic within two years of his beginning as a regular writer about the theater. In December of 1910, one year after he began appearing in it, *The Green Book* described him as "one of the best known and entertaining writers on theatrical topics in America."[37] By praising Nathan to its readers in this way, *The Green Book* was no doubt serving its own interests by making an appeal to its readers. The operative word in the notice is "entertaining" and it was by being entertaining that Nathan initially made his way. Four years later in a similar, if slightly hyperbolic vein, two months after he had begun writing for *Puck*, the magazine listed Nathan alongside Richard Le Gallienne, James Huneker, and Benjamin De Casseres on the title page of its October issue as being "among the writers and artists of international fame who are regular contributors." By 1917, Nathan himself was being written about. He was caricatured this way by John Held in *The Theatre's* November issue:

When you cross the path of George Jean Nathan, *The Smart Set's* funny play reviewer, be sure to wear a scathe-proof suit, for George is the world's champion standing broad scather. He is also, by his own unanimous choice, President of the Amalgamated Self-Haters of the Universe.[38]

Richard Lahey wrote of him in August of 1923:

> George Jean Nathan of *The Smart Set* is the snatch-your-coat-and-beat-it champion of the American theatre. He has never been known to stay for a third act of anything but German tragedies and Columbia burlesques. To peevish managers he explains that the first five minutes of any show lets him know all about it![39]

In 1924, Archie Bell penned an article for *The Theatre* entitled "The Most Hated Man in the Theatre: The Little Sunshine of the Great White Way and Nobody Loves Him but George" that ran in the November issue. The title alone clearly shows the impact of Nathan's critical stance. The article is not unusual and is a response to the celebrity status acquired by "the night watch." In the 1920s articles about critics and their habits became quite common, much more so than they had been in the previous decade. Nathan became as much a personality as any of the stars whose efforts he critically assessed. There are three large files in the Billy Rose Theatre collection devoted solely to news clippings about Nathan from the 1920s through the 1950s. Is there a contrast between the high-living darling of the gossip columnists and the icily detached aesthete? Certainly there is, but Nathan thrived on such paradoxes. Nathan's critical sangfroid appeared to be in constant conflict with the hot-blooded style in which he wrote and it is therefore essential to examine this conflict between style and substance in order to recognize the practical necessities Nathan had to contend with as a professional writer. For it is with these exigencies that the difficulty of assessing the nature of Nathan's authority lies. The journalistic nature of much of his work is particularly difficult to assess because Nathan frequently tried to create the impression that his writing style emerged Minerva-like from his own Jovian brow and that he went through no developmental phase. It can be argued that his highly individual style was apparent from his youth, but adapting that style to mass-market journals would be something of a problem for him. It is not particularly rewarding to analyze Nathan's style as it was embodied reflected in his earliest work in such publications as *Harper's Weekly*, *The Bookman*, or *Outing* because it does not bear any resemblance to his mature style. Nor is there any real transition period between them, as he was entirely dependent on the whims of his editors. One can read the articles published at the same time in different magazines and wonder at the disparities in style and tone. The *Bookman, Burr MacIntosh,* and *Smart Set* articles from 1909–10 are cases in point.

Nathan's earliest published writings are not devoted to drama criticism. He wrote travel features, book reviews, and even descriptions of sporting events. Indeed, from the very beginning of Nathan's magazine career at *Harper's Weekly,* a popular periodical, his work has the homogenized quality that suggests the strong editorial presence of George Harvey and his minions, Edward S. Martin and George Buchanan Fife. Nathan's work is so much of a piece with the other writing in *Harper's Weekly* that it is unrecognizable. In the numerous other magazines for which he wrote from 1906 through 1909, Nathan's work is not particularly notable other than as demonstrations of how adaptable he was as a writer. As his work fits into *Harper's Weekly,* so do articles that Nathan published in more fashionable journals fit into them. They do not differ markedly from the others in those publications; for example, an article entitled "The Greatest Non-Resident Clubs in The World" in the March 1909 issue of *McLure's* is stylistically indistinguishable from the articles that surround it.[40]

It is more significant that an article he wrote for *McLure's* four years later, in 1913, in collaboration with George M. Cohan is not discernibly different in style either. This was after he had become the drama critic for *The Smart Set* and established himself as a well-known journalist, so it clearly indicates that a guiding editorial hand influenced the finished material that *McLure's* published. This article, "The Mechanics of Emotion," was published in *McLure's* in November 1913.[41] It is a fascinating dissection of contemporary theatrical technique. Nathan praised Cohan throughout both of their careers, irrespective of the showman's popular standing. He was a great admirer of Cohan, consistently hailing him for his total understanding of the theater, and of the theater audience:

> George M. Cohan's talent as playwright is founded not upon an observation and understanding of human nature, but upon an observation and understanding of theatrical nature. He is concerned not with man as man, but with man as member of a theatre audience. Human nature, Mr. Cohan shrewdly realizes, ceases to be human nature to a considerable extent soon after handing its ticket to the doorman.[42]

Nathan especially admired Cohan for his complete lack of pretense. Nathan's comments on Cohan are consistent with his ideas

about the importance of artifice. This illustrates Nathan's insistence that the theatricality of drama is its most important element.
Nathan's appreciation of this aspect of drama always informs the
literary emphasis that his criticism seems to have.

The Century and The Bookman are two other widely circulated
magazines for which Nathan wrote features and theatre pieces.
In these high-quality publications, too, Nathan's style is indistinguishable from the writing that surrounds his work. An examination of Nathan's work in general-interest magazines through 1914
when he became coeditor of The Smart Set reveals not a trace of
Nathan's highly personal style. Conversely, the monthly theater
articles he composed for Green Book, Burr MacIntosh, and Puck
from 1909 through 1915 display Nathan's style in nearly full
flower. They are humorous, haughty, and highly personal.

It is clear, then, that Nathan's style was subsumed by the house
style of the particular journal when he was writing articles about
subjects for which he cared little. In other instances, indifferent
editors reworked his writing so that it conformed to their publications' journalistic norms. Nearly half a century later, Nathan recalled the wiles he employed to get into print:

> I found myself commissioned as a writer on the theatre for Outing
> . . . just what a periodical devoted to sports and the wide, open spaces,
> was going to do with pieces about the theatre, I could not figure
> out. . . . I concocted a series of articles on the outdoor life of several
> actors of the period. Since none of them that I could discover had
> any outdoor life other than that involved in going from their hotels to
> the theatre and back again, I simply gathered together all the "stills" I
> could lay hands on which showed them in al fresco scenes from the
> plays in which they had appeared . . . and shamelessly offered the
> photographs as the real thing. Since there were no complaints from
> the readers, it looked as if sportsmen never went to the theatre.[43]

The examples cited above fall within the years of Nathan's earliest association with The Smart Set, 1908 through 1914. In his posthumously published memoirs, just about the only straightforward
praise Mencken gives Nathan is to salute his industry as a free-
lancer. He reports that Nathan earned an average of one hundred
dollars a week in this way. Were it not for the existence of a curious
piece of Nathanian juvenilia, there would be little to indicate that
Nathan developed his style on his own. This is a point of contention because of critic Burton Rascoe's assertions in his "Smart Set
History," that Smart Set editor Willard Huntington Wright was
the most significant force in molding Nathan as a writer. Burton

Rascoe claims that Wright was, in fact, chiefly responsible for shaping Nathan's style of writing. Rascoe was a colleague, friend, and sometime literary rival of Nathan, so he is not writing with any detachment when he details Nathan's *Smart Set* career in "*Smart Set* History." Moreover, he had a serious falling-out with Nathan's coeditor, H. L. Mencken, and in his text it is quite clear that he is determined to build up Wright at the expense of Wright's editorial successors at the magazine—namely, George Jean Nathan and H. L. Mencken.[44] Moreover, Wright had started working on a travel book (*Europe After 8:15*) with Nathan and Mencken prior to taking over as editor of *The Smart Set*. There is little discernible stylistic difference among the chapters (Nathan wrote the ones on Berlin and Paris). Rascoe's assertions that Nathan did not come into his own before he worked with Wright can be refuted if we consider his work in *The Green Book* or *Puck*, to name but two magazines. There is, however, evidence that Nathan's writing style asserted itself even earlier—when he was sixteen years old.

The piece in question is entitled "Love: A Scientific Analysis," and although it is pure pubescent piffle—to employ a Nathanesque construction—there is much in it that suggests the humorous and world-weary style Nathan would later use in his reviews and essays. Isaac Goldberg reprints this "juvenile burlesque" in his study of Nathan. Letters in the Isaac Goldberg collection at the New York Public Library verify its composition. They are letters from Nathan giving Goldberg permission to go through various papers that Nathan's mother had given him from the family's Indiana days, within which trove was "Love: A Scientific Analysis."

It is vintage Nathan at the tender age of sixteen. He uses the names Mr. Beauchamp Kraus and Miss Bermuda Dampjofer (253) for his prospective lovers. The sentences are peppered with arcane locutions and words in foreign languages, slang is mixed with scholarly diction, and there are fraudulent footnotes and references to such pseudoacademic delicatessen as "Professor Hugo Disback's 'Essay on the Intelligence of the Dachsund'" (255) and "Dr. P. P. Gambrinus of Tusculum College," identifier of the "extraordinary condition of *Flora sendis*" (256). This "essay" more than lives up to its epithet, but more important than these laborious attempts at humor are the lists of examples of evidence that Nathan includes in his "analysis."[45]

In *The Smart Set's* "Repetition Generale" and later in *The American Mercury's* "Clinical Notes," Nathan would catalogue American foibles, thereby ridiculing the all-American "booboisie" that both he and Mencken abominated. In 1927, Nathan compiled *The New American Credo,* an inventory of nonsense and buncombe inspired by his earlier work with Mencken. More important are the lists of dramatic situations made to demonstrate a point that were a Nathan stand-by. Indeed, one of his books, *Since Ibsen* (1933), is a "statistical historical outline of the popular theatre since 1900." It consists of one hundred and sixty-three pages of examples of dramatic situations drawn from contemporary plays.

*Since Ibsen* is a tongue-in-cheek text, but Nathan was able to use his catalogue technique for more serious purposes elsewhere. One such instance occurs in a 1935 essay reprinted in *Passing Judgments.* Nathan lists eighteen comic bits from Noël Coward's *Design for Living* that were lifted bodily from old vaudeville routines such as those of, among others, Mae West, Fanchon and Marco, Tony Pastor, the Billy Watson "Beef Trust" Show of 1907, and *The Girl With the Whooping Cough,* a cheapjack farce from 1909. He conclusively demonstrates that Coward has merely substituted evening clothes for baggy pants.[46]

Let us return to the question of Willard H. Wright's influence on Nathan's development as a writer. Nathan began writing for *The Smart Set* in October 1909; Wright edited twelve issues of the magazine from March 1913 through February 1914 and collaborated on a travel book with Mencken and Nathan that was published in 1914. The consonance of style of Nathan's and Mencken's writing is well known, but *Europe After 8:15* was not the only work coauthored by Wright, Mencken, and Nathan. The three created the pseudonymous "Owen Hatteras" for a variety of endeavors in *The Smart Set.* After Wright's departure from the magazine, Mencken and Nathan would be the subject of *Pistols for Two,* a biography penned by "Hatteras." From the close collaboration among these three writers, it seems quite clear that each had a unique voice and furthered equally the careers of the others.

In 1962, twenty-eight years after Rascoe's *"Smart Set* History" appeared, M. K. Singleton's *H. L. Mencken and the American Mercury Adventure* added further confusion to this issue. Singleton draws another comparison between Wright's and Nathan's work, although in a somewhat misleading fashion. He selectively quotes from Charles Angoff's introduction to *The World of George Jean Nathan* and indicates that the "dialectical" nature of Nathan's *The Critic and the Drama* is "comparable to Willard Huntington Wright's *The Creative Will: Studies in the Philosophy and Syntax of*

*Aesthetics.*"[47] But Angoff was not referring specifically to one book by Nathan when he wrote:

> George Jean Nathan cannot properly be fitted into any critical or philosophical school. On occasion he practices the critical impressionism of Huneker, but he can also be profoundly dialectical, as can readily be seen by examining *The Critic and the Drama,* first published thirty years ago [Angoff was writing in 1952] and still one of the most searching works of modern dramatic criticism in English.[48]

Angoff praises Nathan's *Critic and the Drama* rather extravagantly and inaccurately. Nathan would surely have scoffed at the notion of a "dialectical profundity" in his work. Wright, on the other hand, fancied himself an American Nietzsche. And it is difficult to assess Wright's prose style because it is so similar to Mencken's. This difficulty makes Rascoe's aforementioned argument all the more unpalatable. And although Rascoe tries very hard to demonstrate that the barely postadolescent Wright exerted a profound influence on Nathan, his editorial reach far exceeds his historical grasp,[49] For if one examines Wright's body of work— with the exception of his pseudonymous work as S. S. Van Dine— one learns that for all of his erudition and ambition, he was unable to maintain any consistent standards of literary or editorial performance. Wright's decline as a serious writer was swift after he left *The Smart Set,* and it is quite clear that even though he was an interesting, even fascinating character as far as American magazine editing and detective fiction go (as John Loughery's recent biography of him shows), Wright is, at the most, an important encourager and colleague of Nathan, Mencken, and others, and little more.

Singleton's argument about Wright's influence on Nathan tries to demonstrate that Nathan was a critic to whom "theory was interesting but by and large superfluous."[50] There is an ambivalent tone in Singleton's entire assessment of Nathan; on the one hand he disparages his attempts to adapt his criticism to the demands of a mass audience in the widely circulated *American Mercury,* and on the other he maintains that "Nathan's judgments have held up to a considerable degree."[51]

Singleton's evaluation, written in the decade after the critic's death, is contemporaneous with the description of Nathan in the article by Gordon Rogoff, "Modern Dramatic Criticism," in *The Reader's Encyclopedia of World Drama.* Rogoff echoes Singleton when he describes Nathan as the "first [American] critic of any influence, if not stature" and virtually dismisses him as a "clever journalist" who knew next to nothing about acting. Rogoff goes on to make great claims for *The New Republic* critics, Stark Young, Eric Bentley, and Robert Brustein.[52] Rogoff's displeasure with Nathan is of a piece with the academic backlash against Nathan, which Nathan undoubtedly set himself up for. Throughout his career, he routinely chided academe. In this regard, Nathan reflected the antiacademic tenor of his own intellectual generation. Nathan was particularly scornful of professors such as Brander Matthews, Clayton Hamilton, and Walter Prichard Eaton who wrote dramatic criticism. He also dismissed the revered George Pierce Baker as an overrated hackmonger.[53] Nathan was surely reacting to the commercial theater's anointing of Baker. He was also vehemently opposed to academic approaches to theater and to criticism. Thus, it ought not be surprising that it is difficult to secure balanced assessments of Nathan.

As we have seen, the attempts to attribute to others the formation of his tastes and methods and to discredit Nathan himself are not useful. Wright's importance to *The Smart Set* can be readily admitted, but to credit him with influencing Nathan's development as a writer is a dubious attribution. One could more easily stress Nathan's (and especially Mencken's) influence on Wright. And the surviving text of Nathan's "Love: A Scientific Analysis," written when he was sixteen, demonstrates remarkably the early development of Nathan's individual style. It is all the more interesting in that he was able to adapt his style at will almost from the start of his career. It is most likely, though, that his chameleon stylistic efforts were a direct result of his decision to support himself via freelance work at the beginning of his career. Nathan's father died in 1904, and apparently his family's money was controlled by a trust fund which Nathan did not have access to until after his mother's death,[54] So through the 1910s and 1920s Nathan had to earn his living.

Another example of the singularity of his style is revealed by the efforts of the editor of the magazine *College Humor* who, in a letter of 16 May 1928, solicited some of his turn-of-the-century prose for a retrospective issue. Toward the end of Nathan's life, the staff of *The Widow*, the Cornell humor magazine of which he had been an editor, asked permission to republish some of his material in its fiftieth anniversary issue. Their letter of 20 January 1950 shows that the current editor wanted to showcase the publication's most famous alumnus. Both of these solicitations demonstrate that Nathan's earliest writing continued to attract interest.

In the light of such evidence, it seems more reasonable to assert that, at *The Smart Set*, Wright simply allowed Nathan to write as he pleased. After all, Wright was six years younger than Nathan and was completely new to the magazine, whereas Nathan had been a staff member there for four years. And it seems clear that the lack of personal tint in Nathan's early professional writing lies with the editorial procedures of the publications he worked for.

Tracing Nathan's path to *The Smart Set* gives us some perspective on the process of drama criticism (a process that has been virtually ignored, even by journalism texts)—the way in which drama critics create their reviews and the pressures put upon them by editors or publishers and, in some instances, producers or other theater personnel to alter the presentation of their perceptions. Richard H. Palmer's 1988 study, *The Critics' Canon*, addresses this issue in contemporary terms; it is intended to "explain the ways of theatre critics to theatre practitioners," but Palmer's work does not provide any historical perspective.[55]

Nathan got his first newspaper job through the influence of two of his uncles, Charles Frederic Nirdlinger and Samuel F. Nixon. A graduate of Harvard, Nirdlinger had been a foreign correspondent and the drama critic for the *Herald* and was also a friend of the paper's owner, James Gordon Bennett. Nixon, owner of a chain of theaters based in Philadelphia, was a friend of the *Herald*'s managing editor, William C. Reick. Once hired, however, Nathan was on his own. He was assigned to general reporting duties and it was not until near the end of his tenure at the *Herald* that he was allowed to cover the theater. Writing about something that actually interested him revealed clearly to him the general tawdriness of the *Herald*. He was continually cautioned against writing unfavorable reviews, as the entire paper conducted its affairs for the benefit of its advertisers rather than with any concern for veracity or taste. Nathan recalled that "there was a minimum of honesty in dramatic reviewing on the *Herald* in those days. The theatrical syndicate controlled absolutely the dramatic policy of the paper."[56] It is ironic that Nathan's uncle, Nixon, was one of the original partners in the theatrical syndicate. The syndicate would indirectly and directly influence the course of Nathan's career for the next few years. He would leave the *Herald* by his own choice; he would be fired from his position at *Puck* in 1916 because of his refusal to write favorable reviews for syndicate-sponsored shows, regardless of their quality, or to do puff pieces about syndicate stars. Strangely, Nathan seems to have held no grudge against the Syndicate.

He had not been fired from the New York *Herald,* but he probably would not have been retained there much longer anyway. Because of his unwillingness to suit his writing style to the editorial policies of its famous owner, James Gordon Bennett, Nathan's career as a newspaperman was a brief one. He described the house policy thus: "There were so many Don'ts editorially that it would have taken a vaudeville mind-reader to remember them in composing an article."[57] Nathan discovered that he could not function as a writer for daily newspapers and soon learned that the monthly magazine was the best venue for his criticism.

When the time came for him to leave the *Herald,* once again personal contact was to stand Nathan in good stead. He was asked by Lynn G. Wright, an old Cornell friend with whom he had edited the *Sun,* the college's daily newspaper, to serve as drama critic for *The Bohemian* and to contribute features to *Outing.* Lynn Wright was on the staff of the *Outing* Publishing Company that put out the two magazines. All of Nathan's previous commentators describe him as being a drama critic for *Outing* from 1906 to 1908, but a perusal of that magazine reveals nothing with Nathan's byline until 1908. Moreover, during that time he wrote only one article for *Outing* that has anything to do with the theatre. Entitled "The Physical Demands of the Stage," it appears in the April 1909 issue, pages 49–60. It details the various ways in which performers keep fit, and it is, of course, something of a hoax, being the article in which Nathan presented bucolic stills from stage productions and passed them off as authentic outdoor moments in the lives of the stars. *Outing* and *The Bohemian* are sometimes identified as "little magazines," but this is not the case. *Outing* was a magazine that focused almost exclusively on outdoor recreation; it had a circulation of over 100,000 and was a favorite of gentlemen sportsmen during the years Nathan contributed to it. It was the *Sports Illustrated* of its day.

*The Bohemian* had originally been a "little magazine" but it had been bought by the publishers of *Outing* and made into a general magazine by the time Nathan came to write for it. *The Bohemian* was a periodical similar in format to *Munsey's Magazine,* another general-interest journal for which Nathan wrote. It featured fiction and articles about celebrities, the theater, and travel, including a series about the dangers confronting unwitting white women who dared visit New York's Chinatown after dark.

Searching for Nathan's early drama criticism is difficult, especially if we attempt to follow the "chronology" Charles Angoff compiled for his anthology of Nathan's writings in 1952. Everyone

who has written about Nathan since then has taken its reliability
for granted, even though Angoff offers no citations for it, and
even a cursory search through the *Reader's Guide to Periodical Literature* reveals that his chronology is rather flawed. Nor does it
appear that he consulted Goldberg's or Frick's studies which mention several magazines that are absent from his chronology, including *The Bookman* (contributor, 1909–14), *Century* (drama
critic, 1907), and *McLure's* (contributor 1909–13), three widely
read and respected magazines. In any event, most of the writing
he did before 1909 was not drama criticism. A review of the articles he wrote during these years reveals that Nathan spent his
years as an apprentice professional writing about a variety of subjects. In 1909 he wrote an article analyzing the functions of the
Department of the Interior for *Munsey's* magazine. As late as 1916
he would write a series of detective stories for *The American Sunday
Monthly Magazine* in collaboration with police detective William
J. Burns.

It is this journalistic beginning that haunts Nathan the drama
critic. Having spent his first years writing on order for various
editors of general-interest magazines, he developed the ability to
create essays and feature stories even if he had no interest in the
subject matter. Later, when he came into his own as a critic, he
had to write for an audience largely outside metropolitan New
York who would most likely not have seen the productions about
which he was writing. He would concentrate on being entertaining in order to hold his audience. After all, Nathan had come to
write about the theatre not from any particular training in it, but
simply out of a desire to write about it. He would later, in 1923,
describe his reasons for turning exclusively to the theater:

The theatre, as I look at it, is one of the best subjects in the world
from which to fashion a variegated assortment of predicates. It is
almost impossible for the writer on politics to use politics as a hook
whereon to hang his opinions, say, of music or cow diseases. The same
thing holds true of writers on music itself, or painting, or architecture
or sports or science, or archaeology, or economics, religion, or almost
anything else save books. The theatre, to the contrary, by the very
nature of its diverse constituent elements and its peculiar ramifica-
tions offers to the man who writes about it a hundred convenient
opportunities to write con sardini on nearly everything under the
sun, and what a writer craves are such opportunities. What is more,
these digressions from the main theme are not, in dramatic and theatrical criticism, so patently or objectionably out of key as they would
be in other forms of critical exposition . . . I see no reason why objec-

tion should be made to me for using a single line of a play by Mr.
Samuel Shipman to work off my opinion of unipolar induction, sexual
hygiene, the political situation in central Siam, or anything else.[59]

What emerges from Nathan's self-analysis is that his first priority
seems to be the art of writing, rather than any sense of aesthetic
mission or ordination. Implicit in his explanation, though, is his
attitude that the theater is the most interesting of the arts because
it most directly influences the emotions and yet requires intellectual explication and criticism. The phrase "intelligent emotionalism" recurs in his work from his first use of it in *The Critic and
the Drama* in 1922.

Nathan's description of the wide spectrum of topics available
for the theatre critic to write about while he dissects a play indicates most clearly his roots as a journalist. He does not regard
the theater as something that exists in isolation but as something
that is to be discussed as a part of society. Nathan gained an
unfortunate notoriety for his aloofness and for stating that his
motto was "be indifferent," but in actuality, for all of his grandiose
posturings, he is very much concerned with the realities of life as
reflected in the theater. By this I do not mean that Zola-esque
naturalism was his ideal (he disliked most of Eugene Brieux's
work); rather, that he demanded that plays be honest and, more
particularly, that they be honestly presented and free from pretense on the part of producers or performers.

Furthermore, Nathan's consideration of his national—as opposed to metropolitan—audience caused him to shape the articulation of his views in this way. So there is more to Nathan's use of
humor in his theater reviews than the notion that he had to spice
up his commentary in order to make the theater section of the
magazine attractive to *Mercury* readers nationwide,[60] for there is
more than laff-larding behind Nathan's methods of appealing to
his audience. During his *Smart Set* years, Nathan was a national
figure, alongside Mencken. Both men were humorists as well as
editors and critics. Humor is not ancillary to Nathan's style, it is
central to it.

Another device that surely attracted his readers' attention was
Nathan's dictum: "Be indifferent." Nathan both inspired and responded to contemporary sensibilities. After all, the 1924 Knopf
advertising copy for his books decreed he was a man to know,
"especially for the rising generation." As for Nathan's relation to
the flappers and their escorts, one need only recall the "nonchalance" that Murad cigarette advertising bruited for confirmation

of Nathan's cultivated credo. He wanted to be read, and he knew how to write about the theater and himself at the same time. Nathan's unabashed personalizing of his reviews gave theater criticism an intensity it had lacked before. Clearly, this is what his audience wanted—not that Nathan pandered to a mass readership. He is representative of his era; columnists of every sort crowded the newspapers and magazines of the 1920s. The byline personalized journalism as never before. For his part, though, Nathan perfected a complex balancing act. While writing prose that sometimes overheated, he projected a coolly detached persona. He was successful and true to his own aesthetic code at the same time. Whether he was "true to himself" is irrelevant.

Through the close of the first part of Nathan's career, circa 1930, when he left the *Mercury* and parted professionally with Mencken, he is set on a critical path that marks his criticism as at once practical, even as it is impressionistic. By "practical" I mean that Nathan's appraisals were based upon the plays as he found them in the commercial Broadway theatre. This is one reason Nathan is historically interesting: his almost exclusive concern with the Broadway theater is from our *fin de siècle* perspective, is archaeological. We no longer regard this limited aspect, even of the New York theater, as the sole venue for the American theater. In this sense there is an unconscious economic bias to consider in Nathan's critical emphases. And to examine the basis of his critical reach is to study the rise and fall of the Broadway theater as the proving ground of the American theater.

At this point a brief return to the very beginning of Nathan's career as a drama critic will reveal the sort of difficulties with which he had to contend from the outset of his career. Before Nathan could use the theater as a sounding board, he had to experience directly the vagaries of daily journalism's internal and external pressures. Recalling that he had worked on the staff of the New York *Herald* for a year before he was "drafted by the drama department to serve as a fourth-string reviewer," on the evening of 29 January 1906, Nathan reminisces in *The Theatre Book of the Year 1950–1951:*

in those days there were sometimes three or four, indeed even five or six, openings on a single evening. On my return to the office, Thomas White, chief of the department, asked me, before I sat down to confect my review of the show [*Bedford's Hope*], what my opinion on it was. I replied that it seemed to me to be an excellent melodrama of the blood-and-thunder species and that the audience had stood up and cheered it. White received the news with a superior and pitying smile. "Young man," he said "no such melodrama can possibly be as good as you say, consequently don't say so in your notice." I said it nevertheless to the extent of some eight hundred words which, when they appeared in print the next morning, were not only cut down to about a hundred but drastically edited.

While White was nominally the *Herald*'s first-line drama critic, the factual first-stringer at the time was John Logan and I inquired of him if what happened to my copy was a common procedure on the paper. "Always remember," he whimsically replied, "that the *Herald* is a very fashionable paper and nothing that takes place below Twenty-third Street can ever be much good."[61]

(Nathan's memory fails him here. There is no such review of *Bedford's Hope* in the *Herald* during that week. The show opened on 16 January.) As the location of the performance of *Bedford's Hope*, the play he claimed to have reviewed, was the Fourteenth Street Theatre, a comment he made two decades later in the *American Mercury* of May 1926 is quite interesting. He attacked the self-consciously avant-garde theaters who believed that "everything south of Fourteenth Street is drama; everything north of Fourteenth Street is not."

From the beginning of his career to the end, Nathan was resistant to any sort of "fashionable" dramatic trends or editorial pressures. Even though he adjudicated from a distinctly elevated Broadway perch and was friendly with producers such as Charles Frohman and Arthur Hopkins, ten years after the onset of his magazine career, he ran into trouble with the Theatrical Syndicate. Nathan did not oppose the Syndicate because of their business practices; indeed, he made no specific charges against any theatrical producers (Hollywood producers were quite another matter) so much as he attacked particular plays. Nathan's memory, usually cited as prodigious (by Lillian Gish, Harold Clurman, Charles Angoff, H. L. Mencken, and many others), seems conveniently to have been blurred when in 1921, in *The Theatre, The Drama, The Girls*, he wrote that "no theatrical manager has ever swindled me."[62] Only six years earlier, he had been denied complimentary theater tickets by Klaw and Erlanger. A letter in the Cornell collection from J. Clarence Hyde, "general representative to Messrs. Klaw and Erlanger," dated 1 March 1916, reads in part:

I have received your letter of even date. In reply I would say that your name does not appear upon the Klaw and Erlanger first or second night complimentary lists. Klaw and Erlanger simply do not consider you in the nature of a guest. If you wish to buy tickets for their theatres, that is your privilege. My reply to the second question in your letter is that Klaw and Erlanger do not maintain what you style a "black-list."[63]

This letter, combined with the fact that Nathan was fired from *Puck* in the same year because of his negative reviews, clearly indicates that Nathan was no friend of the Syndicate. Erlanger, a friend of Nathan Straus Jr., *Puck's* owner, prevailed upon Straus to fire Nathan. In addition, Erlanger was able to persuade the Philadelphia *North American* and the Cleveland *Leader* to stop carrying Nathan's syndicated weekly letter on the drama that they had been running since 1912. Nathan was not the first critic to lose his job because of theatrical managers. In 1909, the venerable, if senescent, William Winter had been hounded from the New York *Tribune* after the newspaper's managing editor, Roscoe Brown, complained that his reviews "did injury 'to some of our advertisers.'"[64] What is interesting about Nathan's difficulties in 1916 is that they took place almost exactly one year after the celebrated fracas between Alexander Woollcott and the Shuberts had broken out.

In the *Times* of 17 March 1915, Woollcott wrote a mixed review of the Shuberts' show *Taking Chances*, saying that overall it was "not vastly amusing." Two lawsuits later found Woollcott himself barred from all Shubert theaters. New York State's highest tribunal, the Court of Appeals, ruled on 22 February 1916 that it was the Shuberts' right to prevent anyone from entering their playhouses, provided that they were not doing so based upon reasons of "race, creed or color."[65] Woollcott's career was helped immeasurably by the incident. The *Times* gave him a byline and he became a celebrity in his own right.

The Shuberts were notorious for banning critics. They banned Acton Davies of the *Sun* in 1914, but he obviously did not take this personally, as he promptly went to work for them. Through the years Percy Hammond, George S. Kaufman and, of course, Walter Winchell were kept out of Shubert theaters. Winchell quipped that since he'd been barred from Shubert openings he would wait three nights and go to their closings. As was the case with Woollcott, Winchell became better known and more widely read after his battle with the Shuberts. In 1928, the Marx brothers' *Animal Crackers* featured a character based on Winchell. The columnist conspired with the Marx brothers to break through the security net the Shuberts had set up. Winchell was smuggled into the theater heavily disguised (including a hump on his back). Once backstage, he was made up like Harpo, and he watched the show from the wings. Such an episode demonstrates that in the war between producers and the press, the critics will always win.

Nonetheless, the Shuberts were only following the example set by the Syndicate. In 1905, Alan Dale was prohibited from entering any syndicate-controlled houses. The Syndicate also pulled all of its advertising out of Hearst newspapers. Dale's experience was not a career boost. It is likely that his editor, Arthur Brisbane, the most pompous figure in the history of American journalism, coerced Dale into appeasing the Syndicate. By 1909 Dale's style had changed and Syndicate advertising returned to Hearst papers.[66] In 1916, Klaw and Erlanger were no longer theatrically dominant, but they remained prominent in New York theatre. Within a month of the ruling by the Court of Appeals, they took the opportunity of the Shuberts' victory over Woollcott to put pressure on Nathan. They could not completely silence him, though, as he was then coeditor of *The Smart Set*. As the Dale episode shows, newspaper critics were entirely subject to their editors, but by 1916 Nathan had established himself as one of the foremost critics on Broadway. Within ten years, Knopf advertisements would claim that he was the most widely read and frequently translated critic in the world.

Nathan had begun his ascent to the crest at the high tide of magazine publication in America. Magazines flourished in the years between 1890 and 1914 because of technological advances. Linotype machines, half-tone engraving, and the development of high-speed printing machinery enabled more publications to reach more readers at a faster rate and at a lower price than ever before. At the turn of the century, the amount of advertising increased tremendously, providing a new source of revenue as well as a source of pressure for periodicals. As competition among journals became fiercer, the need to attract readers forced editors and publishers to resort to novel ways of securing readership.

Eltinge Warner, owner of *The Smart Set*, would provide Nathan with his best critical venue. Warner's magazine, published "for minds that were not primitive," rode the wave of the periodical publishing boom from 1900 until 1930. From its pages would come the essays, later published in Nathan's first books, that would so excite Gordon Craig and Bernard Shaw. Here Nathan would be able to make dramatic criticism a thing in itself, as his contemporary Randolph Bourne would do with American literary and social criticism. H. L. Mencken's preeminence as a critic remains

well known and controversial, so there is no need to elaborate
on his contemporary influence. Now almost forgotten, Bourne
insisted that an "impossibilist élan" must infuse criticism, elevating
it beyond "reviewing," even beyond "commentary." The critic must
employ the most exacting standards, standards demanded by
criticism itself, not by the art form being scrutinized. Thus, the
critic becomes a vital, if not essential, part of the community. Nathan clearly possessed the élan elucidated by Bourne. Bourne
reached maturity well before the 1920s, as did Nathan and Mencken; it is unfortunate that the ballyhoo attendant upon the Lost
Generation has obscured Bourne, Nathan, and Mencken's prewar
assault on the genteel tradition.

At the time Nathan came to write for *The Smart Set* it aimed to
stake out a readership based on the individual personalities of its
writers. Critic and magazine were perfectly suited for one another. And an examination of Nathan's *Smart Set* years will enable
us to proceed into the next phase of his career.

**Nathan and Mencken at the outset of their collaboration circa 1909 (from the George Jean Nathan Papers, courtesy of Cornell University Library).**

An Underwood and Underwood Studio photograph of Nathan from the early 1920s (from the Louis Sheaffer Papers, courtesy of Connecticut College Library).

**Nathan and Mencken photographed by Irving Penn in 1947 during their widely publicized reunion (from the George Jean Nathan Papers, courtesy of Cornell University Library).**

Here is a rare view of the private Nathan, in a photograph possibly taken by Eugene O'Neill, when he visited the playwright at Château du Plessis with Lillian Gish in 1929. Carlotta Monterey O'Neill is on the right (from the Eugene O'Neill Papers, courtesy of Yale University).

O'Neill, Gish, Nathan and the O'Neills' dog "Blemie" (from the Eugene O'Neill Papers, courtesy of Yale University). The O'Neills considered Nathan the dog's "uncle."

**Nathan and Lillian Gish at Château du Plessis in 1929. "Blemie" is at the left (from the Eugene O'Neill Papers, courtesy of Yale University).**

Nathan with actress Anna May Wong in a Carl Van Vechten photograph, probably taken in 1939. This glamorous glimpse is a perfect example of how Nathan wanted himself perceived (from the Carl Van Vechten Papers, courtesy of Yale University).

# 3

# Nathan in the Critical Arena: The Criticism of Criticism

ONCE NATHAN HAD ACHIEVED A POSITION AS A PROFESSIONAL writer from which he could offer criticism and commentary according to the dictates of his own sensibilities and aesthetic whims, he regularly began to take issue with other drama critics. From *The Smart Set*'s pages he attacked critics for their shoddiness of style, for theatrical boosterism and, most of all, for doing what he perceived to be disservices to the art of criticism. Any writer who did not demand the most from the theater and who did not recognize that his or her first duty was to dramatic criticism itself was liable to be taken to task by Nathan. Nathan is usually recognized for the support and enthusiasm he showed for playwrights—Eugene O'Neill, Sean O'Casey, William Saroyan, and Paul Vincent Carroll—but he has not been adequately acknowledged for his services to drama criticism itself. Only his fellow drama critic, Elliot Norton, has tried to give him his due:

> Nathan himself, while hitting out ferociously at playwrights, actors and producers whom he considered incompetent or fraudulent, had been doing a good deal to improve the quality of drama criticism by taking it seriously and by formulating its function in one essay after another. He had also hammered at the inadequacies of his colleagues.[1]

There will never be a theatre named for him, but it is most fitting that the highest award an America drama critic may receive is the George Jean Nathan Award, the terms of which Nathan established in his will. It is awarded annually to a drama critic whose writing serves both the art of the theater and the art of criticism. Even though many actors, designers, and directors had a pronounced antipathy to Nathan, there was never any doubt that he loved the theater. He may not have always liked much about whom and what he saw in it, but no one ever accused him of attempting

81

to destroy the theater as an institution, an accusation all too frequently, if carelessly, made against many drama critics today. Of
course, in Nathan's day the theatre was still viable. The sensitivity
of the theater community today is entirely understandable given
the theatre's vulnerability.

When Nathan became coeditor of *The Smart Set* in 1914, he was
able to define the role of the drama critic and discuss in a significant way what the function of a drama critic should be. Nathan
was able to offer his thoughts on the function of drama criticism
and of drama critics in the late summer numbers of *The Smart
Set,* when the New York theaters were closed. Nathan did not limit
his dramaturgical fulminations to the summer and fall issues,
however, as it was his wont to intersperse his random thoughts on
dramatic criticism whenever and wherever he saw fit. During
these years he developed much more confidence and became increasingly disputatious. In so doing, he was instrumental in setting
in motion the critical currents of the time and, in effect, fighting
for what he believed American drama ought to represent and
doing what an American drama critic ought to do.

*The Smart Set* was, by all accounts, a unique periodical. It was
an offshoot of a high-society scandal sheet called *Town Topics*
owned by a Colonel William D'Alton Mann and it was never quite
able to free itself from a disreputable aura. Mann was rumored
to supplement his magazine revenues with fees secured via black-
mail. The story went that he would obtain damaging information
about society figures and threaten to publish it unless he was paid
off. As his magazines were written almost entirely by those members of New York's "four hundred" with literary ambitions, no
one doubted Mann's access to information. Such allegations were
never proven; nevertheless, the effluvium of scandal lingered over
*The Smart Set* until it folded.

The format and advertising of the magazine added to its overall
tawdriness. Notices for patent medicines were prominent features
of *The Smart Set*'s advertising copy, and such things as "stomach
reducers" and "healing tobaccos" were peddled with gusto in its
pages. Its cover featured a depiction of a sneering devil and bore
such slogans as "The Aristocrat Among Magazines," "For Minds
That are Not Primitive," "A Magazine of Cleverness," and "The
Only Magazine with a European Air." Irrespective of any *Smart
Set* authorial pretensions of deathlessness, the magazine itself has
almost literally disappeared, save for those volumes preserved in
microfilm collections. It was printed on the cheapest grade of
paper. As a result of its paper's excessively high wood pulp content

the periodical files of *The Smart Set* have almost completely deteriorated. It is one of the scarcest of all magazines.

*The Smart Set*'s reputation as a roguish, voguish publication could not overcome the fact that its table of contents usually featured writing by some of the most forward-thinking and artistically adventurous writers in the United States and Europe; James Joyce, Joseph Conrad, Willa Cather, Leonid Andreyev, Theodore Dreiser, and Edna St. Vincent Millay were among the authors who appeared in *The Smart Set* during Nathan's time there. Mencken complained that advertisers falsely believed that *The Smart Set* was exclusively a fiction magazine. Prestigious firms shied away from such journals, so Mencken and Nathan's most impressive, regular advertising account was Bromo-Seltzer. *The Smart Set*'s downmarket advertising must have been a source of ironic laughter for its self-consciously chic readers. Edmund Wilson, writing toward the end of his life after an intervening half-century of extremely distinguished literary achievement, recalled the impact of *The Smart Set* on his own intellectual development:

> In the spring of 1912, just before graduating from prep school, I somehow happened to pick up a copy of *The Smart Set*, a trashy-looking monthly, and was astonished to find audacious and extremely amusing critical articles by men named Mencken and Nathan, of whom I had never heard. I continued to read *The Smart Set* through college, at first with a slight feeling of guilt, for it was making fun of everything respectable in current American drama and literature.[2]

*The Smart Set* was the perfect forum for Nathan because its primary focus was "beautiful letters," as Mencken put it. A journal that published fiction, verse, drama, satire, and critical articles, it was commonly assumed that *The Smart Set* actively solicited material from authors whose work had been rejected by every other American periodical.[3] Indeed, the entire magazine was a sort of commentary, as the editorial choices that Nathan and Mencken made were deliberately undertaken to send groundswells through the mainstream of American culture. The efficacy of Nathan and Mencken's editorial policy is verified by a 1923 observer who felt that its "success was all too complete," due to the "*Smart Set* vernacular, with all its assumptions," being "utilized (without acknowledgment) by half the critical writers of the country."[4]

During much of the time he wrote for *The Smart Set*, Nathan's reviews were also being published in two other monthly magazines, *Judge* (1912–19) and *The Bookman* (1909–14). He also appeared in *Puck* (1914–16), the Associated Sunday Magazines

(1909–14), and through the National Newspaper Syndicate (1912–29) by the week. It is important to keep this in mind in light of some of the difficulties various commentators have assumed that Nathan had. They argue that he had to devise ways in which he could make his reviews interesting and worthwhile for readers after the fact of a show's opening or closing.

As for Nathan, once he was coeditor, he could at last write and publish as he pleased. Writing in a monthly enabled him to make his own way through the theatrical season in such a way as to render the immediacy of his opinions less important than the way he presented them. No doubt the fact that he was himself in a position to be a dramatic and literary arbiter, through the choices he made of authors for his magazine, added to the weight of his authority. Nathan published dramatic work not only by Eugene O'Neill but also plays by S. N. Behrman, Djuna Barnes, F. Scott Fitzgerald, Max Bodenheim, Ben Hecht, and James Branch Cabell, among many others. Nathan was continuing what had been a normal feature of the magazine, a one-act play in each issue, but the fact that *The Smart Set* remained a place of publication for playwrights made Nathan more than simply a retailer of his own opinions. Through the publication of plays he could show the world the sort of drama he thought was good.

In his *Smart Set* history Carl Dolmetsch details the annual schedule that Nathan followed through the year: November through May, feature articles that were reviews of current productions; June, a recapitulation of the entire season; July and August, discussions of European theatre; and September and October, essays on drama criticism and the theater in general.[5] Dolmetsch's purpose in summarizing Nathan's publishing agenda is part of a larger attempt on his part to somehow justify Nathan's critical procedures. Dolmetsch indicates that Nathan was operating under a sort of handicap because he was not writing morning-after reviews. He goes on at some length describing how Nathan's monthly writing assignment was a "predicament."

> His articles had to be composed at least a month in advance of publication and, although he had leisure to polish phrases and clarify impressions without the pressures of midnight deadlines that beset his newspaper colleagues, he was in the unenviable position of being a "second-guesser" who must find something fresh to say about plays that had already been discussed in the dailies and weeklies. Even so, there always remained the chance that, by mid-month, he would be caught feeding a dead horse, so to speak—lavishing extended discus-

sion upon some play that had already closed! Finally, in addressing a
national audience, most of whom lived outside the metropolitan New
York area, his commentaries had to appeal to those yearning readers
in the corn rows for whom Broadway might be as fantastically inacces-
sible as, say, Katamandu.[6]

Dolmetsch is on firmer ground when he offers analysis of Nathan's criticism itself than he is when he offers a justification for
Nathan's critical technique. Although it may be hard to imagine
Nathan specifically attempting to reach an audience of "readers
in the corn rows," it is not impossible to conjure an image of RFD
enthusiasts snickering over *The Smart Set*'s waggeries.

After all, given the monthly format of the magazines he wrote
for, that must have been the case for at least a portion of his
readership. Nevertheless, it does not mean that Nathan was in
some sort of critical "predicament." Many argue that Nathan was
somehow suffering under a burden to produce his articles. What
these scholars have forgotten is that Nathan *wanted* to write in
this way; he eschewed daily journalism. And even though he wrote
weekly articles throughout his life, he much preferred the
monthly format. It is always overlooked that in 1932, when he
founded his own journal, the *American Spectator*, it was a monthly.

Later in his life, in an article he wrote in 1952 especially for
Angoff's anthology, *The World of George Jean Nathan*, entitled "On
Monthly Magazines," he defines what he thinks a good magazine
should be. From these thoughts we may extrapolate what he as-
sumes a good article should be:

> A monthly magazine [is] something halfway between a newspaper and
> a book. The only kind of such magazine that interests me editorially,
> however, is one that tends to be nine-tenths book to but one-tenth
> newspaper. The daily journalistic point of view that afflicts even some
> of the better monthly periodicals has been responsible for lowering
> their one-time position in the cultural world. . . . The curse of timeli-
> ness has laid its heavy hand on magazine editing, with the result that
> a magazine which in an earlier era could be read with some satisfac-
> tion some months after its publication date presently becomes flat and
> stale a few days after its appearance. . . . This is no argument in favor
> of arty magazines. . . . Nor is it an argument for an ivory tower atti-
> tude. It is simply a single editor's belief that a magazine worth its salt
> should forgo the common editorial preoccupation with journalistic
> immediacy. . . .[7]

The last thing Nathan was concerned with in his writing was "immediacy" or "timeliness."

The eight theater books Nathan published from 1915 through 1924 represent much of his best work: *Another Book on the Theatre* (1915), *Mr. George Jean Nathan Presents* (1917), *The Popular Theatre* (1918), *Comedians All* (1919), *The Theatre, the Drama, the Girls* (1921), *The Critic and the Drama* (1922), *The World in Falseface* (1923), and *Materia Critica* (1924). The comments Nathan makes on critics and criticism in these other works demonstrate clearly his attitudes about the importance of criticism for its own sake. The twenty-one theater books Nathan wrote after the mid-1920s were written after he had consolidated his position in the American theatre. What is more, by the 1930s, Nathan had clearly established his point of view. His methods were having an impact and an influence on criticism itself, as is attested to by a pair of contemporary commentaries. The *Nation* declared, "we may say of Nathan's dramatic criticism what he himself says of Shaw—that he has brought, aside from his own contribution, the gift of independence and courage to other"[8] and the *Saturday Review of Literature* held Nathan wholly responsible for removing pedantry, Comstockery, parochialism, and fraudulence from America's drama criticism.[9]

From a historical perspective, looking at Nathan's comments can allow us to know more about drama criticism as a thing in itself. The usual use that is made of Nathan's drama criticism is simply quotation. Snippets of his reviews are offered as examples of how certain playwrights, performers, or theatrical trends were perceived in their own day. The issue of Nathan's position and the framework of his criticism are ignored.

Another, better use that should be made of Nathan's work, however, is to look at his comments on criticism. These are the thoughts of a working journalist as opposed to those of a theorist or an academic. By studying his words, we may learn how aesthetic principles are retailed on the Rialto; by this I mean we experience the play of ideas within a context of direct journalistic and theatrical exchange. Nathan's critiques were reassembled in book form at the end of the season, and it is the usual case to disparage such efforts at authorship as paste-pot jobbery, but it is not useful to condemn Nathan for such endeavors. After all, a library of critical reactions to the American theater during the first half of the twentieth century has been preserved as a result of this method. Rather than bemoan its format, we would do better to work with what we have and, in using the materials Nathan left for us, develop a method of dealing with drama criticism.

As previously noted, it has often been the fashion to dismiss drama criticism because it lacks the qualities that theater historians crave and literary historians savor. Without going over again why it is important to consider these materials in and of themselves, let us review some of Nathan's commentary on the task of the drama critic. A chronological progress is most convenient here, so the selections will be presented in the order in which they occur in Nathan's works.

Nathan's first book of drama criticism, *Another Book on the Theatre*, was published when Nathan was thirty-three. It has the youthful and energetic tone that never diminishes as he gets older. He always sounds like a person of great authority. We may not necessarily accept his authority, and his attempts at achieving a youthful *gravitas* may not always be successful, but nonetheless, there is an appropriate worldliness in Nathan that is wholly lacking in his contemporaries.

From the first pages of this text Nathan *seems* facetious but is not. It would never be Nathan's way to heavy-handedly propound his ideas before his public; his style might pull no punches and call attention to itself, but not his ideas. In the Introduction and Apology of *Another Book* Nathan explains why he is *not* a drama critic.

First, I believe that drama is *not* one thing and literature another. The two, I absurdly believe, may be, and from the soundest critical point of view *are* on perfectly friendly terms. Second, I believe ridiculously that, in the main, acting is acting only in so far as it is ocularly reasonable and effective and that therefore, in many species of roles, "types" are absolutely imperative. Character acting I exclude inasmuch as character acting is not acting at all, but merely a slick knack for making-up. If acting is not meant to be ocularly impressive, why the theatre? Why not sink your spine in a mellow chair and *read* the play? . . . I believe . . . that poor George Shaw is our most talented living playwright; that the late Clyde Fitch was a laughably overestimated fellow; that the late Stanley Houghton was another; that the Hungarians are writing the most imaginative plays of the hour; that Raymond Hitchcock is as adroit a *farceur* as Sacha Guitry; that Granville Barker is, in considerable measure, an artistic mountebank; that Arnold Daly is the best actor on the American stage. . . . That musical comedy should be a frank appeal to and stimulant of the sex impulse and should aim to be nothing else; that there is no such thing as the mystery called dramatic technique. . . .[10]

Nathan continues in this vein, listing all the criteria of taste that separate him from every other drama critic in the country. He concludes this section with lines that seem rather uncharacteristic: "I am a progressive. Our theatre as you know, isn't" (xi). In one sense, Nathan truly was progressive. He *never* waxed nostalgic for the theater of the past. Even when he was a septuagenarian he never derided the contemporary theater for not measuring up to the theatre of his youth.

Farther along in the Introduction and Apology, he ponders why we should even bother with criticism of the theater, and then he responds to his own doubts with the admission that he must continue to challenge the American theater with mockery until it does "original" things such as present a play in which Maude Adams is "ruined" or John Drew plays a character who "ends unhappily."[11]

Later in *Another Book on the Theatre*, Nathan expounds upon a favorite theme of his—that criticism must be personal. He rejects entirely the notion that impersonal criticism is even possible. Criticism that is allegedly objective is not criticism, but "reporting." Nathan maintains that the difference between criticism and reporting is that reporting consists of "recording what one has seen and heard" and criticism entails "the recording of deductions made from what one has seen and heard."[12] Nathan elaborates on this belief in virtually all of his later works. The public persona he developed is an integral part of his criticism because of such attitudes. Other critics may not be so candid about the ways in which their personalities or peculiarities inform their criticism; but, in light of the current questioning of objectivity by scholars of everything from literary theory to quantum theory, Nathan's frankness seems to be all the more honest.

This is not to make a claim for Nathan's perspicacity solely on latter-day theoretical quibbles over the nature of reality but merely to emphasize that one aspect of Nathan's methodology has come into academic fashion, if not quite into the academic fold. This aspect of Nathan merits mention only because it must be stressed that part of the controversial nature of Nathan's criticism stems from his strong personality. To many, he is objectionable for this reason if no other.

In Nathan's next book of criticism, *Mr. George Jean Nathan Presents*, published in 1917, he devotes an entire chapter to the primary problem he faces as a critic. Its title is descriptive: "The Dramatic Critic and the Undramatic Theatre."[13] This chapter is a response to the ongoing controversy over the role the critic has in the theater. Nathan, as usual, sounds flippant, but he is actually stating the truth about the theater as it is. He bolsters his argument with some statistics supplied by Clayton Hamilton, a most unusual ally for Nathan to select, considering that Hamilton was often a favorite target of Nathan's satire.

He begins his essay with the simple statement that the "mere journalistic reporting" type of criticism should not have a place on Broadway. He goes on to explain this point, saying that "to report the result of a first night performance, particularly on Broadway, is to report a murder in terms of the flowers placed by relatives on the deceased's coffin."[14] As anyone who has regularly attended opening nights knows, this is perfectly true. To gauge the success of a play based upon the audience's reaction at a premiere is absurd, as said group of people is so eager to enjoy the proceedings that it falls over itself in order to present a favorable impression, knowing, perhaps subconsciously, that part of its demonstration is entirely for the benefit of the critics.

Hamilton, Nathan informs us, adduces that a "person of intelligence and taste who casually takes a chance on going to a play is likely, twenty-two times out of twenty-three, to have his intelligence insulted and his taste offended." Nathan applauds Hamilton's findings and tallies his own; he tells us that during the past six seasons he can think of only 25 or 26 out of the more than 600 shows presented that have "merited approach by the critic seriously interested in drama." As for the remaining productions, Nathan lists them: "trick melodramas, fussy farces, mob mush, [and] leg shows."[15] Of course, Nathan is not writing of his critical demission with this chapter. On the contrary, he proceeds to give reasons why criticism must continue to fight against the theater's main enemies, the low tastes of its public and most of its managers, and the "Anglo-Ohio" mentality of its moralizing, blue-nosed critics.[16]

The following year, 1918, Nathan published *The Popular Theatre,* a survey of the various facets of mass entertainment in Nathan's time. There are chapters dealing with vaudeville (both "big-time" and "small-time"), motion pictures, and comedians as well as such "legitimate theatre" topics as playwrights, performers, and audiences. In the thirteenth chapter he offers a description of the "typical season" of the popular theater, in this case the season of 1916–17. He describes ninety-seven evenings at the theater, from 31 July 1916 through 15 May 1917, on which date he repairs "to the Glen Springs Sanitorium."[17] Nathan's catalogue of the theatrical season is pointed satire against the entire commercial theater. He mocks its every aspect, from Shakespearean revival ("watched Mr. Robert B. Mantell give his celebrated performance of the role of Macbeth in his presentation of Shakespeare's *Merchant of Venice*") to musical comedy (*Oh, Boy!*, the Wodehouse-Bolton music show, "had *two* pretty girls. Therefore exceptionally good entertainment.")

By setting up the Broadway theater in this way, Nathan is making the point that it is ridiculous to treat the "popular theatre" as though it were wholly—or even partially—an artistic endeavor. In support of this attitude, he offers a quotation from Clayton Hamilton's ecstatic ode to J. M. Barrie's *A Kiss For Cinderella*:

> If you have tears, by all means go and shed them as a sort of exquisite libation to the latest masterpiece of Sir James Matthew Barrie, Baronet (for services to mankind); but, if you have not tears, by all means stay away and make room for the rest of us who want to blow a kiss to Cinderella.[18]

Nathan's response to Hamilton's reaction is an example of his belief that art should be "hot" and criticism "cold." He retorts:

> Since the play seems to the present somewhat less impressionable writer to be a work considerably inferior to Miss Eleanor Gates' *Poor Little Rich Girl*, and more greatly inferior still to Barrie's previous plays, he has decided to stay away, as requested, and allow the moist M. Hamilton this extra room wherein to blow kisses.[19]

It is well known that Nathan was particularly fond of chastising his colleagues, and this aspect of Nathan's work is offered up as evidence of his lack of genuine concern for the theater. Nathan is chastised for carping over presumed faults of his colleagues when he should be finding things to praise at the theater. Overlooked are Nathan's intentions. He sought not merely to engage in personalities but also to question the methods and criteria of his fellow critics. By questioning their means of assessing drama, he was offering an evaluation of the criticism of his time that was an indirect means of presenting his own definitions of good dramaturgy. Nathan demanded that those who criticized must be held accountable to the needs of criticism itself, not to the needs of the theatre. When Nathan discussed other critics, he did so primarily to reveal the weaknesses of criticism that chimerically attempted to "serve" the theater. We may question Nathan's beliefs about the function of criticism, but we must counter any demands that a critic must first and foremost "serve" the theater with the response that a critic in service to the theater belongs on the payroll of a theater company as a dramaturge or publicity director. He or she does not belong in a public critical forum.

As evidence to support this contention, the examples of Kenneth Tynan and Robert Brustein may be offered. Tynan gave up criticism while he worked at Britain's National Theatre. He was controversial because of what he wanted the National to present in its repertoire, and he created a lot of difficulties for Laurence Olivier and Lord Chandos, but Tynan catalyzed a great deal of drama while at that theater. At no time did he seem to be serving anything but the National Theatre's agenda as he saw it. After he left the National—even though he departed under very strained circumstances—and returned to writing criticism, his integrity was unthreatened. Robert Brustein, on the other hand, has compromised his critical voice by continuing to serve as artistic director of the American Repertory Company and the drama critic of *The New Republic*. No matter how altruistic his aims may be, there will always be those who will perceive him as serving his own theater's agenda whenever he praises or dispraises a past, present, or future member of his company—not to mention a rival theater.

Nathan argued throughout his career that "destructive criticism" was the best, if not the only, form of "true" criticism. In the book that follows *The Popular Theatre*, *Comedians All* (published in 1919), he devotes the third section of this text (pages 13–28) to a discussion of what destructive criticism is and gives examples of what it is not. He says,

> That any fool can find fault is, of course, perfectly true. But that any fool can find fault accurately, soundly and searchingly is a horse of another colour. . . . The extraordinarily capric [*sic*] quality of the mass of journalistic criticism in America is due, not as is generally maintained, to the desire of its writers to please by indiscriminate praise, but to the utter incapacity on the part of these writers to dispraise. . . . [T]he omnipresent note of eulogy is attributable less to the commentator's wish to eulogize than to the recognized fact that . . . gush is immensely more simple than diatribe. Every critical writer knows well the truth of this. When he is lazy, he writes praise; only when his mind is alert and eager does he find himself capable of fault finding. The art of the careful, honest and demolishing *coup de grace* is an art calling, firstly, for an exhaustive knowledge of the subject under the microscope, secondly, for an original and sharply inventive analytical turn of mind, and thirdly, for a wit and power over words that shall make them whiz through the printed page.[20]

Nathan then presents two cases of pseudodestructive criticism and a contrasting example of pseudoconstructive criticism.

Nathan selects pieces from the New York *Globe* (a fading paper
with only four years to live) and the *Evening Post* (at that time a
liberal standard-bearer) as examples of pseudoconstruction and
one from the *Evening Telegram* (in rival publisher Henry Villard's
famous phrase "that pink drab of lowest journalism") as an example of pseudodestruction. Each example is a review of *A Sleepless
Night* by Jack Larrie and Gustav Blum. This play was a negligible
farce that opened on 18 January 1919 and played for seventy-
one performances. (Featured in the cast was Carlotta Monterey,
Eugene O'Neill's future wife.) Nathan dissects each review, revealing its inconsistency, ignorance, and internal contradictions.

The *Globe*'s reviewer commented that the play had elements of
satire that caused the audience to "giggle" when it should have
been "laughing out loud and blushing." Nathan's response:

> in his very first sentence he says that the piece is a farce comedy [but]
> he finds fault with the farce comedy because the farce comedy
> achieves something that *farce* is not supposed to achieve. Which, obvi-
> ously, is not far removed from criticizing *A Wife Without A Smile* be-
> cause it achieves something that *Charley's Aunt* is not supposed to
> achieve.[21]

And he discredits the *Post*'s attempt at fault-finding by reminding
readers that the same critic, the redoubtable J. Ranken Towse no
less, who called *A Sleepless Night*'s story "silly and preposterous"
had commended the plot of *Saturday to Monday* as "interesting
and reasonable." Nathan remonstrated that the plot of both plays
was "fundamentally the same."[22] On the pseudoconstructive side,
Nathan chastises the *Evening Telegram* review for such facile conclusions as "The various actors did their roles to perfection. The
production was staged under the capable direction of Oscar
Eagles."[23]

As noted above, Nathan does not excuse these writers on the
grounds that they have too little time in which to compose better
critiques. And to prove that even magazine writers are prone to
the same sorts of errors, he trots out a selection from one of his
favorite whipping boys, Clayton Hamilton, who was then writing
for *Vogue*. He quotes from an article Hamilton wrote praising the
French dramatist Henri Lavedan as "one of the foremost repre-
sentatives of contemporary French dramatic authorship." He then
takes it apart for the inaccuracy of Hamilton's pronouncements
about Lavedan's high standing in France: "By no first-rate critic
in or out of France has Lavedan ever been recognized as of the

company of Rostand, de Curel, Hervieu, Donnay, Lemaitre—or even de Caillavet and De Fleurs." He counters Hamilton's assertion about Lavedan's great popularity in the United States: "Lavedan's plays, contrary to Mr. Hamilton, have—with a single exception—*not* 'enjoyed unusual success in the commercial theatre of this country,' but—Mr. Hamilton may learn if he will engage the records of the late Charles Frohman—lost a fine pot of money."[24] In this example of what Nathan terms critical "flap-doodle," Hamilton is further chided for his recurring exaggerations and his all-too-selective memory. One must admit, though, that Nathan's reference to so many French playwrights in his fusillade against Hamilton is *de trop*.

Later on, in *Comedians All*, Nathan breaks down American dramatic criticism into two classifications, "college professor" and "newspaper." He sums up the former as being "founded on"

(1) an almost complete lack of knowledge of the actual theatre and the changes wrought therein in the last decade, (2) a stern disinclination, confounded with poise and dignity, to accept new things and new standards, and (3) a confusion of the stage with the tabernacle pulpit.[25]

He finds that the "newspaper" school has

(1) a desire to attract notice through the eloquent championship of the dramaturgic under dog or (2) a desire to earn [a] salary in peace and comfort by championing all the upper dogs. . . . I doubt if I exaggerate unduly when I say that neither of these critical schools has in the last dozen years expressed a single thought, a single philosophy or a single recommendation that has assisted an American producer or playwright, however eager and willing, to improve upon his labors or elevate his standards.[26]

With these examples, Nathan demonstrates that he is most emphatically not engaging in personalities for the sake of a cheap laugh or to simply insult a rival. Moreover, he indicates that a good critic, even as he or she hopes that the theater will improve, must be aware of the theater as it is and have knowledge of both highbrow and lowbrow entertainment.

Nineteen years later, in 1938, Nathan would reverse his woeful assessment of American drama criticism in the chapter "Afterthoughts on Criticism" in *The Morning After the First Night*. Therein he declares that there has been a great improvement in drama criticism: "Our critics have changed and our theatre has changed for the better with them."[27] He especially approves of the New York Drama Critics' Circle and maintains that it is something that has the potential to do much for the improvement of the American theatre.

Nathan liked to assert his influence with playwrights, producers, and directors and discuss it in his articles. But in general, acting was the least of his concerns as a critic. Typically, in 1921's *The Theatre, the Drama, the Girls,* Nathan explains why he eschews extensive commentary on actors:

> Dramatic criticism advances as its concern with the actor recedes. Extended criticism of actors is a subterfuge for concealing a confined knowledge of drama. . . . The critic who treats of the history of the theatre in terms of its great actors is like the historian who treats of the world's wars in terms of their great generals. This is the superficial, the showy, the gilt and glitter melodrama method. . . . The actor is essential to the performance of drama. Catgut is essential to the performance of music. . . . To argue that [the actor] is an artist is to corrupt the word artist with half-meanings. . . . His imagination can at the highest reach only the imagination of his dramatist's power; his emotion can flow only in the degree that his dramatist has turned on the faucet. If he is a good actor, he can serve his dramatist. But he can never be so good that he improves on his dramatist. I speak, obviously, only of dramatists who are artists. Almost any fairly competent actor can improve upon a hack playwright. . . .[28]

He goes on to accuse American dramatic criticism of being "actor-ridden." As an example of this, he quotes a "subjoined spasm" by Alexander Woollcott about Elsie Janis. Woollcott confesses that his ecstatic review of Janis's singing and dancing is being "solemnly reported by one who finds it difficult to keep from growing incoherent in the process." To Nathan the spectacle of American theatrical criticism "struck dumb with wonder and projected into a foaming fit by a vaudeville performer" is disgusting.[29]

Nathan's next volume, *The World in Falseface,* 1923, is one of his most important books. It is this book, though, that contains the foreword that haunted him ever afterward. In that foreword, he reiterates flippancies such as "what interests me is the surface of life," but also offers the blithe assertion that:

> if all the Armenians were to be killed tomorrow and if half of Russia were to starve to death the day after, it would not matter to me in the least. What concerns me alone is myself, and the interests of a few close friends. . . . Such, I appreciate, are not the confessions that men

usually make, for they are evil and unpopular confessions. My only apology for them is that they are true.[30]

Most of Nathan's "defenders" (Goldberg, Angoff, Frick, and Simpson) either expurgate this passage or slough it off as merely "Nathan being Nathan." Only Thomas Quinn Curtiss attempts to deal with it. He recalls that it has been the basis for "most of the attacks" on Nathan, from Alfred Kazin to the Ku Klux Klan.[31] Curtiss feels that Nathan changed his mind later in life, and offers as proof a selection from "I Believe," the chapter Nathan contributed to *Living Philosophies* in 1939. Therein Nathan stoutly maintains that he is against all of fascism and most of communism, and that it is impossible to be a pacifist, given the world's present climate:

> certain convictions that I entertained in other and younger days have undergone some alteration. . . . No man can live through the upset and agony of our time and remain insensible to it. The sounds of barbaric cannon, the cries of starving and helpless masses of men, the tears and curses of humanity reach even to the remotest ivory tower. And the human mind, however independent and self-frontiered, must find its aloof contemplation invaded and shattered by them. . . .[32]

Curtiss does well to let Nathan speak for himself, but this humble—especially for Nathan—expression is not altogether satisfactory. Nathan was, after all, a man of forty-one when he wrote the earlier quoted passage, and therefore to ascribe its excesses to the folly of youth rings just a bit hollow.

Less satisfying, though, is Angoff's attempt to make Nathan out to be a model citizen. In *The Tone of the Twenties*, he describes Nathan as voting regularly and serving delightedly and frequently on juries.[33] Nathan must have served on a jury at least once; he was unable to visit O'Neill in California in 1939 because of jury duty.[34] Angoff, however, is not always a reliable authority. One may or may not accept Angoff's critical opinions, but his first-hand accounts have been questioned by some commentators.[35] Given the animosity Angoff displays toward Mencken in his book *H. L. Mencken: A Portrait from Memory*, it is not surprising that Angoff would do what he could to contrast Nathan with Mencken. It seems that Angoff emphasizes Nathan's observance of his civic duties in order to accentuate Mencken's contempt for such things.

Nathan's disregard, in the infamous passage, for the plight of the Armenians and the Russians was surely an arbitrary reference. It is most likely that he selected those nationalities of the latest newspaper headlines he had read. Mencken's alleged anti-Semitism and racism are currently the subject of much debate, but Nathan has not been accused of any racism lately, although he has recently been characterized as homophobic, and with some justification. However, my purpose here is not to attack or defend Nathan for his personal beliefs.

Nathan's personal beliefs are, nonetheless, relevant to this study in two ways. First, they offer a genuine glimpse into Nathan's perception of himself and into what he held to be a person's absolute value. Nathan based his standards on two things: work and friendship. In this sense Nathan is absolutely elitist, yet when we recall his exchange with Goldberg over the issue of his own Jewish identity, the fact that Nathan at no point in his writings ever makes any serious references to family members is all the more interesting. It leads to us to the second relevant point. For all the anti-Babbitt zealotry, which he shared with Mencken, Nathan is very much an advocate of the self-maker. But by stating so bluntly, in the first pages of *The World in Falseface*, that his personal concerns are eye-of-the-needle narrow, Nathan sets himself up for a contradiction a few pages later, when he describes why drama criticism is the ideal forum for his views.[36] As noted earlier, he believes that because of the "diverse constituent elements of the theatre," drama criticism can be used for a great variety of purposes. It is possible, of course, that with his cold-hearted statement about his imperviousness to massacres and famines, Nathan simply wished to make it absolutely clear that politics and social issues had no place in his life which was to indicate that he was in that much better a position to be a critic.

The passage is undeniably offensive and we can suspect that when Nathan wrote it, he was fully aware of its shock value. He wanted to be outrageous. He certainly succeeded, but then apparently thought the better of it; hence, the muted apology in "I Believe." Nonetheless, as Curtiss informs us, such a self-consciously Byronic "among them, but not of them" stance attracted much contemporary rancor. This was not the only such statement he made, as we have seen in his motto, "Be indifferent," and he repeated variations on the same theme throughout the 1920s.

The accusations Walter Lippmann made against him in the March 1928 *Vanity Fair* may be taken as a summary of the *mundus contra* Nathan attitude. Lippmann protests that he will "never learn to live as beautifully as Mr. Nathan."

> I do not agree with [his] opinion that his humorous disesteem for politics is due to his superior tastes; I think it is due to an inferior

education, to a somewhat lazy incomprehension of what politics deal with and to an imagination which is defective in dealing with realities that are complex, and physical, and illusive. . . . Mr. Nathan is far from being wholly dumb. To my tastes he knows the theatre as well as anyone from 34th to 59th Street. He knows it better than I shall ever know politics. I sincerely admire him. I think that in addition to being a very shrewd critic he has created a character called George Jean Nathan that is as interesting as any I have ever seen for a long time on any stage. I think, too, that he is by way of being a connoisseur of human folly, not a connoisseur of the first order for he lacks education and sympathy, but nevertheless a man of unusual tastes, a sort of gourmet with dyspepsia. He is not a man of the world, but at least a man of his own world. But when he talks about matters he doesn't understand he talks through his hat with a very loud voice.[37]

It is a note of wistful irony that Lippmann is now as obscure a figure as Nathan, and Lippmann's worldview now seems as quaint as Nathan's. Moreover, there is a compelling point of consonance between the two men; Lippmann maintained an absolute silence about the Nazis' treatment of the Jews throughout his career and, as Nathan had done, he completely dissociated himself from his Jewishness. It is not the intention here merely to discredit Lippmann's criticism, but it is necessary to deal with Lippmann's commentary with some perspective. Previous writers have ignored statements like Lippmann's or merely reprinted them, dismissing them with a Nathanian shrug. Nathan himself projected the image that he was arrogantly impervious to any negative reactions to himself. But what is significant about this criticism is that it is just as much of its time as Nathan's jaded utterance and that it comes from an equally rarefied sentience. This is even clearer when amplified by the following letter from Edmund Wilson, who knew Nathan slightly and occasionally worked with him. Wilson is writing to Lippmann after the appearance of the *Vanity Fair* article:

I like and admire George Nathan, but I was rather glad to see you take a crack at him in *Vanity Fair*. I suppose that Nathan's opinions on politics are merely a shadow of Mencken's and that Mencken is the real enemy in this regard, but I think it is a good thing to have somebody take a stand against the point of view expressed in the passage you quoted. I feel very strongly myself that America has been unfortunate since the war in being obliged to take all the indifferentism and defeatism of Europe and that it is high time we set out ourselves to supply some sensible ideas about society and life in general. Dos Passos, one of the young American writers who has been carrying on ever since the war and who has been unaffected by the European malady that I speak of above, was saying to me the other day that he thought the indifference to politics on the part of the literary and artistic people in New York was extremely sinister, because it was merely the first step in a process which subsequently involved the discarding of almost every other sort of interest, too, so that there was nothing left except a nonsensical Algonquin joke or an arid poem. I seem to see signs of a rally against all that state of mind which has been one of the causes for the eminence of Nathan and certain other people.

As you are working constantly in the political field, you are perhaps not aware of the extent of the detachment of literature, since the war, from all sorts of public affairs and social questions, but I think that in pillorying that particular opinion of Nathan's you have said something very much to the point for literary people in general.[38]

Lippmann and Wilson give us perhaps the best insight into why Nathan was perceived as he was. Wilson, born in 1895, was thirteen years younger than Nathan and mistakenly assumed that Nathan's ideas were somehow a product of postwar malaise. At that stage in his career he had conveniently forgotten the Nathan he had read in his prep school days. Lippmann, born in 1889, was only seven years younger than Nathan and seems to have been closer to the mark. Neither savant, however, seemed to be able to comprehend Nathan's indifference to politics. Their attitudes are of interest to cultural historians for another reason: behind their hostility to Nathan's lack of concern with politics lurks an almost Rousseauvian disdain for Nathan's theatrical expertise. Lippmann's employment of the false humility trope is particularly transparent. Not only does Lippmann restrict the perimeters of theatrical knowledge to a few blocks of New York City, he praises Nathan's theatrical omniscience but then proceeds to disparage his intelligence, education, and imagination. He gives Nathan credit for knowing the theater better than anyone else, but to Lippmann the theatre was a rather shallow endeavor in comparison to the unsoundable depths of politics. So for Lippmann, the high priest of "the American century," to credit Nathan, the "dyspeptic gourmet," with being the theater's greatest exponent is to salute him for chronicling small beer indeed.

How different from Wilson's and Lippmann's is the sensibility represented in the opening of the final book of Nathan's *Smart Set* years, *Materia Critica* (1924):

As a critic, it has never been my aim or purpose to convince anyone, including myself. My sole effort has been to express personal opinions grounded upon such training and experience and the philosophy deduced therefrom as I may possess. . . . I please myself to believe that the critic who has another aim is a vainglorious and often absurd figure. . . . Criticism is the prevailing of intelligent skepticism over vague and befuddled prejudice and uncertainty. . . . When the critic ceases to have self-doubts, he ceases to be a critic and becomes a pedagogue.[39]

Nathan's critical method is difficult to describe because it is essentially amorphous. One cannot codify Nathan's formulas, give an approximate word count of his average review, or present a series of definitions as they occur in his works. Nathan's criticism is as varied as the plays he reviews, and this variety is in itself one of his critical credos.[40] As the passage above reveals, the only aspect of his criticism that is entirely consistent is his exacting standard for theater critics.

The drama critic must be a historian of the theater, a student of literature, a philosopher, and a possessor of the most delicate sensibilities. And he or she must be prepared to employ these talents fully at every theatrical exhibition and dramatic spectacle. Later on in *Materia Critica,* Nathan explains that the drama critic must not be limited to any one type of theater: "*Shuffle Along* has its place in the theatre, and in criticism perhaps no less, equally with *Connais-toi* and *Heartbreak House.*"[41]

Nathan's development as a critic parallels the development of American drama criticism as a whole. It was fortunate that he began writing when he did, as he was able to be part of two important developments in American culture. Nathan was a very young participant in the prewar aesthetic movement in America (a movement exemplified by James Huneker). Nathan was an established critic when Eugene O'Neill was able to attract the attention of the entire world. Nathan's use of his influence in the theater is particularly well known in O'Neill's case, but he did not limit himself to assisting O'Neill. Throughout his entire career he sought out producers for promising playwrights. Among Nathan's papers at Cornell letters spanning four decades give evidence of his labors on behalf of playwrights. Not only that, he was also frequently asked by producers for advice on prospective properties. To give but two examples of producers who solicited his advice: a letter written by Winthrop Ames on 20 June 1919 asks him about young playwrights[42]; and twenty-nine years later, on 16 March 1948, Richard Aldrich importunes, "We are anxiously looking for scripts, so if you run across any that might survive a

New York City opening night, we would appreciate a word from you."[43] Even movie producer Carl Laemmle asked for potential movie scripts from Nathan in 1919, an unusual request considering that Nathan loathed the movies from their inception.

Nathan read play scripts all the time, and there are entire boxes of manuscripts in the Nathan collection at Cornell, examples of the playwriting efforts that were constantly sent to him by hopeful dramatists. And he read not only the efforts of amateurs; F. Scott Fitzgerald and Sinclair Lewis submitted versions of their plays to him, too. Nathan read Fitzgerald's *The Vegetable* and thought rather well of it and he gave Lewis advice about the dramatization of Lewis' novel *It Can't Happen Here*.

Letters in the Cornell Collection reveal that in May of 1939 William Saroyan sent him a draft of *The Time of Your Life*. Afterwards, Saroyan thoroughly revised it according to Nathan's suggestions. He wrote to Nathan on 2 June 1939, "I am just now finished with making the changes in the play which we talked about and I feel now that we have a much improved piece of work—on all counts."[44] Saroyan eventually dedicated the play to Nathan. In the published correspondence between Sean O'Casey and Nathan, there are several references to the latter's willingness to make use of his contacts in the press and the theater to secure a favorable reception for O'Casey's *Purple Dust* and *Within the Gates* in New York. And contrary to recent allegations that he was somehow out to sabotage Tennessee Williams's career, on 5 April 1945, Nathan wrote Alfred Knopf and asked him to consider publishing Williams's work.

Not everyone was delighted with Nathan's procedures. Critic John Mason Brown resolutely refused to read scripts that were sent to him by producers, and he rather enjoyed this difference in attitude between himself and Nathan.[45] George S. Kaufman and Edna Ferber had a more serious reason to dislike Nathan's working methods: he gave a negative review to the manuscript of their play *Dinner at Eight*. On 25 October 1932, Ferber and John Peter Toohey, the press agent who ballyhooed the Algonquin Round Table, wrote Nathan that he was "a law unto himself." Ferber and Toohey also told Nathan that Kaufman considered him "tricky and underhanded."[46] Kaufman felt that although it may have been Nathan's right to say whatever he liked about *Dinner at Eight*, "it was dishonest of him to read the play beforehand." Nathan admitted in his article that he was commenting on a manuscript and not reviewing a production,[47] but one can see Kaufman's point.

In a random series of recollections recorded in *The Theatre Book of the Year 1950–1951*, Nathan discusses some of the plays and producers with whom he was directly involved. He mentions that he twice tried to get a producer for Eugene O'Neill's *Anna Christie;* he failed with Edgar Selwyn but succeeded with Arthur Hopkins. He brought Paul Vincent Carroll's *Shadow and Substance* to the attention of Eddie Dowling, *The Time of Your Life,* to the Theatre Guild, and Maurine Watkins's *Chicago* to Sam Harris. He recommended "that Laurette Taylor, who had not acted for many years, be cast in the role [of Amanda Wingfield] for which the producers had tentatively cast Jane Cowl." He also tried to get Somerset Maugham to dramatize his short story "Miss Thompson." Maugham failed utterly to see the theatrical possibilities in the story, but Nathan managed to persuade director John D. Williams to find a way to develop the story into a play. In spite of Maugham's myopic misgivings, "Miss Thompson" became *Rain.* Nathan adds as an afterthought that he could not share in the enormous profits each of these plays reaped because "it is expected of a critic that he be financially immaculate in his dealings with the theatre."[48]

It is said that Nathan was slipping during the 1930s and 1940s, but we can see that even in the latter part of his career, Nathan did what he had done in its beginning. It cannot be denied that in some ways, Nathan was out of step with the times and that his contempt for "the little red writing hoods," as he termed the leftist playwrights of the day, placed him at odds with much of the radically politicized theater of the 1930s. But to peremptorily dismiss him as an incipient William Winter is to ignore the support and encouragement he gave to plays by William Saroyan, Sean O'Casey, William Inge, and Arthur Miller. Nathan did not despise the plays of John Howard Lawson because Lawson was a leftist, he despised them because they were bad plays. It is worth noting that Nathan's first extended criticism of Lawson was written in 1926, well before the "red" decade. Nathan addresses Lawson's posturing preface to his play *Nirvana:*

One fears that Mr. Lawson is a student of such profound scientific documents as Sir Arthur Conan Doyle's "The Coming of the Fairies," to say nothing of the works of Mary Baker Eddy and Camille Flammarion. . . . "Viewing the mental uncertainties of today," proceeds our young philosopher, "I am convinced that there is a religious need not satisfied by any of the current forms of worship." In other words, what is needed to resolve scientific uncertainties into certainties is a new theology. I content myself with a polite silence.[49]

Even a conventionally "good liberal" like Charles Angoff admitted, in 1966, that Nathan's animosity toward Clifford Odets, the representative politically committed 1930s Broadway playwright, has been thoroughly vindicated.[50] In this instance, Angoff's comment is valuable because elsewhere he had assailed Nathan and Mencken for their lack of response to the political consciousness of the 1930s. Perhaps the most asinine attack Nathan received was in 1938 from a *New Masses* stalwart pen-named Robert Forsythe, his real name being Kyle S. Crichton. Doubtless "Forsythe" was burning from Nathan's merciless exposé of his dual career as Forsythe the little red writing hood and Kyle S. Crichton who "went to Hollywood on behalf of a capitalist-owned weekly to compose articles on beautiful stars at a luxuriant weekly fee, and with all expenses paid. He had the royal suite at the Beverly-Wiltshire Hotel, with a valet in constant attendance. . . ."[51]

Forsythe's counterattack, the chapter entitled "Winken, Blinken and Nod" in *Reading from Right to Left*, is devoted to running down Nathan and Mencken. (The title is an allusion to a widely circulated satirical poem of the 1920s, "Mencken, Nathan and God.") The tone of the piece is harsh, even cruel. It is also relentlessly self-righteous in a way that Nathan, even at his most supercilious, never was. In addition to berating him for having written for three magazines that had ceased publication, Forsythe racks Nathan for the failure of *The American Spectator.*

This final magazine-founding effort of Nathan's has generally been presumed to be a publishing debacle. The conventional wisdom has it that Nathan's last attempt to realize his dream of a "blue review" was undone by the *Spectator*'s skylarking tone, which was in complete discord with the Depression. This is a flawed assessment for a variety of reasons. Many comparable magazines did well during the early 1930s; *The New Yorker* and *Esquire,* hardly renowned for their grim resolution, were nonetheless able to overcome the hard times of the decade, and they continue to this day, so blaming the *Spectator*'s demise on the Depression is unsatisfactory. Letters in Cornell Collection indicate that Nathan and his *Spectator* were victims of financial chicanery. The major stockholders in the *Spectator* were Raymond Long and Richard R. Smith, two men prominent in publishing circles throughout the 1920s. A letter of 9 July 1932 to Nathan from Smith details the financial misfortunes that beset Smith and Long's ventures after the stock market crash. The upshot of the letter is that Long has deserted his obligations by fleeing the country and that Smith is now bankrupt so there was never any capital foundation for the *Spectator.* One year later, on 10 August 1933, a letter from Nathan to Smith inquires whether there is any hope that he might ever retrieve any of his money. It is clear, then, that *The American Spectator* was doomed even before its first issue; that it lasted as long as it did is remarkable. Nathan's excuse for the journal's demise was that he had simply gotten tired of it.

In his diatribe, Forsythe writes of Nathan as though he were on his deathbed. "The anguished cries of the senile are nothing new in life," is his valedictory comment on Nathan's presumed critical stasis.[52] It is significant though, that even at a time when Nathan is thought by some commentators to have become less influential, he is still the object of controversy.

It is even more significant, however, that he was consistently able to attract praise from serious writers throughout his entire career. As we have already seen, Bernard Shaw and Gordon Craig were enthusiastic about him, and so was Thomas Mann. On 27 November 1948, ten years after Forsythe's assault, Mann wrote Blanche Knopf, the wife of his publisher and director of the publishing house. It is probable that he had been asked by the Knopfs to provide some sort of promotional statement. Mann singled Nathan out for his "rich and amusing vocabulary of displeasure," explaining that "what differentiates him from the many others who try to imitate his crushing negativism, is the unmistakable fact that a true, deep and sensitive love of the good and the spiritual forms the background of his witty ill-humour." Mann's instinctive understanding of Nathan's enduring and essential hope for the theater, in spite of his exhortatory excesses, is further revealed when Mann says, "He is at his best when he derides the commercialization of great and serious art, as in the case of Strindberg's *Dance of Death."* Mann is referring to an adaptation of this play called *The Last Dance,* by Peter Goldblum and Robin Short, which Nathan had recently lacerated.[53] The play closed after seven performances. Finally, Mann concludes that Nathan never takes himself too seriously: "I also love his self-irony which occasionally softens his mercilessness."[54]

Nathan had matured but not mellowed, by any means. It was perhaps premature of Lippmann to posit in 1928 that Nathan had "created a character called George Jean Nathan," but twenty years later this was definitely the case. In the Nathan collection there are many requests, dating from the 1930s through the

1950s, for the use of his name in song lyrics and in movie scripts. No doubt Nathan reveled in the role of theatrical elder statesman, and he made the most of his nearly legendary status.

There is much more to Nathan than his star player status at the Stork Club, where he frequently supped after the theater in its exclusive Cub Room, surrounded by the likes of Walter Winchell, Ernest Hemingway, Marlene Dietrich, and Dorothy Kilgallen. He remained, in spite of such diversions, a hard-working critic until just before his death. Even after a series of strokes left him unable to write, he managed to dictate his reviews, as the letters in the Nathan Collection at Cornell transcribed by his wife, Julie Haydon, reveal.

If we take a look at some of Nathan's contemporaries, we see that for the purposes of commercial theater, the American theater had the right critics at the right times and in the right places. There were fifteen newspapers serving New Yorkers during that time, and there were more than two hundred openings in a season, eleven on 26 December 1927 alone and two hundred sixty-nine in the latter half of that season. All this made for a great deal of boisterous competition. Of course now it seems almost unthinkable that the *New York Times* was not the only newspaper that mattered, that its critic was not only just one of many, or that weekly magazines considered the theater more important than the movies. But Nathan is closer to us than we might think. He wrote for the sake of criticism and he wrote for his readers. Today, the emphasis of virtually every professional critic writing is on somehow advising theatergoers whether a show is worth the price of the ticket. At its worst, this practice degenerates into a thumbs-down/thumbs-up consumer guide approach. Editors *demand* that critics write for a given periodical's readership rather than for the good of theatrical art.

Other modern critics have attempted to make changes in the theater or have come to criticize it via a working acquaintance with the theater; Harold Clurman and Kenneth Macgowan are examples of this approach. Nathan's approach to drama criticism and the way in which he conducted his career serve, for good or ill, as the benchmark for all of his successors because his first allegiance was to criticism itself, rather than to "the theatre."

Nathan was a professional writer and for much of his career, an editor; he was never a booster. The American drama critics who came to prominence after Nathan began his career, such as Alexander Woollcott (who started at the *New York Times* in 1914), Heywood Broun (who began writing for the *New York World* in

1921), Robert Benchley (who first reviewed for the old *Life* in 1920), and Percy Hammond (who moved to the *New York Tribune* from Chicago in 1921), among others, were all working journalists assigned to the theater because of their proven writing abilities, not because of their theatrical expertise. These men wrote drama criticism because they wanted to be professional writers. Nathan wrote professionally because he wanted to be a drama critic. Heywood Broun's stint as a critic was only a stopover between sports writing and the creation of his crusading column "It Seems to Me." Robert Benchley used his theater reviews as a conduit for his drolleries. Indeed, of this entire group, only Percy Hammond functioned primarily as a drama critic. Hammond had been a newspaperman for twenty-five years before he came to New York as critic for the *Tribune*. He had been the drama editor of the Chicago *Tribune* and his caustic critical style succeeded in getting him barred from the Shuberts' theaters there. Hammond was a widely quoted and caustic stylist; he said of a certain musical "that I have knocked everything except the knees of the chorus girls and God anticipated me there."

Alexander Woollcott started at the *New York Times* and after a thirteen-year career at several New York newspapers went on to aggrandize himself and his tastes as a critic-at-large (a calling for which he certainly had the width, if not the height). Eventually, Woollcott left daily journalism altogether to write for the new weekly, *The New Yorker* magazine, thence to become radio's "town crier" and, ultimately, Kaufman and Hart's "man who came to dinner." He acquired phenomenal celebrity bruiting books such as *Good-bye Mr. Chips* and making a spectacle of himself at the trial of Bruno Hauptmann. Even though Woollcott's childhood dream had always been to be a drama critic, he gave it up because he found it too limiting. He had come to realize that he wanted to be a star in his own right. Eager for the spotlight, he tired of chronicling on-stage goings-on, even though his self-conscious and effusive style made the critic himself the focus of his readers' interest rather than the particular play or performer under scrutiny. Woollcott's 1928 departure from theater reviewing was precipitated by his intemperate panning of O'Neill's *Strange Interlude* before it had opened, a feat he managed to achieve by obtaining a rehearsal script. Almost immediately thereafter, Woollcott gave up regular reviewing to begin his "Shouts and Murmurs" column in *The New Yorker*, in which he addressed any subject that captured his interest. Woollcott never intended to influence criticism, nor had he ever attempted to have any impact on the theater as an institution. His entire career was focused on making himself an institution, and in this he succeeded brilliantly.

The most influential critic to emerge after Nathan's maturity was the most important of Woollcott's successors at the *New York Times*, Brooks Atkinson. Atkinson had been educated at Harvard and had enrolled in George Pierce Baker's Drama 47 Workshop. After being graduated, he was an English professor at Dartmouth College for a year and a reporter on the *Springfield Daily News* in western Massachusetts. Then he found work as the assistant drama critic for the *Boston Evening Transcript*. Atkinson's apprenticeship under the legendary H. T. Parker, known as "H. T. P." or "Hell-to-Pay," gave him lasting admiration for the craft of newspaper reviewing as well as respect for the intelligence of his readers. Nathan may well have reminded Atkinson of Parker.

The Bostonian was a waspish and singular character. He wrote in a style that could be orotund in one passage, pithy in the next. Parker had little patience with dullards. Once, two nonstop talkers sat behind him on an opening night and through his teeth he rumbled; "They are making so much noise on the stage that I can't hear a word you are saying."[54] H. T. P. looked upon theater criticism as a vocation and practiced it from 1903 to 1934. For two generations of Boston theatergoers he was, in poet David McCord's phrase, "a small and bitter gargoyle above the Brahmin sea."[55]

Atkinson remains the most beloved American drama critic of all time, a genial pipe-smoker reduced to tears by the umbrellas-in-the-rain finale of *Our Town*. He wrote for the general public, for casual theater enthusiasts. Dubbed "Manhattan's Thoreau" by John Mason Brown, Atkinson's New England nostalgia and liberal convictions were central to his criticism. When the United States entered World War II, he insisted on becoming a war correspondent and went abroad. He was awarded a Pulitzer Prize for his reports from Russia. After the war he returned to the drama desk and, true to his beliefs, he was an early opponent of Senator Joseph McCarthy. His four decades of reviewing won him the admiration of everyone in the theatrical community. When he retired in 1960, the Mansfield Theater was renamed the Brooks Atkinson, quite a significant tribute, given Richard Mansfield's historic status as one of America's greatest actors.

When we reread Atkinson's reviews today, they stand in sharp contrast to Nathan's. They are relaxed and detached. Atkinson's reviews reveal that the *Times* had become the paper of record for the New York theater. Their tone is authoritative without being assertive. Given Atkinson's great reputation, we might expect more from his reviews, but they offer little substantive commentary. Atkinson's concentration on keeping his temper and maintaining the perspective of the average theatregoer broadens his perspective in a way that limits his effectiveness. Atkinson was no crusader. He accepted whatever was acceptable to his readership. To contrast Atkinson's professional style with Nathan's, let us consider the events surrounding the first production of Thornton Wilder's *Our Town*. It is also worth looking at the comments of Stark Young and John Mason Brown in this context.

It is a theatrical legend that Atkinson's support for Thornton Wilder's *Our Town* saved that play and rescued an American classic from oblivion. It may be that, save for Atkinson, no one in New York gave the play an unqualified rave, but we must recall that the only unmitigated pan the play *ever* received was from the *Variety* reviewer who savaged its initial Princeton tryout.

Brooks Atkinson's New York colleagues were charier than he. Nathan, writing in *Scribner's,* a general-circulation literary magazine, declared it more of a "theatrical stunt" than a play; "a sparse Sino-American paraphrase of Andreyev's *The Life of Man.*" But even Nathan conceded that there were, no doubt, audiences who would succumb to the emotional appeal of the play.[57] He also correctly predicted that *Our Town* would win the Pulitzer Prize, even though he successfully worked to prevent it from winning the New York Drama Critics Circle Award. Stark Young, writing in the liberal, politically minded *New Republic,* did not think enough of the play to give it any special emphasis in his article. He was particularly perturbed by "the worst pantomiming [he had] ever seen." Nonetheless, Young was impressed by the third act's "device of the dead appearing in a stage image that is unforgettable."[57] Conversely, John Mason Brown, writing for the *Evening Post,* then a left-leaning newspaper, had only one difficulty with the play: its final act. He said that Wilder "chills the living by removing his dead even from compassion." Otherwise, Brown deemed it "one of the sagest, warmest and most deeply human scripts to have come out of our theatre."[58]

The play's real struggles had less to do with critics than with backstage conflicts. On its tryout tour in Boston, the play opened in the same week as Orson Welles's modern dress, "fascist" *Julius Caesar.* Both this production and *Our Town's* absence of scenery prompted agitation on the part of the unions. The play's producer and director, the infamous Jed Harris, had to fight, with his fists as well as with legal tactics, to bring up the curtain. The play was a modest success, but it took the life out of his career. The difficulties he had in mounting the production caused him to withdraw from financing his own shows and marked the end of the era of showmanship in serious playmaking.

Desperate for a hit, Harris had taken no chances with the play. He courted Alexander Woollcott to whom Wilder had dedicated the play. No stranger to logrolling, Woollcott did everything he could for the drama. Ultimately, Harris counted on the fact that Brooks Atkinson was famously fond of plays that were set in the New England of "the good old days." (Nathan had ribbed Atkinson for this in print.[59]) Later in his life, Harris took to retailing the anecdote that he had cajoled Atkinson into attending a rehearsal of Wilder's play.[60] Such a story is far beyond the apocryphal. Atkinson, who was literally "the conscience of the *New York Times*," would never have violated his own ethical code and allow himself to be so used by a producer.[61] Atkinson praised the play, and his sincere admiration for it established its claim to being one of the great American dramas. *Our Town* had a successful run of 347 performances in New York but went on to a rather disappointing tour.

Atkinson's reaction to and assessment of *Our Town* have stood up well, but this is just about the only occasion on which Atkinson's view stood out so markedly. Nathan, for once, sided with the majority of his colleagues. The entire story of the first production of Wilder's play is instructive, as it reveals that many of the assumptions about contemporary critics are incorrect. They were neither bewildered by the play's use of Chinese theater techniques, nor were they lulled by the play's seeming sentimentality. On the contrary, most of their commentaries recognized the existential dilemma Wilder had dramatized.

Absence of scenery was not the only thing *Our Town* had in common with other plays that season. It was one of several preternatural plays. Picking up on a perceived trend, the elegant fashion magazine *Vogue* devoted an entire feature to *Our Town* and two other plays, Paul Vincent Carroll's *Shadow and Substance* and Paul Osborn's *On Borrowed Time. Vogue* was startled by a theatrical season highlighted by such "morbid" themes as these dramas offered.[62] In the 1938 season, *On Borrowed Time* was as successful as Wilder's play, and *Shadow and Substance* was only slightly less so. Yet it was Steinbeck's *Of Mice and Men* that won the New York Drama Critics Circle Award that year (in spite of Nathan's high regard for *Shadow and Substance*).

One critic who was certainly Nathan's equal in his love for and knowledge of the theatre was the professor, playwright, and novelist Stark Young. He is the most important critic to make his mark after Nathan began his career. Young remains one of the most respected reviewers of the American theater. He brought erudition untinged by pedantry to drama criticism. A polished stylist particularly skilled in describing acting, Young is still almost universally respected and admired. He was famous for his courtesy and sensitive judgment. Young was the *New Republic's* drama critic from 1922 to 1947, save for an unhappy one-season stint at the *New York Times* (1924–25). He also worked at *Theatre Arts* as associate editor from until 1940). In contrast to his contempt for Woollcott, Nathan maintained a cordial relationship with Young. Indeed, Nathan's contemporary eminence is best summed up by this colleague, who wrote several warm and enthusiastic letters to Nathan. The earliest letter is from 1925, the last from some time in the 1940s. Unlike Nathan, Young is a critic who was almost universally admired. Like Nathan, though, Young found himself unable to function as a daily reviewer and did not enjoy his one-year stint at the *New York Times*. He returned to the monthly *New Republic*, which was, interestingly enough, also a journal for which Edmund Wilson and Walter Lippmann wrote. Young remained there until 1947, when he resigned in a dispute over editorial policy.

Young's letters to Nathan have a curious tone. He was a year older than Nathan, but there are moments when he seems much younger, sounding like an apprentice begging a favor of the master. No doubt this is due to Young's well-known and justly admired courtesy. In a sense, though, he was Nathan's junior, in that Nathan had been a critic for fourteen years before Young began his career at *Theatre Arts* and the *New Republic* in 1921. At first, Young wrote to Nathan to express his strong feelings about Nathan's "personal distinction," and to salute his success on the occasion of the first anniversary of *The American Mercury* in a letter dated 10 August 1925. Young is particularly delighted to have this opportunity to write to Nathan as he has apparently wished to do so for some time. On 27 November 1932 he apologized to Nathan for the *New Republic's* attack on *The American Spectator;* he wanted Nathan to know that he "completely disassociated himself" from the position taken by the magazine.

In 1942, in a letter written at the time the Lunts were performing in *The Pirate*, he commends Nathan's erudition. Young had apparently enlisted Nathan's aid in showing up the rather shabby behavior of the Lunts and S. N. Behrman. The Lunts had solicited a play from Young and he wrote one for them about a pirate and a lady, but they had refused to accept it. The Lunts then turned to playwright S. N. Behrman, who was given Young's "buccaneer script." Behrman found a creaky German comedy, *Der Seeräuber,* on the same theme and so created his *Pirate.*

In his column, Nathan commented that Behrman's title was doubly accurate. He pointed out that S. N. Behrman's version of *Der Seeräuber* had been far more than merely "suggested" by Ludwig Fulda's thirty-year-old play, as it used the title, the situation, virtually the entire plot, the location, the characterizations—even the characters' names—of the German original.[63] Complimenting him on the appropriate application of his knowledge, Young told Nathan that he was the only American critic entitled to speak on German drama. In a letter, Young continued,

> [your] article seems a masterpiece in every respect. Nobody else in town could write it in the first place; and in the second place no other theatre writer would ever know all that authoritative data. And in the third place, nobody else would defy chatter, threats and libel suits as you have done. . . .[64]

Finally, in an undated letter probably dating from sometime in the early 1940s, Young says of Nathan's career;

> It astonishes me that you who once did so much for an obviously living American theatre can still do so much for a theatre that now just spins around here and there and threatens to die on us. Though I suppose nothing dies. At any rate you show signs of nothing but life, and I am all for you.[65]

Young and Woollcott were Nathan's major rivals for different reasons. Young's background and learning challenged Nathan's status as the best-read critic. Woollcott's grandstanding could crowd anyone's limelight, and he demanded attention constantly. These three reviewers were the most important critics of the 1920s, yet each lived something of a hidden life. Nathan kept his Jewishness secret. Young was a homosexual determined to remain in the closet. Woollcott's sexual ambiguity and pervasive emotional insecurities were completely masked by a bizarrely adhesive public persona composed of acerbated treacle. The choices each of these men made did not necessarily harm their criticism, but their public functioning is emblematic of mainstream American culture and its demands. Their decisions about the conduct of their lives inform us about the twentieth-century conceptions of the "man of letters" and the "man about town." Certain eccentricities of manner and demeanor were appropriate because they made good copy. Superficial flamboyance was welcomed; more intimate departures from accepted norms of conduct were not. This is hardly a revelation, but the decade of the 1920s is particularly important in this regard, for it was the era when critics themselves became celebrities. Nathan and Woollcott embraced fame; Young shied away from it. Ironically, today Young is the best remembered of the three; he is the critic most respected by historians. Nathan is attended to mainly by O'Neillians or Mencken scholars. Woollcott survives as a stage character in a Kaufman and Hart comedy. Nonetheless, the ambiguous relationship each one of these critics developed with American culture is compelling; each chose to play the part of the critic, while being to his own self untrue.

Nathan's enduring status among his fellow critics is worth noting briefly. John Mason Brown, who reviewed for the *New York Evening Post* (1929–41) and *The Saturday Review* (1944–53), among other publications, diligently educated himself to become a drama critic. All through his years at Harvard, where he worked with George Pierce Baker, he studied the history of the theater and its literature with one purpose: that he might one day criticize it professionally. Nathan no doubt smiled at Brown's high-minded attitude, but he nonetheless encouraged the younger critic and earned his lasting loyalty. As Brown records in *Two on the Aisle* (299–302) and elsewhere, Nathan was not merely "the Dean of Critics" in his later years. He gave thoughtful encouragement to many of his worthy colleagues from the 1920s until the end of his days.[66]

Brown was not exactly Nathan's protégé, but he was clearly influenced by Nathan to a great extent. Brown's use of his knowledge of theatrical history and stage conventions as applied in his whimsical, yet pointed, series of "letters from green room ghosts" is an example of Brown's following Nathan's lead. What is more, Brown's editing, with Montrose J. Moses, of *The American Theatre as Seen by its Critics 1752–1934* is a testament to the place secured by criticism as a result, in no small part, of Nathan's labors. The prominence given Nathan in this collection constitutes Brown's and Moses's recognition of those labors.

Nathan's role in the foundation and early years of the New York Drama Critics' Circle best indicates the prestige he had among his fellow critics. Press agent Helen Deutsch instigated the Critics' Circle and served as its first executive secretary. In 1936 she sent a letter to the twelve leading critics in New York suggesting that they ought to confer an award of their own in response to the Pulitzer Prize committee's giving the best play award to Zoë Akins's adaptation of Edith Wharton's novel *The Old Maid*. Nathan's displeasure over Akins's award is indicative of his integrity; according to Mencken, the author was one of his intimate friends: "Nathan used his influence to get Akins her first hearing."[67] Nathan's efforts on behalf of actresses were no secret on the Rialto, but he aided productions of plays solely on the basis of their theatrical merits. Nathan's voice had long been loudest in protest against the Pulitzer committee's choices. Nathan never forgave the committee's shameless about-face of 1923 when it awarded Hatcher Hughes, a lecturer at Columbia, the prize for *Hell-bent fer Heaven*, a hyperreligious, pseudofolk drama. Determined that his Columbia colleague should win the prize, Brander Matthews browbeat the committee into reversing its initial, unanimous vote for George Kelly's *The Show-off*. In 1925 Nathan assailed the choice of *They Knew What They Wanted* and protested the following year when the prize was given to George Kelly for *Craig's Wife*. Nathan's antipathy to the Pulitzer committee continued after the Critics' Circle was formed. He wrote: "What they know of the theatre and drama might comfortably be put into a quinine capsule, with plenty of room left to spare for a copy of the Lord's Prayer, a tinted photograph of Major Bowes, and one of Anna Held's pink garters."[68] In 1943, John Anderson, critic for the *Journal-American*, told Helen Deutsch that Nathan had sought redress for the Pulitzer blunders for "a long time before you came along."[69] Anderson was helping Deutsch to fend off attacks claiming that she had organized the Circle strictly as a boon for her clients. Such a suspicion had been aroused the first year of the Circle's existence when Maxwell Anderson, her client and neighbor, was awarded the first Critics' Circle Prize. Nathan was elected the second president of the Circle and served from 1937 to 1939.

As we have seen, Nathan valued criticism above all else. The nature of Nathan's personal approach to criticism caused him to be attacked and misunderstood. Nonetheless, there was always a core of support for the critic throughout his lifetime. By establishing the inalienable right of the critic to have his own personality, Nathan led the way for the slightly less personal, greatly less impassioned criticism of the present. If Nathan seemed to go out of fashion in the 1930s, it was only that he was simply not part of the leftish trend in the theatre. As he had before, when David

Belasco's brand of realism was all the rage, he watched, waited, fought against the current, and prevailed.

The most important aspect of Nathan's career remains his definition of what the drama critic should do. He had established his definition by the middle of the 1920s. Two contemporary reviews, one of *Materia Critica* and one of *The Autobiography of an Attitude*, reveal how well Nathan had disseminated his critical beliefs. Both writers attest to Nathan's status as "the perfect dramatic critic" and make it clear that his methods had crystallized by 1925. Of *Materia Critica*, one unsigned review said:

> In George Jean Nathan, then, we have the perfect dramatic critic, the archetype, the *Kritiker an sich* as Kant might say. He is the complete man of the theatre, his mind is as uncontaminated with irrelevancies as that of politician with ideas or that of a professional moralist with a sense of decency or fair play. Everything human is alien to him, unless it concerns the theatre, of which his love is profound and extensive and of which he never tires. . . . The mere journalists loathe him . . . the younger intellectuals apply to him their usual naive test, namely the absence of any display of classroom learning, and conclude that he is just a super lowbrow.[71]

A year later, speaking of *The Autobiography of an Attitude*, Robert Malcolm Gray comments:

> It is curious how the Nathian [*sic*] philosophy or attitude already becomes traditional and therefore a little old fashioned. . . . Here the manner does not seem to be so amusing as it used to be. It is as if the author had reached the pass of imitating himself, and the effect is sometimes galvanic rather than lively.[72]

Close examination of Nathan's later work reveals that he is restating and reapplying ideas and attitudes that he had promulgated during the 1910s and 1920s. Nathan's critical presence is important through the 1930s, 1940s and 1950s, but he is no longer defining the role of the critic in the theater so much as he is refining it. Having reviewed some of the salient statements Nathan made about the function of the critic and some of the responses he received, it is now best to turn to Nathan's only excursion in the theoretical realm, his 1922 volume, *The Critic and the Drama*.

# 4

# The Limits of Impressionism

As ARE MANY THINGS CONNECTED WITH GEORGE JEAN NATHAN, HIS book *The Critic and the Drama* is a misunderstood entity. It is held out by his admirers to be his great treatise on the aesthetics of the theater and ridiculed by his detractors as a halfbaked philosophical screed. While he was writing it, Nathan had this to say about his work in progress: "It is at bottom an attempt to substitute a more liberal aesthetic evaluation for that offered by Croce, together with an appraisal of criticism in America."[1]

What Nathan meant by "more liberal" than Croce is explained in the completed text. Nathan is not satisfied with Crocean intuition because it is, in his eyes, something that gives too much freedom of interpretation to the artist and too little freedom of expression to the critic.[2] The paradoxical nature of such a philosophical proposition appears to indicate that something is amiss here. Nathan is not only refusing to play by the rules of logical argument he is out to break every single one of them.

That Benedetto Croce was the most influential aesthetic philosopher of the turn of the century is something that only partisans of George Santayana will dispute. Nathan can be considered a partial subscriber to Croce's aesthetics, at least as far as drama is concerned. Croce rejects the notion of applied formalism to art in general and to plays in particular. He dismisses entirely the concept of imposing theoretical criteria on individual plays in order that one might render a dramatic work of art a "tragedy." Surely Nathan's approach to criticism would seem to fit into Croce's larger philosophical endeavor. That it is possible, though, to make Croce's aesthetic more "liberal" is open to debate. Clearly, Nathan is on shaky ground when he does battle with the likes of Goethe and Croce, but in this text, he is not engaging in controversy so much as he is making a tactical retreat. Or, to put it in strategic terms, he is waging guerilla criticism via internal theoretical subversion.

114

It is quite likely that much of what Nathan writes in the "Aesthetics of Jurisprudence" chapter of *The Critic and the Drama* is not, in fact, completely serious. For instance, Nathan's epigraph to the book begins, "Of all the arts and half arts even above that of acting is the art of criticism founded most greatly upon vanity. . . ." Ostensibly reasonable Nathanesque dicta these, and to describe, as Nathan does a few lines later, "the ineradicable vainglory of criticism" as one of its fundamentals is no doubt honesty on Nathan's part.[3] Within the larger context of objective theoretical inquiry though, it hardly seems the proper tone in which to undertake a book of dramatic aesthetics.

Nathan's book is divided into six chapters: "Aesthetic Jurisprudence," "Drama as an Art," "The Place of the Theatre," "The Place of Acting," "Dramatic Criticism," and "Dramatic Criticism in America." The entire book is not facetious, but the opening passages and much of the first chapter have more than a hint of tongue in cheek about them. This is not to disparage *The Critic and the Drama*, but to put it in its proper place alongside Nathan's other volumes. For in virtually every one of his books, he effortlessly mingles serious invective with frothy expostulations. In the second section of "Aesthetic Jurisprudence," Nathan states outright that he does not "believe finally in this or that 'theory' of criticism."[4] He then proceeds to enter into what was in the early 1920s a major critical controversy on both sides of the Atlantic: the brouhaha over the Goethe-Carlyle and the Spingarn-Croce theories of aesthetics neither of which, by the way, may be said ever to have actually existed.

Nathan's coeditor, H. L. Mencken, started this critical altercation when he reviewed Joel E. Spingarn's book *Creative Criticism* and subsequently expanded his review into an essay, "Criticism of Criticism of Criticism," which was published in his first series of *Prejudices* in 1919.[5] Isaac Goldberg, the biographer of both Mencken and Nathan, who was also a drama scholar, devoted part of a chapter of his 1922 book, *The Drama of Transition*, to this contemporary aesthetic controversy.[6] Reviews of Goldberg's book spawned other articles until 2 May 1923, when Spingarn intervened with an article of his own, "The Growth of a Literary Myth." Therein, he sketched the development of the Croce-Spingarn-Goethe-Carlyle theory of criticism from an imaginary "monster into an important reality."[7]

Spingarn describes how he casually employed two stray quotations from Carlyle and Goethe in one of his essays in *Creative Criticism*. These remarks in combination with Spingarn's lifelong study of Croce were given equal weight by Mencken. Spingarn demonstrates quite clearly how Mencken misread him entirely. When he turns to Nathan and his alleged use of the socalled Goethe-Carlyle theory, it is Spingarn's turn to misread.

Nathan refers to the Goethe-Carlyle theory on pages eleven through nineteen and spends most of his time disparaging it as yet another inefficacious "theory." Nathan describes it thus:

> The critic's duty lies alone in discerning the artist's aim, his point of view and, finally, his execution of the task before him. . . . This is not a "theory" of criticism so much as it is a foundation for a theory.[8]

As the chapter progresses, though, it becomes quite clear that Nathan is creating an epistemoeschatocritical pastiche. He confesses

> There may not be contradictions in the contentions here set forth, I am not sure. But I advance no fixed, definite theory of my own; I advance merely contradictions of certain of the phases of the theories held by others, and contradictions are ever in the habit of begetting contradictions. Yet such contradictions are in themselves apposite and soundly critical, since any theory susceptible of contradictions must itself be contradictory and insecure. If I suggest any theory on my part it is a variable one: a theory that, in this instance, is one thing and in that another.[9]

Perhaps this is Nathan's attempt to bring pataphysics to the United States. For surely this is the Nathan of "Why Our Drama is Backward," *The Avon Flows,* and *Bottoms Up.* The first is his reconstruction of Augustus Thomas's play *Indian Summer,* in which he completely reverses the drama's action in order to render it more comprehensible.[10] The second is his conflation of *Romeo and Juliet, The Taming of the Shrew,* and *Othello,* which dramatizes what would have happened if Romeo and Juliet had lived. The third is a little volume of parodies of popular dramatic conventions, subtitled "An Application of the Slapstick to Satire." No doubt this is the Nathan who claimed a master of arts degree from the University of Bologna, as detailed in *Pistols for Two,* the Mencken-Nathan biography penned by "Owen Hatteras, D. S. O." (in reality, Mencken and Nathan themselves, of course). It would be perfectly in keeping with Nathan's temperament and in harmony with his past and future writings for him to have confected an aesthetic study that is something of a hoax.

Toward the end of "Aesthetic Jurisprudence" he takes on Spingarn directly, referring to his essay on "Creative Criticism" as "a particularly clear example of the manner in which the proponents of the more modern theories of criticism imprison themselves in the extravagance of their freedom."[11] Nathan refutes the notion that it is of use for the critic to regard each work of art as a separate entity unless each "work of criticism be similarly a unit, a thing in itself."[12]

Fortunately, the remainder of *The Critic and the Drama* is much more reasonable. Incidentally, *Vanity Fair* nominated Nathan for its hall of fame when *The Critic and the Drama* was published. This most sophisticated magazine selected him that year "because the *Mercure de France* has said he is the greatest dramatic critic America has produced since Poe." *Vanity Fair* also cited his coeditorship of *The Smart Set,* but chose him "chiefly because in his new book he explains the seriousness of his critical position."[13] Obviously, *Vanity Fair*'s editors missed the waggish tone that much of the book retained, even as Nathan succeeded in making his more serious points. Indeed, what better and more characteristic way could there be for Nathan, the consummate antitheorist to mock the latest trend in critical theory than to nonsensically appropriate its diction.

What is more, Nathan expresses opinions in the later chapters that he will expand upon throughout his life, whereas he never again indulged in the hypothetical excrescences of "Aesthetic Jurisprudence." In the second chapter's discussion of drama as an art, he asserts that drama is a "democratic art in constant brave conflict with the aristocracy of intelligence, soul and emotion."[14] He advances farther along in this line of thought later in the chapter:

> All great art is democratic in intention, if not in reward. Michelangelo, Shakespeare, Wagner and Zola are democratic artists, and their art democratic art. It is criticism of Michelangelo, Shakespeare, Wagner and Zola that is aristocratic. . . . To appraise a democratic art in terms of democracy is to attempt to effect a chemical reaction in nitrogen with nitrogen. . . . No great artist has ever in his heart deliberately fashioned his work for a remote and forgotten cellar. . . .
>
> It is as ridiculous to argue that because Shakespeare's is a democratic art it must be criticized in terms of democratic reactions to it as it would be to argue that because the United States is a democracy the most acute and comprehensive criticism of that democracy must lie in a native democrat's reaction to it.[15]

Nathan articulates his own aristocratic aesthetic with this argument and implicitly makes the case for his own critical methods.

In the chapters on the place of the theater and of the actor, Nathan addresses his concerns with the design of the theater building and his lack of concern for the individual actor. Nathan does not believe that one theater is better than another, nor does he consider it valid to separate historical theater such as the Greek and Elizabethan stages from the twentieth-century Grosses Schauspielhaus or the Julian Eltinge theatre.[16] As for acting, Nathan's antipathy to allegations about the art of acting has already been discussed; here he dismisses it as "less an art, than the deceptive echo of an art." (*Critic and the Drama* 103).

In the book's penultimate chapter Nathan upends the most commonly accepted "virtues" of criticism. He begins with "honesty." Unfortunately, because most critics are "blockheads," what they "honestly" believe is worthless. (115) He moves on to "enthusiasm" and dismisses it as merely "an attribute of the uncritical" and "an endowment of immaturity." (117) He continues with "detachment." Nathan says that to ask a critic to become detached from his criticism is "like asking an actor to keep himself out of his role." (121) Another deadly virtue is "sympathy"; regarding this, he declares that the critic must have, not sympathy, but "interest." Nathan maintains that "sympathy and enthusiasm, unless they are *ex post facto*, are precisely like prevenient prejudice and hostility." (123) The scourge of "constructive criticism" is the most insidious virtue of all:

> As a result of this conviction we have an endless repertoire of architectonic advice from critics wholly without the structural faculty, advice which, if it were followed, would produce a drama twice as poor as that which they criticize. Obsessed with the idea that they must be constructive, the critics know no lengths to which they will not go. . . . They constructively point out that Shaw's plays would be better if Shaw understood the punctual technique of Pinero, thus destroying a *Caesar and Cleopatra* to construct a *Second Mrs. Tanqueray*. . . . One can't cure a yellow fever patient by pointing out to him that he should have caught the measles. One can't improve the sanitary conditions of a neighbourhood merely by giving the outhouse a different coat of paint. (124–125)

As usual, Nathan propounds his view that a critic must adjudicate plays as they are in the theater. Nathan's insistence on the proper function of criticism shows us that he is not content with things as they are, for although he insists that the critic should take things as they are, the critic must not leave them that way. Nathan concludes *The Critic and the Drama* with a survey of dramatic criticism in America. Americans, he says, practice "Mason jar criticism, a labeling and bottling process" (145) of the drama's disparate elements. And American criticism is doomed to "follow the bellcow, the bellcow is personal cowardice, artistic cowardice, neighbourhood cowardice, or the even cheaper cowardice of the daily and to a much lesser degree periodical press." (147–148) Here Nathan is lashing out against the lingering puffsterism that continued to plague drama criticism in the 1920s. He flogs his colleagues for enslaving themselves to the box office and for writing down to their audiences. He inveighs against the insularism of the theatrical and critical communities. He concludes that at best, American drama criticism is cushioned by a plushcovered provincialism that is blissfully unaware of its parochial shortcomings, and thus is in "a state of stagnant optimism." (151).

Apparently Nathan thought at one time of revising this work, for among the miscellaneous manuscripts in the Nathan Collection at Cornell is an unbound edition of *The Critic and the Drama* that has been reassembled and filled with marginal notations and emendations. Most of the changes consist in updating the references Nathan makes to theatrical people, plays, and so forth. He reorganizes the chapters thus: "Aesthetic Jurisprudence" remains the first; "The Place of Acting" is moved from fourth to second; "Dramatic Criticism," which now has included in it the chapter on American criticism, is moved from fifth to third; "The Place of the Theatre" goes from third to fourth; and "Drama as an Art" is removed from second to last place. Nathan also decided to turn the epigraph into an envoi.

Internal evidence suggests that he undertook these revisions circa 1934. On page 78, Nathan has crossed out "eighteen" and changed it to "thirty," this in reference to the number of years he has been a critic (the original was published in 1922). The cuts and alterations increase from the back of the book to the front, and there are almost no changes in the first two chapters. He cuts out the references to "commercial Puritanism." (127–128) and to the ridiculous restrictions imposed on the public expression of emotions. (136) Considering the problematic nature of Nathan's own Jewishness, a note at the foot of page 144 is troubling. He is discussing Pinero and the line reads," . . . Pinero, while treating of British impulses and character, is himself of ineradicable Portuguese mind and blood. . . ." In the margin he has written, "=

Jewish" and has indicated that this is to be inserted between "Portuguese" and "mind." Pinero's PortugueseJewish background is a matter of record, but Pinero's genealogy is not the issue. What does matter here is why Nathan should have made such an emendation. The passage in question deals with "personal criticism." Nathan is explaining how it is impossible to separate one's own personal characteristics from one's criticism and, furthermore, that it is impossible to leave out the personality of the performer or the playwright from drama criticism. For Nathan to consider that Pinero's Jewishness is significant is to contradict everything that he had written to Goldberg almost ten years earlier. Perhaps Harold Clurman was right after all. If Clurman *was* right, it would make much of Nathan's indignation (in the "Dramatic Criticism in America" chapter of *The Critic and the Drama*) about the yokelization of American society almost poignant. He comes off sounding much less like a slightly ruffled peacock and much more like someone who is afraid of being tarred and feathered. Thus, the selfdirected barb that he was the selfappointed "president of the Amalgamated SelfHaters of the Universe" recounted by John Held in 1917 takes on another, rather bitter, resonance.

A comment Nathan made about himself and first-night audiences sheds further light on the critic's ambivalent attitude about himself (an ambivalence that has been ignored by everyone except H. L. Mencken). Writing in 1924 about the theatre as a "social occasion," Nathan says:

> The theatre is always a trifle silly at these times, like a newly rich pork packer who puts on spats and takes up French. It fills its seats with a lot of rich Wall St. Jews (who are driven to regard the theatre and the opera house as a social quarters by virtue of barriers set up against them in more private and exclusive guilds), a somewhat lesser number of *Social Register* pushers, and a few eminent visiting foreign firemen. . . . That I, for example, often so pretty myself up on such occasions is surely no tribute to my good manners and gentlemanliness, and most certainly not to my respect for the profession of dramatic critic, but rather a mark of cheap affectation that seeks, by so uniforming itself, to avoid conspicuousness and, in the avoiding, makes its entrepreneur no better than the swine he affects to spit on.[17]

The reference to "Wall St. Jews" is, of course, obliquely amplified by the mention of "pork packers" and "swine." Certainly Nathan knew what was and was not kosher. Such bizarre psychological encoding signals a field day for Freudians and nevertheless confirms the suspicion that Nathan, if not a tortured soul, was at least a conflicted one. There are those who would connect Nathan's shattered self with his inability to fashion a coherent critical theory, but such facile linkage smacks of crude psychologizing.

The "Aesthetic Jurisprudence" chapter of *The Critic and the Drama* is unsatisfactory as a serious theoretical disquisition, but it is nonetheless an adequate explanation of why theories are not useful for drama critics who are journalists. It is, however, an appropriate presentation of Nathan's aestheticism. The chapter and the remainder of the text are also good indicators of Nathan's influence and prestige at that point in his career.

If the early 1920s represent the high point of Nathan's standing as a critic, what then, is to be made of the remaining three decades of his career? Significant changes in Nathan's professional position radically altered his place as a critic. When he ceased to be coeditor of *The American Mercury* he was no longer able to arbitrate on the national literary, political, and social scenes as he had been doing. He lost his forum for explicit social commentary and editorial decision-making. Not that any of those had mattered to him essentially, but nonetheless it is undeniable that when he lost his place at the *Mercury*, he lost face. So more than ever Nathan turned to the world of the theatre. It became the sole sphere in which he exercised his talents. That he wanted to do more is evidenced by his abortive *American Spectator* enterprise. Nathan stayed at the heart of Broadway and was as influential as ever, but he was now exclusively a Broadway figure, whereas previously, he had been a national one. In any event, Nathan's backstage activities belie the assertion that he was somehow fading out of the picture. Nathan may have ceased to blaze, but through the 1920s, 1930s and 1940s, he was as fiery a presence as ever. In 1931 his name was in the headlines when he was called to testify in a plagiarism suit brought against Eugene O'Neill. Georges Lewys claimed that O'Neill's *Strange Interlude* was cribbed from her novel *The Temple of Pallas-Athenae,* and she sued the playwright. "Nathan in Court Tilt Aids O'Neill Defense" was the 17 March *New York Times* headline for the story covering the critic's testimony. O'Neill won the suit handily. Nathan's courtroom responses, and even the questions put to him, demonstrate that he was a most respected drama critic and a highly regarded man about town. On the stand, Nathan was asked about and explained such things as O'Neill's dramatic technique, his and O'Neill's discussion of the legs of Lotta Faust, how much he drank, and why he sported his handkerchief in the upper right pocket of his jacket.[18]

Nathan would have had another good reason to peruse that particular page of the *Times* on that day. His cousin, Fred G. Nixon-Nirdlinger, had been shot and killed by his wife, Charlotte, in their apartment on the French Riviera. This man was the son of Nathan's uncle Samuel Nixon-Nirdlinger, the theatre manager. Fred Nixon's wife had killed him in self-defense after a violent dispute. The story was in the headlines for months. Obsessed with Charlotte, Nixon-Nirdlinger had been insanely jealous of his wife, divorcing her and later remarrying her. The couple's two children, one aged three and the other aged eighteen months, were in the apartment when the murder took place. Nathan is never mentioned in any of the stories detailing the murder or the subsequent trial in Nice in which Mrs. Nixon-Nirdlinger was acquitted. This is not surprising, but what is a bit odd is that there is no reference to the murder in Nathan's papers. Nathan had admitted to both Isaac Goldberg and Constance Frick that Samuel Nixon was his uncle, so it cannot be that he kept the Nixon-Nirdlinger side of his family a secret. Nor did Nathan keep his friends away from his family (as Harold Clurman implies). In assorted letters to Nathan and others, H. L. Mencken devotes some attention to the death of Nathan's brother Fritz during the 1918 influenza epidemic, the death of Nathan's mother, and the failing health of Nathan's sister-in-law, Marguerite (with whom Mencken apparently stayed in contact throughout his life). It is possible that Nathan was simply not concerned with his cousin's death, or perhaps the scandalous nature of the murder and the trial were so distressing to him that he excised any references to them from his life.

The following year, Nathan's name even resounded through the halls of Congress. In 1932, Representative William Sirovich of New York, the chair of the House Committee on Patents, Copyrights and Trademarks, was in the midst of hearings on a bill that would have regulated drama criticism, among other things. But on 11 March, he left his own committee to testify on a taxation bill. He called for a reduction of the tax on theater tickets. To support his amendment, he discussed the dire state of the theater. The Depression was blamed, but Sirovich identified a threat almost as dangerous as the economic debacle: drama critics. "They are flippant, irreverent, they believe it is smart to deprecate and only deprecate. . . ." However, Sirovich reserved his wrath for the columnists who review plays and "live on the lowest type of dung. . . . These men are not dramatic critics. . . . They are a passing phase of mental depravity. . . ." No doubt this refers to Walter

Winchell's cohorts, not to mention Winchell himself, as he was a charter member of the New York Drama Critics Circle. But what is surprising is that almost a sixth of Representative Sirovich's three-and-a-half pages of testimony is devoted to an encomium to George Jean Nathan.

> At the highest rung of American dramatic critics stands a most unusual gentleman, a man with a great many of whose views I am in disagreement, but for whose character, idealism, and scholarship I have the highest respect. . . . His aesthetic and artistic standards give him that isolation of eminence which can never be approached in real life. . . . Mr. Nathan's genius is . . . that of an honest, able, fearless, and courageous critic.[19]

Sirovich goes on to call Nathan "the high priest of the intelligentsia of the theatre" and "the outstanding spokesman of his profession." He concludes his remarks by demanding that Nathan purge drama criticism of its malefactors, quoting Nathan himself: "it is incumbent upon dramatic criticism itself to ridicule out of it, to cannonade out of it, to murder out of it all its mountebanks, shysters, and pretenders."[20]

In the middle of the decade, Nathan's ten-year campaign on behalf of Sean O'Casey bore fruit; in 1934 he helped get O'Casey's *Within the Gates* a Broadway staging. Nathan first sent it to the Theatre Guild, but they turned down O'Casey's script. Undaunted, Nathan was able to persuade two independent producers, John Tuerk and George Bushar Markell, to take on the play. O'Casey himself came to New York to oversee rehearsals, and the critic and the playwright finally met. They spent many evenings together during O'Casey's three-month stay. Nathan escorted O'Casey to soirees and supper clubs. After these jaunts, they frequently talked till dawn in Nathan's rooms at the Royalton. No relationship in Nathan's life was as incongruous as this one, but it was warm enough for O'Casey, the dedicated Marxist, to call Nathan "a communist" on the basis of his devotion to the best in art. For his part, Nathan placed O'Casey's work with the greatest dramas of the century. Nathan's devotion to O'Casey demonstrates the integrity of his critical judgment. That so notorious a snob and reactionary could so enthusiastically endorse a radical proletarian artist like O'Casey speaks for itself. It also undermines the notion that he was insensitive to the social consciousness of the 1930s. What Nathan was insensitive to was dubious drama wrapping itself in the red flag of "commitment" or "activism." To assume that Nathan's allegedly reactionary politics influenced his criticism is a superficial assessment of his mature attitude.

The playwright's successful support of William Saroyan in the late 1930s and into the 1940s further reveals that Nathan had lost none of his acumen. On the negative side, he had enough influence to prevent Thornton Wilder from being awarded the Critics' Circle prize for *The Skin of Our Teeth* at the end of the 1942–43 season. Nathan, along with John Anderson, the critic of the *Journal-American,* was accused of "browbeating" his colleagues into voting against Wilder. Even so, this was but one episode in what was a significant literary contretemps. It is now almost forgotten that in a two-part article, "The Skin of Whose Teeth? The Strange Case of Mr. Wilder's New Play and *Finnegans Wake,*" published in the *Saturday Review of Literature* shortly after the play opened, Joseph Campbell and Henry Morton Robinson had convinced the nation's middlebrow readers that Wilder had virtually plagiarized his play from James Joyce's *Finnegans Wake*.[21] The high-brows were convinced otherwise, as Edmund Wilson argued for the playwright's innocence in his essay "The Antrobuses and the Earwickers," published in *The Nation*.[22] Wilson's defense notwithstanding, Wilder's curious failure to respond to the charges hurt his reputation. Nathan, never a fan of Wilder's work, gleefully pilloried the production, saying of the playwright, "When it comes to being a Joyce, Mr. Wilder remains nine parts Peggy to one part James."[23] Although he singled out Tallulah Bankhead's performance as one of the best of the year, Nathan made sure that it did not win the Critics' Circle Prize.

Nathan's relationship with Saroyan is not quite of a piece with those he had with other playwrights. In 1929, writing in *Overland Monthly,* Saroyan fired a broadside: "The American Clowns of Criticism—Mencken, Nathan and Haldeman-Julius."[24] Saroyan attacked Nathan for his intolerance and his seeming irrationality. He did give him credit, though, for being one of the four funniest writers in English (the other three being Ring Lardner, Robert Benchley, and Stephen Leacock). Clearly, Nathan took the assault well. Ten years later he kept Saroyan from giving up on the theater altogether. In 1939, After Saroyan's *My Heart's in the Highlands* had met with critical hostility, save for Nathan and John Mason Brown's enthusiasm, the playwright had determined to "brush the dust of Broadway from his boots forever." Nathan called Saroyan on the morning of his presumptive departure and invited him for lunch at "21." That afternoon, Saroyan explained to Nathan that he wanted to write another play, that, in fact, he knew he had one inside him. Saroyan was so shaken by the drubbing his first effort had been given that he needed a firm commitment his play would be produced before he could actually write it.

Nathan planned on much more than simply bucking up the writer's sagging confidence. He went to work arranging the most auspicious meeting possible between Saroyan and Eddie Dowling, the actor-turned-director-and-producer. As president of the Critics' Circle, Nathan was able to arrange for Saroyan to be awarded a "most promising playwright" citation. Nathan went so far as to organize the seating at the awards dinner. Dowling was seated across from Saroyan. The producer congratulated Saroyan and told him he would buy his next play "sight unseen." Saroyan took him at his word and wrote *The Time of Your Life.*

The play was Saroyan's greatest success. It was also the play that made Nathan's break with Lillian Gish quite clear. Saroyan had conceived the part of the prostitute, Kitty Duval, as a role for Gish. Nathan had even taken him to dinner at her apartment after *My Heart's in the Highlands* had closed. But after Dowling and the Theatre Guild had agreed to produce *The Time of Your Life,* Nathan once again invited the playwright to lunch at "21." Julie Haydon was there too; she did not say a word during the meal. As they got up to leave, Nathan indicated Miss Haydon and simply said, "Here's your Kitty Duval."[24] Later, after a dreadful New Haven tryout, Nathan managed to persuade the Guild and Dowling that the play should go on. He suggested that Robert Lewis be dismissed and that Dowling and Saroyan himself take on the direction. Nathan's advice was taken here and elsewhere during the play's difficult pre-Broadway performances. *The Time of Your Life* eventually achieved a healthy run and went on to win the Critics' Circle and Pulitzer prizes—though Saroyan made a big show of refusing the Pulitzer. Nathan had done everything in his power to ensure the play's success, but he could not keep Saroyan's ego from sabotaging his own playwriting career. Nathan was close to him through the early 1940s, but Saroyan failed to be a consistent dramatist.

Nathan's relationship with the greatest American dramatist to emerge after World War II is problematic. Recently, allegations have been raised that Nathan behaved unethically and unscrupulously toward Tennessee Williams. Yet these accusations are themselves testimony to Nathan's perceived influence. The charges reveal that Nathan was still a powerful influence in the American theatre. It is unfortunate that his influence has come to be understood in a negative context. An examination of his discussion of

Tennessee Williams sheds light on Nathan's mature style and offers evidence that he was flexible about his own critical priorities. He would be the first person to admit that he slighted the actor in favor of the playwright, but occasionally he would devote the full thrust of his review to a discussion of acting. A particularly interesting example of Nathan's understanding of acting is his discussion of Laurette Taylor's performance in *The Glass Menagerie*. It demonstrates not only Nathan's sensitivity to the exigencies of the individual performance vis-à-vis the entire portrayal of a character, but it also serves as evidence of the virtual impossibility of adequately discussing a particular performance without taking into account the entire production of a particular play. Nathan does not miss the chance to belittle the acuity of his too-eager-to-please colleagues. The controversy that has arisen over Nathan's activities vis-à-vis this play as well as the density of his commentary on Laurette Taylor's performance warrant full quotation.

Three seasons ago, the late Laurette Taylor's portrayal of the mother in *The Glass Menagerie* was hailed, and deservedly, as one of the finest examples of the acting art that our contemporary stage had ever seen. But I wonder how many of her eulogists knew why it was what it was, that is, aside from its readily to be discerned and appreciated aspects. Did they know, for instance, that she on this occasion profited herself by rejecting Coquelin's dictum, "The first duty of a player is respect for his text; whatever he says must be said as the author wrote it"? Far from doing any such thing, she threw a lot of the Tennessee Williams script to the winds and adapted and rephrased it, very ingeniously, to her own personal acting ends. Did they further know that her performance varied markedly from night to night, that it was never the same, and that she skillfully maneuvered it to the different reactions of successive audiences?

Did they appreciate her dexterity in timing her laughs so that they would not suffer from what coughing there might be in the audience? Did they know that what seemed "natural" in her performance was frequently the result of audacious ad libbing? Did they understand that seldom was her articulation and modulation of a line of dialogue the same, and that in this regard she followed her instinct as to a particular audience's character and receptivity? Did they comprehend, in short, that what they regarded, and correctly, to be the top acting performance of its year was not one performance but successively all of a dozen or more, that its entrepreneur had directed herself in it without aid, that she created a character out of bricks and straw supplied only meagrely by the playwright, and that she literally acted the role which itself did not in any way even faintly resemble her and which in sum, for all its embroideries, remained Laurette Taylor from first to last? She did not, as the expression goes, lose herself in the part. She lost, and with uncommon beauty and effect, the part in Laurette Taylor.

Where, in such a case, do the stern critical principles regarding the art of acting find themselves?[25]

Such a passage reveals Nathan at his best. Even if we do not agree with him, his knowledge of the particular performance and of theatre in general enables the critic to make his point seem unassailable. It is vintage Nathan, as well. He *dares* his readers to disagree with him via his stream of rhetorical questions. This is not merely a device; each question is a validation of Nathan's drama criticism. This is so because each question shows his readers what lies behind the assertions he is making about Laurette Taylor's performance and the assertions he is making about the assessments of that performance by "her many eulogists." It should not be overlooked, however, that Nathan is praising Laurette Taylor's performance at the expense of Tennessee Williams's play.

Nathan's role as a behind-the-scenes player is particularly evident with *The Glass Menagerie*. As soon as Eddie Dowling, who was producing and directing, got hold of the play, he showed the script to Nathan and solicited his advice. Nathan was immediately drawn to the script because he saw the role of Laura as a perfect showcase for actress Julie Haydon's talent. (Nathan married Miss Haydon in 1955 after a courtship that lasted a decade and a half.) Nathan also believed that Laurette Taylor would be perfect as Amanda. This is another instance in which Nathan slighted Lillian Gish. Williams had wanted her for the part and had written it with her in mind. Nathan used his considerable influence with Dowling to secure the roles for Haydon and Taylor. Dowling obviously had great respect for Nathan. The critic had previously involved himself with Dowling's productions of *The Time of Your Life* and *Shadow and Substance*. Julie Haydon starred in both of those shows, as well. Nathan certainly never apologized for his closeness to Dowling, and he frequently wrote laudatory columns that singled him out as the only visionary producer in the American theater.

Partisans of Tennessee Williams sometimes attack Nathan for his support for script revisions of *The Glass Menagerie*. Williams denied that the script was changed after the play opened in Chicago, but in letters and in his *Memoirs*, he accuses Nathan and Dowling of unsolicited coauthorship.

Nathan got together with Eddie and between the two of them they composed a drunk scene for Tom that they thought was the only

possible salvation for the play. . . . This "drunk scene," obviously composed in a state which corresponded, was given to me as a *fait accompli*
the next day. . . . I said to myself, "This is the living and the dying
end."[26]

Nathan wrote about the changes the play went through and, as
we have seen, praised Laurette Taylor's ad libbing. He also asserted that Williams "rewrote the drunk scene no less than four
times under Dowling's supervision."[27] That the play was substan-
tially revised is clear, as Williams's manuscripts reveal. In any
event, Nathan left the "credit" to Dowling, but his own involvement in the script was an open secret amongst Main Stemmers.
Lyle Leverich's recent biography of Williams questions Nathan's
ethics. If Williams agreed to add the drunk scene that he and
Eddie Dowling had written, the playwright "could rely on Nathan's support."[28] Playwright Robert Anderson, who came to
know Williams later in his career, worked with the same production company, The Playwrights' Company, and who had the same
agent, Audrey Wood, wrote to this author:

> I know Lyle [Leverich]'s book, but I can't believe that any deal was
> made about making changes in the script in exchange for a good
> review. . . . I think I would have heard if Nathan had done any strong-
> arming of Tennessee. . . .[29]

The only thing Nathan consistently cared about in his entire life
was drama criticism. It does not follow that he would have compromised his integrity for the sake of throwing his weight around.
Leverich also asserts that Nathan was jealous of Laurette Taylor's
great success in the play. She *was* unquestionably the star of the
show. How then can Nathan's long tribute to Taylor be accounted
for? Leverich offers no evidence for any of his accusations against
Nathan; he speculates that homophobia and fear that Williams
would usurp O'Neill's crown drove him to belittle the younger
playwright. Such *ad hominem* accusations are, of course, unanswer-
able. No one could doubt that Nathan was intolerant of homosex-
uals, nor was he was ever shy about making his influence felt, but
to strike a corrupt bargain would have vitiated everything Nathan
had worked for in his four decades as a critic. What is more, if
he did do a dirty deal, he failed to keep his part of the bargain.
Nathan's review was hardly an unqualified rave.

Nonetheless, even as he dispraised the playwright, he hastened
to admit that Williams's importance as the primary author of the
production's success should not be overlooked. Nathan was never

again as respectful toward Tennessee Williams, though. In his *Memoirs*, Williams calls Nathan "my nemesis" when discussing *Menagerie*'s New York premiere.[30] For his part, Nathan seems to have found the playwright pretentious and ignorant of stage history.[31] He chides Williams for employing old-hat expressionist devices that Piscator had used decades earlier, but he neglects to mention that Piscator had been a mentor of Williams. Of course Williams's antipathy to Nathan and to critics in general is well known. Williams had not always been so leery of Nathan's advice. Recognizing the critic's preeminence, in 1940 he specifically sought out Nathan's opinion of his early play *Battle of Angels*. Nathan apparently read the manuscript and found it unusually promising."[32]

Because Williams's and Nathan's early ambivalence toward each other quickly veered toward active dislike, it would not be too speculative to identify Nathan as one possible source of the paranoia that afflicted Williams throughout his later career when he was convinced that a cabal of O'Neill adulators was sabotaging his career. But to take such paranoid imputations seriously is to unjustly defile Nathan's critical integrity. It has been argued that Nathan somehow kept other playwrights down—particularly Williams—in order to keep O'Neill's reputation aloft. This ignores the support the critic gave to William Saroyan, Sean O'Casey, and Paul Vincent Carroll. Playwrights aside, in the 1940s, Nathan devoted much of his energy to boosting Eddie Dowling. And this led to a dispute between O'Neill and Nathan. In 1946, Nathan persuaded O'Neill, who persuaded his producers, the Theatre Guild, to allow Dowling to direct and star in *The Iceman Cometh*, O'Neill's first Broadway production in twelve years. Dowling was quickly overwhelmed by the task and left the role of Hickey to James Barton. O'Neill was extremely dissatisfied with the "business" Dowling had attempted to add to the play. Dowling was eventually forbidden to add any blocking that was not specifically indicated in O'Neill's script. The production was not a success and O'Neill blamed Dowling, in part. The playwright regretted having let Nathan influence him in choosing Dowling. He complained, "Nathan may know plays, but he doesn't know actors and directors."[33] Besides, it could only have helped Nathan's career to "discover" another great American playwright. It is more likely that Nathan simply disliked Williams's later dramas and was unable to appreciate what the dramatist was trying to do. He is certainly not alone in identifying *The Glass Menagerie* as a singular achievement.

Aside from his grudging endorsement of *The Glass Menagerie*, Nathan failed to support Tennessee Williams's subsequent work. Thus, William Saroyan would prove to be the last of Nathan's "discoveries." Nevertheless, his attitude toward Arthur Miller demonstrates that he was critically flexible as he grew older. Nathan was not initially enthusiastic about Miller. He was not impressed with *All My Sons* or later with Miller's adaptation of *An Enemy of the People*, but he was quite taken with *Death of a Salesman*. His essay on this play is an outstanding example of his ability to consider a play not only in its own context, but as part of drama as a whole.[34] Nathan's thoughts on *Death of a Salesman* and his response to Miller's "Tragedy and the Common Man" are among his most cogent later essays. Nathan praises the play while pointing out that director Elia Kazan's "favorite occasional melodramatic emphasis on the box-office's behalf is clear."[35] He asserts, though, that the play's "innate, silent power" overcomes the "hearty yawping" and "pawing embraces" that show us Willy's love for Biff and Lee J. Cobb's resorting to "kicking up his heels in a gazazka" in order to demonstrate Willy's younger self. But he salutes the "complete honesty in most of the characters" and the "absolute honesty" of its theme.[36]

Through the 1940s Nathan's energy was undiminished. He jousted with Gilbert Seldes in the September and November pages of *Esquire* in 1945. Nathan dreaded the advent of television; Seldes was prepared to welcome its possibilities. Nathan rejected outright any suggestion that the theatre could be challenged as an art form by television. This was an echo of his lamentations about film and radio. Nathan's insistence throughout his career that the theatre was its own place and should be discretely observed deserves further attention.

In 1946 he gave high praise to the revival of *Show Boat* and did so in a way that called into question the "superlatives visited upon some such more recent exhibits as *Oklahoma!*"

> and above all, while it is not the only show of its kind that has done so, it confidently invites response without resort to those vaudeville specialty acts, arty ballets and other irrelevancies which are included in most musicals. It recognizes its beginning, middle and end, and it sticks more or less resolutely to them.[37]

The recent revival of *Show Boat* and the concomitant reverence and controversy the musical has attracted would no doubt have caused Nathan "to smile and wonder." Moreover, Nathan's continuing appreciation for older musicals is not a result of his inability to appreciate the so-called integrated musical. On the contrary, it is simply that his knowledge and experience kept him from being bedazzled by what was merely new wrapping for an old package. Certainly no historian of musical theater accepts any longer the notion that *Oklahoma!* was the first integrated musical.

Keeping in mind Tennessee Williams's imputations that Nathan wanted to commercialize *The Glass Menagerie*, Nathan's reactions to William Inge reveal the critic's keen awareness of how plays can be shaped by directors, especially by such anointed figures as Joshua Logan and Elia Kazan. Nathan had been impressed by Inge's *Come Back, Little Sheba* and his commentary on the play once again belies any sense that he was somehow out of touch with postwar theater. Nathan praises the play for its sincerity and honesty. He applauds Shirley Booth's and Sidney Blackmer's acting as well as Daniel Mann's direction which "met the script head on and does not in any way try to prettify it." Always eager to show up a trend, Nathan facetiously informs the Theatre Guild that they would have been "commercially wiser" to have engaged Jo Mielziner rather than Howard Bay for the set design.

> [I]t might have guaranteed the play a much more popular reception by getting . . . one of his fancy scrim, colored-lighted sets, with maybe some off-stage soft music added. The notices would have been ten times better, and Inge would have undoubtedly have been hailed as a new Tennessee Williams or Arthur Miller.[38]

Yet Nathan actually finds it "reassuring" that the Theatre Guild produced Inge's play. He castigates the Guild for having ignored new American playwrights (such as Williams and Miller whom he calls "talented novices,") but hopes that its "taking a chance on Inge is "a token of its future conduct."[39]

A few years later when Inge's next effort made it to Broadway, Nathan was less impressed by *Picnic* the play, but more sympathetic to Inge the playwright. Nathan reports that Inge was besieged throughout *Picnic's* production process and "bombarded by 'hundreds of suggestions' from outside sources and was prevailed upon to incorporate many of them into his script."[40] Nathan suspects that Joshua Logan's direction, in contrast to Daniel Mann's restrained staging of *Come Back, Little Sheba*, pumped up the drama's emotional hydraulics.

> [The] production operating with a vengeance in behalf of the popular box-office is so over-elaborated one has a suspicion that what was very

probably a play as relatively simple and affecting as something like "Home Sweet Home" has been orchestrated Hollywood-wise for the Philharmonic Symphony Orchestra reinforced by a Sousa Band, the Seventh Regiment Fife and Drum Corps and the Andrews Sisters. While there periodically emerges from it clear evidence of Inge's faithful observance of life, sharp appreciation of character and gift for beautifully accurate dialogue, there are many more times when the playwright seems to be shoved into the background by way of allowing the director to make a name for himself. . . . [E]verything nevertheless points to the fact that it had a quality that was in greater part edged out of it in the campaign to Broadwayize it into a financial success.[41]

It is interesting that both Lawrence Langner and Joshua Logan were quite proud of the changes they had pressured Inge into making. Logan goes on at some length in his memoirs, detailing the evolution of the play.[42] To say the least, he is uncharitable toward Inge and more than generous to himself and to Langner. The controversy over *Picnic* was no secret, and Nathan was not alone in recognizing that Logan's passion for directorial interpolation was particularly fervid this time around. Harold Clurman's essay written for the program of *Summer Brave,* Inge's 1975 revised version of *Picnic,* makes it clear that in the 1953 production "the more sombre significance" of his work was tossed aside, and thus "Inge was downgraded as a mere purveyor of hit shows." Clurman calls *Picnic* "sunny" and *Summer Brave* "bittersweet."[43]

It is interesting that Clurman and Nathan came to virtually the same conclusions about Inge's work. Both agreed that a restrained and honest play had been turned into a sensationalized "adult" drama. It is especially relevant that Nathan and Clurman can be found to agree not merely on a particular play, but on *how* their points of view are consonant. Both focused on Logan's direction as it affected the playscript. What is more, Nathan and Clurman were not alone in taking issue with Logan's direction. For his part, Clurman is one of the most admired men of the American theatre. He is respected as a director and as a critic. In the early 1950s, he was not quite at the midpoint of his career. Nathan was nearing the end of his. Clurman was a veteran of the Group Theatre, and the passion and political commitment he brought to his work sharply contrasted with Nathan's languid detachment. Nonetheless, Clurman clearly had great respect for Nathan and consistently singled him out as the outstanding American drama critic of his time. He even brought up Nathan for support when explaining some of the difficulties he had while directing *The*

*Ladies of the Corridor.*[44] If Nathan can appreciate aspects of Williams, Miller, and Inge and retain the respect of Clurman and Young, how can he be said to have fossilized in the 1940s and 1950s?

Nathan's measured praise of Inge and his analysis of the show-shop mentality that still afflicted 1950s Broadway demonstrate that Nathan retained his critical acuity. The only reason such pronouncements do not seem fresh is that Nathan had been making them for half a century. We could easily substitute the name David Belasco for Joshua Logan in Nathan's discussion of directorial flourishes. It is not Nathan's fault that in many ways Broadway success had the same paradigm throughout the first half of the twentieth century. It is ironic, though, that it is Nathan who is deemed "old-fashioned." We can readily question whether Nathan was out of touch in the 1950s. I would argue that this is something of a latter-day judgment imposed upon him. No doubt, after Nathan's health failed in 1956 his turn as a star had almost become a vanishing act, but prior to that he had maintained his edge.

To demonstrate Nathan's continuing prestige even in his twilight years, one need only review the comments of Kenneth Tynan or Eric Bentley. These particular critics' careers were beginning as Nathan's was concluding. Tynan clearly appreciated Nathan's method and persona, even when he took issue with him, as he did in "The State of Dramatic Criticism," the first chapter of his first book.[45] Tynan took issue with what he determined to be Nathan's aloofness from the practice of art. And he took contemporary critics to task for attending too closely to "Nathan's resounding apothegm: 'Art and the artist are ever youthful lovers: criticism is their chaperone.' "[46] Writing at his career's outset, Tynan rejected the "appalling minuteness" of this precept, but three years later declared, "I can imagine his arguing that the critic is performing a function in some respects higher than that of the dramatist. . . . Nathan's vivacity is quite unimpaired." For all his modish leftism, Tynan was at heart star-struck, and no doubt he was attracted by Nathan's glamour. In this respect he has more in common with Alexander Woollcott than one might think. (A contemporary exemplar of star-struck criticism is, of course, John Lahr.) Nonetheless, Tynan is the greatest English drama critic of the second half of the century. What, then, do his reactions tell us about Nathan as he was regarded at the close of his career? Much indeed, because once again we find Nathan to be entirely in the swim of contemporary currents and still able to both attract attention and command respect. Tynan's belief that Nathan was too coolly detached[47] is at odds with Nathan's usual arraignment, that his "hot impressionistic style" was one of the things that made him seem dated.[48]

It would *seem* that no better opponent of Nathan as a critic could be offered up than Eric Bentley, who so famously failed to like O'Neill. Nonetheless in Bentley's first book he paid tribute to Nathan. He was not entirely admiring and was rather dismissive of what he deemed to be Nathan's representative American attitude; nonetheless, he seemed to accept Nathan on Nathan's own terms, even when he seemed to dismiss him as having "the aesthetics of a school marm."[49] (It is interesting that both Bentley and Tynan used what are now sexist epithets to disparage Nathan's premises. Tynan had called his aesthetics those of a "spinster.")[50]

Bentley managed to crystallize Nathan's aesthetic sense (and by extension the midcentury "American intellectual scene") in a series of fascinating antitheses. "[I]ts peculiar brands of stuffiness and unstuffiness, preciosity and antipreciosity, real tough-guyism and pseudo tough-guyism, all emanating from the same excessive self-consciousness and *malaise*" are its outstanding characteristics.[51] Nathan, Mencken, and even the progenitor of all show business columns, Walter Winchell, not to mention many later literary theorists and academic critics, all may be characterized by this almost schizoid attitude that Bentley details. Nathan certainly wanted to be taken seriously as a drama critic, but he would have no truck with theory nor would he accept anyone who was a self-proclaimed artist. Thus, Nathan was guilty as charged when it came to Bentley's implication that he radiated the sort of easy anti–intellectualism that corrodes American culture.

Yet is this altogether a fair characterization? Not quite. Nathan presented commentary on mainstream American theater. He was a popular writer writing about popular theatre, so to hold him up to a standard of intellectualism is particularly inappropriate. It is, though, entirely fair of Bentley to demand something more of Nathan. We may question exactly what Bentley expected of Nathan when he said of the American critic,

Nathan's aesthetic is a rationalization of his own talent which is for (a) advertising and (b) debunking. A critic on Broadway could have done no greater service than to have advertised Sean O'Casey (or even Eugene O'Neill if we remember what the alternative to O'Neill is on Broadway). To have debunked Pinero, Brieux, Maxwell Anderson, is something; to have summed up Sir James Barrie as "the triumph of sugar over diabetes" is almost everything. If Nathan is not a great critic of drama, indeed not, as he boasts, a critic of good drama at all, he has been a great fighter against all kinds of nonsense. He consistently puts his critical colleagues to shame with his superior taste and brains. . . . He also believes in testing the bad by the standards of the good; and he usually knows what *is* [Bentley's emphasis] good too.[52]

What was Nathan *not* doing that a critic could do? There is only so much a journalist is capable of. Comments such as Bentley's would seem to damn Nathan for his decision to remain a Broadway drama critic. As we saw thirty years earlier in Nathan's career, he was regarded by those closest to him as "too good" for Broadway. All of this begs the question: What would have happened if James Huneker had successfully prevailed upon Nathan to move to Paris?

The sort of criticism Bentley and Tynan were writing in the 1950s was personal in a way entirely different way from Nathan's. Both writers seemed part of a new generation; both would be voices for political theater. Each critic proselytized the English-speaking theater world for Brecht. Nathan was dubious about Brecht's work. He disparaged both *The Private Life of the Master Race* and *Galileo* as plays and as productions. The theater he compared these works to was the Central European theater of the 1920s. Nathan never saw the Berliner Ensemble and he made no valid contemporary references to Brecht's rivals. Nonetheless, we must concede that Nathan's comparisons were somewhat pertinent, as Brecht began writing in the 1920s, but Bentley's criticism caught the imagination of serious readers in a way that Nathan's no longer could. The readers who respected Bentley no doubt saw themselves as, or actually were, people who would be acting in or directing the plays Bentley praised. Bentley, as was the case with Harold Clurman, could be seen as a theater practitioner who was also a critic. It is simply unimaginable to expect someone to read Nathan in this way. As much as Nathan knew about and wrote about the practical aspects of staging and performing, he has never been accepted by historians as really one who knew anything about the stage. He is dismissed as "merely" literary. For all his admiration of Nathan, Bentley saw only that side of Nathan's criticism.

Tynan would seem to be closer to Nathan in tone and technique, but his famous declaration that he "doubted whether he could love anyone who did not wish to see *Look Back in Anger*" was self-revelatory in a way that Nathan never could be. Tynan's criticism was personalized in an entirely different style than was Nathan's. Nathan was resolutely detached; Tynan flamboyantly *attached* to performers, playwrights, and causes. Tynan's politicized criticism would have been anathema to Nathan. As we have seen, Nathan had his favorites, but strove to project an aura of reserve. Nathan's seemed out of place in an era where commitment to something other than one's self seemed paramount. Thus Tynan, the critic *engagé* par excellence, came to prominence as Nathan's career drew to a close.

Walter Kerr's criticism for the New York *Herald Tribune* and later for the *New York Times* was and is the most highly regarded newspaper criticism of the 1950s and 1960s (save by Eric Bentley and Robert Brustein who were often impatient with Kerr's proprieties). Kerr, like Atkinson, had a theater named after him. Kerr's background as a director and professor was similar to that of Stark Young. Like Young, he also wrote for the theater. Kerr was widely respected because he made his standards so clear. Kerr was regarded as a scholarly critic, but he wrote with a journalist's talent for attention-getting opening lines. Kerr's eminence came from his emphasis upon the play under discussion rather than on his own opinion per se. He had respect for Nathan and believed that he was the most knowledgeable critic of his time. Kerr and his wife were also very close to Nathan personally. Yet Kerr felt that Nathan was unable to change his style of writing to accommodate the changes that overtook the theater after World War II.

I would argue that it was not so much a different theater that Nathan was unable to come to grips with; rather, it was the total success of his own critical methods. Nathan's theatrical battles had all been won. It was journalism that had changed. The Broadway theatre no longer commanded the attention of the nation. For its part, the Broadway theatre was more insular than ever and was all too familiar with Nathan. He had been the most erudite and demanding critic for two generations. Kerr's use of his background and knowledge gave his views great authority, just as Nathan's did, but Kerr's was a new view. Also, he projected patience and tolerance, whereas Nathan brooked no opposition. Kerr was deemed a constructive critic. He wrote during a time when the theater seemed to be in decline. Nathan's self-styled destructive approach could not be tolerated in such an era. More importantly, Kerr wrote for the two most important establishment newspapers. One need hardly mention that if Kerr had continued as a magazine critic writing for the Catholic journal *Commonweal*, there would not be a theater named for him today.

Like Brooks Atkinson, Kerr was a neogenteel critic. He oppugned the excesses of the 1960s. Nonetheless, in his way, unlike Atkinson, Kerr was most definitely a personal critic. One of Kerr's most provocative statements was his summation of theater in the 1960s: "I don't know which attitude staggers me more—today's almost total distrust of the theater or today's almost total trust of the theater."[53] Such a paradox is just the sort of argument Nathan was wont to make. We could well question Kerr's contention that Nathan could not understand playwrights such as Brecht or Beckett. It is true that Nathan dismissed *Waiting for Godot*, calling it "the little play that wasn't there," but Kerr himself was certainly no champion of Beckett. He was not even comfortable with Chekhov, considering his influence detrimental to modern playwriting. Why is it then that Nathan was so readily perceived as being out of touch? Again, there is no profound aesthetic or sociological reason, it is simply that Nathan had been around for so long that he was unable to cause any excitement.

Three years after Nathan died, John Simon began writing for the *Hudson Review*. Many of the accusations made against Simon echo those made against Nathan. Simon was only superficially similar to Nathan. He was as demanding as Nathan, but the premises upon which Simon's demands were based were far more literary than Nathan's ever were. Simon's criteria were based on his reading of the text. Nathan's standards came from his half century of seeing shows. Simon demanded that the playwright be served; Nathan demanded that the theater be served. Nathan sought theatrical entertainment, broadly conceived; Simon rarely found his narrowly conceived vision of dramaturgical integrity in the plays he reviewed. Yet Simon, too, showed Nathan's influence: he was unabashedly personal and gloried in *ad hominem* and *ad feminam* attacks—though in this respect he outdid his predecessor in both order and degree.

Let us conclude this chapter with the coda of Nathan's career. In November of 1951, Nathan's prestige earned him the cover of *Theatre Arts* magazine. The magazine announced that the "foremost" drama critic in the world would contribute a monthly article "exclusively" for *Theatre Arts*. Sadly though, Nathan's health began to break down in the middle of the decade. He had several stokes, and arteriosclerosis left him too weak to attend opening nights. In 1956, he ceased his syndicated weekly column altogether. A month before he died, he published his reminiscences of F. Scott Fitzgerald, Sinclair Lewis, and Theodore Dreiser in *Esquire*. His last piece of dramatic criticism, "The Stage as Self-Poisoner" was published posthumously in *Theatre Arts* in July 1958.[54]

# 5

# Nothing if Not Critical

IN EXAMINING GEORGE JEAN NATHAN'S CAREER AS THE FIRST MOD-
ern American drama critic, we see that his lack of any dramaturgical agenda or theoretical constants was not really a hindrance to
his development as a critic. On the contrary, it was central to
his approach. Furthermore, we must recognize that his ongoing
concern with the methods and materials of drama criticism itself
constitutes a particularly significant aspect of his work. Nathan's
work is of use to historians of American theater and culture as
well as to readers of dramatic literature.

It is of value because no other critic of the time left so many
explanations of what he was trying to do with his criticism. Nathan
never attempted to convince, but he was concerned with honestly
presenting his own temperament as an effective reflector of the
art of the drama. Nathan was an influential editor and important
arbiter of literary taste during the years when he coedited *The
Smart Set*, but this is ancillary to his historical status as a drama
critic.

Nathan's half-century-long career is the best example we have
of how an American drama critic functions and of what an American drama critic can do with his career. Every other commentator
on Nathan has emphasized his service to playwrights, both American and European, and no doubt this is a great accomplishment.
As we have seen, though, the most consistent, indeed, the only
consistent thread running through the tapestry of Nathan's works
is his ambition to raise the level of drama criticism in the United
States. Nathan's most pressing critical objective was to make drama
criticism a serious and worthy endeavor. From the start of his
career, he repeatedly confronted his colleagues with what he perceived to be their shortcomings. Earlier, I described Nathan as a
Wildean "critic-as-artist." This he most certainly was.

Nathan's criticism is emphatically not, as is too often argued, a
response to the spirit of the 1920s. That is not to deny, however,

that Nathan was a major American literary figure of that time. The fictional portraits of Nathan presented by F. Scott Fitzgerald and Charles Angoff in their novelized treatments of the literary milieu of the 1920s, *The Beautiful and Damned* and *Summer Storm,* show the powerful image he projected. Nevertheless, although Nathan may have been among the jazz babies of the Lost Generation, he was by no means of them. He came from a different era, an older tradition.

What is more, the sacred-cow-tipping that Nathan participated in was largely over by the time the doughboys came back from France. Nathan never settled down, though, nor did he ever find a comfortable niche. He too much enjoyed keeping his public guessing ever to become predictable. Witness the closeness of his friendship with Sean O'Casey and his almost paternal concern for William Saroyan, two undeniably proletarian playwrights.

As much as Nathan was able to remold his criticism when he chose to, there were certain personal fixations in his work. Typically, for Nathan, they form a paradox. Even when he was a very young critic, the distinct aura of wisdom-beyond-his-years lent a virile decadence to his prose. Brooks Atkinson once described Nathan as genuinely embodying "the nineteenth century *Yellow Book* conception of a gentleman."[1] By comparing Nathan to the famous periodical that gave its peculiar hue to the 1890s, Atkinson revealed how well he understood his colleague. Indeed, in one of the few sober moments in *The Critic and the Drama*'s "Aesthetic Jurisprudence," Nathan gave a nod to "the often profound Wilde."[2] Having delineated Nathan as a Wildean critic-as-artist, perhaps a glance at Wilde himself is now in order. The following passage from Wilde's "The Soul of Man under Socialism" demonstratesas Nathan's facetiously alluding to Croce, Spingarn, Goethe, and Carlyle in *The Critic and the Drama* does not—the authenticity of Nathan's aestheticism because it is in some ways a prefiguration of Nathan's own critical practice:

> If a man approaches a work of art with any desire to exercise authority over it and the artist, he approaches it in such a spirit that he cannot receive any artistic impression from it at all. *The work of art is to dominate the spectator: the spectator is not to dominate the work of art* [Wilde's emphasis]. The spectator is to be receptive. . . . And the more completely he can suppress his own silly views, his own foolish prejudices, his own absurd ideas of what Art should be or should not be, the more likely he is to understand and appreciate the work of art in question. This is of course, quite obvious in the case of the vulgar theatregoing public of English men and women. . . .[3]

Doubtless, Nathan would vehemently disagree with Wilde's specific thoughts on drama that follow these remarks. Wilde deemed it necessary to sit through all four acts of a play in order to comprehend the fullness of its artistic value, even if the first three acts are of dubious merit. As we have seen, Nathan prided himself on deducing a play's worth as quickly as possible: "The reviewer who can't make up his mind accurately as to a play's worth immediately after it's finished hasn't any mind to make up."[4]

Nonetheless, Wilde's emphasis on the spectator and his requirement that the intellectual mode of perception be entirely relaxed so that one may receive the work of art as a thing in itself is completely in sympathy with Nathan's "intelligent emotionalism." He certainly would have felt at home in Wilde's fantastical "nation of art critics." Nathan makes frequent reference in his criticism to the importance of the visual in the theater. For him, "theater" is most importantly. "the viewing place." For his part, though, Nathan could not be content simply to "receive" the work of art and leave it at that. He would insist on *perceiving* it as well; he was, after all, a professional critic. Wilde saw himself primarily as an artist even when he wrote criticism, so he could be content with just the reception of a work. Nathan's chief concern was with the way a piece was recognized and understood; he would not have been able to consider reception alone an adequate aesthetic goal.

In the previous chapter I suggested that Nathan's attitude that theatre versus the cinema merits special consideration. Although Nathan is certainly no theorist anticipating Grotowski, there is more to his anticinematic stance than mere theatrical snobbery. Not much more, but he does say some provocative things about the special nature of theatrical as opposed to cinematic performance. In 1932 Nathan dismissed the argument then gaining some currency that talking pictures would sweep away the theater altogether. In 1932 Nathan make the startling prediction that by 1937 the damage the cinema had done to the theater would have abated and "the theatre will flourish as it has not in a generation."[5] By 1937 the Group Theatre, the Federal Theatre Project, and the New York Drama Critics' Circle had been established. Nathan championed neither the Group nor the Federal Theatre, but the long-term influence of both of them on the American theater cannot be denied. Writing in 1936, Nathan argued that the cinema's "insistence upon purely physical action" contrasted more sharply than ever with "the stage's increasing insistence upon cerebral action."[6] Naturally, Nathan cannot help making elitist arguments on behalf of the theater, but if we consider the reality of the size of the theater-going public, we must recognize that it is, in fact, an elite. The theater ceased to be a mass art with the advent of the movies. Some theater people and critics may delude themselves otherwise, but the theater is, on the whole, for the few. Nathan makes extravagant and misleading claims for the theater later in his career, but even as he makes the broadest assertions for the stage he hones an essential truth about how theater diverges:

> The very virtue of the stage is that it doesn't show such details [as the film version of *Life With Father* could]. The drama wisely dismisses all such items as irrelevant and immaterial. The screen simply clutters itself up with them by way of supplying to the audience what the film people think it can not sufficiently imagine, like a child drawing a picture of a cow and labeling it a cow for extra safe measure. The drama is a process of selection. The screen is a process of over-embellishment.[7]

This is not to make any claims for Nathan as a legitimate film critic, or even to credit him with an unconscious theoretical bent. It is merely to highlight that Nathan had the good fortune, more often than not, to be correct. Unfortunately, however, because Nathan was so rigorously unsystematic, it has been most convenient to cast him aside. Even so, with almost any dramatic critic,we are tossed into a zero-sum game: one reader's thought-provoking theory is another's mind-numbing formula.

Indeed, we have seen that the theoretical constructs Nathan elaborates in *The Critic and the Drama* are largely irrelevant to his actual critical practices. They are interesting, however, when contrasted with the perorations of academic critics such as Clayton Hamilton and Brander Matthews. Nathan directed much of his youthful venom against these two critics who, as Nathan saw it, were far too concerned with their own blueprints of dramatic carpentry. He dispensed with such dramaturgical considerations and was, in every sense, a freestanding critic. Brander Matthews was undoubtedly a pioneer in the study of drama, and every scholar of the theater owes him a debt of a gratitude, but to Nathan he was an incompetent drama critic because he could get out from beneath the weight of his own critical presuppositions. He was at best a "textbook critic." Hamilton was even more convoluted than Matthews, as we have seen through Nathan's quotation of some of Hamilton's slightly overwrought moments of critical discovery. To find Nathan wanting because of his antiformalism is to apply an extraordinarily inappropriate criterion to him. For historians of the American theater, in particular, Nathan's works are of interest because he labored so hard to make the criticism of American plays a valid occupation. In "The Absent Voice: Drama and the Critic," an English scholar of the American theater, C. W. E. Bigsby, addresses some of the lingering questions concerning criticism and the drama. The body of Bigsby's essay is concerned with some of the problems connected with applying critical theories such as deconstruction and semiotics to the theater, and with what precisely a "dramatic text" is. His conclusion, however, is particularly relevant both to what Nathan tried to do during his lifetime and to the neglect and misunderstanding his work has been subjected to since his death. Bigsby asks whether critics can

> continue to regard the American theatre as culturally marginal, peripheral to the concerns of the critic, whether that critic be committed to an exploration of the structure of language, the generation of character, the nature of readership, or the aesthetic response to ideological fact. . . . The aim is not to arrest that mobility, to deny drama's protean quality by generating normative versions, critical models which are stable because inert, but to acknowledge the legitimacy of analysis, of readings of a text which is in truth only a pretext for a performance that will in turn constitute a new text.[8]

Nathan's affinities with the critical dilemmas that Bigsby puts forth here are obvious. "Protean" is certainly an apt word to describe Nathan's critical stance, but there is more to the relationship between what Bigsby outlines above and what Nathan's career means for us today than mere descriptive similarity. The neglect and even scorn that have been Nathan's fate are analogous to the treatment of drama and all its constituents. The "immobile, normative" models that Bigsby cautions against are of a piece with the very methods that Nathan rejected. The "stable models" reverenced by Matthews and Hamilton are exactly what Nathan anathematized throughout his career.

Finally, Nathan's vaunted elitism must be seen in contrast to his perception of drama as a democratic art. In no way, however, is it to be assumed that his criticism was of, for, and by "the people." Never was there less a Lincolnesque figure than Nathan. But he did believe that the drama was essentially a democratic art form. To Nathan, it was an art intended for a number of "people assembled in an illuminated hall." Although drama is not normally created to be performed before a mob, any audience by its very nature is a mass, and Nathan most certainly valued the perception of the individual critic over the reception of the mass audience.

Nevertheless, he recognized that it was for the audience that the work of dramatic art was created, not for the exclusive appreciation of the drama critic.

It is the critic, though, who must function as the aristocrat, as the reverend seignior, surveying the breadth of the theater with complete detachment. Thus, he is at odds with Stark Young who contended that the finest theatrical art was far beyond the sensibilities of most people and in accord with Walter Kerr who maintained that truly great drama can emerge only from a truly popular theatre. For if Nathan sometimes behaved as though his seat on the aisle were a throne, he was always aware that he was seated in the midst of the madding crowd.

The historical status of Nathan as the first modern American drama critic raises questions about the evaluation of drama criticism itself. Further study has to be made of other drama critics in terms of their careers as critics, rather than in terms of the playwrights or performers they championed. Questions also must be asked about the perception of the drama critic by the historian, for if the traditional uses of drama criticism are not entirely adequate, how are we to use drama criticism appropriately? Objective investigation of the nature of journalistic drama criticism would remedy some of the misapplication to which it is often put. Nathan's criticism is especially useful; in this respect, it is specifically the work of a journalist addressing "critical" issues.

Historians would do well to examine Nathan's commentaries on his colleagues and comparatively assess various drama critics. Nathan's caustic critiques are not universal scholarly models, but they do indicate how historians might begin to assay the critical techniques of other reviewers. Finally, Nathan's career indicates to us that if we entirely dismiss drama criticism as a legitimate part of theater history, we risk rejecting a particular means of understanding contemporary reactions to the theatre. Historians should endeavor to understand the peculiar exigencies of drama criticism and be able to comment on the implications of such critical exigencies.

With the recent increase in American popular theatre studies, Nathan's comments about vaudeville, cabarets, and burlesque are gaining currency. This is a bit ironic, given that during his lifetime he was often satirized or mocked by his contemporaries on the basis of his daunting erudition. His predilection for learnedisms and for referring to all of the languages he knew and to his personal acquaintance with the European theater was the usual basis for parodies and put-downs by his opponents. Nonetheless, Nathan will continue to appear in the occasional bibliography, most likely because of his ability to recognize that there is no real hierarchy of the performing arts. The forwardness of this outlook is startling when we consider Nathan's perceived public persona. Yet reviewing the work rather than the man shows us that one of his most sustained efforts in analysis is a lengthy disquisition on producer George Lederer's contribution to the perfection of the "leg show."[9]

Such a predisposition toward popular entertainment is, of course, fully revealed in Nathan's early work, *The Popular Theatre*, in which he dissected every aspect of his subject. Nathan's critical gaze was always wide-ranging, if not always penetrating. In this text he took on producers, directors, performers, press agents, ticket brokers, theater managers, anyone involved with the theatre business. He fully engaged his readers with each aspect of the theatre business.

*The Popular Theatre* is not unique in Nathan's body of work. When Nathan considered the theater he did so from his own perspective, but he also took into account the contextual factors of the entire realm of the theater. In this way he was writing in a much more inclusive way than are even the most avowedly democratic critics are in our day. By creating such a plateau on which to place his critical tableaux, Nathan truly practiced the *art* of criticism. There was no method for him to draw on; his life was his method. His "hot, impressionistic style" enabled him to survey with the sneer of cold command the theater and its denizens, both on stage and in the audience.

How did Nathan engage his readers in spite of his toplofty sneer? He did so by sliding down the firehouse pole and lying about with rubber chicken and slapstick. He took up the cudgels by naming names; he never refrained from a fight or shirked his duty as the "bad boy" of criticism. Today when critics mention almost anything personal they are accused of *ad hominem* attacks or of indulging in personalities.

Engaging in personalities was one of Nathan's critical tenets. It was this self-conscious presentation of himself that kept his prose so animated. Another stylistic element energized his writing; when Nathan wrote of the theatre of the past he did so only rarely with what might be termed nostalgia. Even as he approached old age, he never bemoaned the current state of the theater in terms of the past. When he gave up his theatre book of the year series in 1951, he did so because he found himself unable to complete his calendar of "especially interesting performances." It was not because there were none to equal the great stars of the past, but because the current season was, in his view, astoundingly abysmal.

A typical Nathan review or, rather, Nathan's pattern of review-writing can be assessed, for if he had no critical system that was consistently applied, he did employ certain habits of style and diction with regularity. He varied them, to be sure, but nonetheless followed them throughout his career. The most successful of these was the catalogue a list of qualities of a given show or performer, followed by an explication of why said performer or show was not quite what it appeared to be or was lately being bruited to be. This technique was used with devastating effect in discussing Noël Coward. The catalogue allowed Nathan to be both erudite and clownish. The form undoubtedly shows itself off, but there is an insistence of tone about it that grabs our attention. Nathan's habit of exhaustively calculating the influences on or lack of originality in a given show or individual performance presents the critic at his best. This is Nathan's outstanding way of revealing his authority. He foregrounds his background in such a way as to make his argument irresistible.

Nathan's other consistent tactic was to hurl invective and otherwise engage in personalities. The most famous example of this was his attack on Alexander Woollcott, but Nathan also sallied forth with broadsword and "gravy-bomb" (a Nathanism) against such critics as Clayton Hamilton and the playwright cum press agent cum critic Channing Pollock. He also never hesitated to attack performers on what seemed a personal level, although he reserved his most potent venom for fellow scribes.

Nathan's most noted stylistic trait was his singular diction—his coinages, neologisms, learned borrowings, and so forth. At this he rivaled Winchell and Mencken. He created collective nouns: "Rialtors," "jerkwater solons," "boobletariat," "six-day sock-wearers," "schnitzels of buncombe," and "one-building universities." He castigated "delicatessen" as in the "pfui opus," the "hick-prickers," "hazlittry," "soup-coloraturas," the "marmalade explosion," the "barrack of balderdash," and all manner of "flapdoodle."

Nathan's self-confidence was unbounded, and hard to take sometimes, but the unabashed absence of any apologies for it could make it a redeeming quality. And these stylistic constants mark Nathan as a member of his generation of journalists. He would no doubt shrink from this categorization, but he came of age during a new era in magazine and newspaper writing. Nathan the journalist and critic never merely reported the newsworthiness of the theatrical event by saying, "Now I've seen it, here's what I think." Instead, Nathan recreated the entire milieu of the Broadway theater for nontheatergoers. Such writing paralleled that of the Broadway columnists who recreated the world of night clubs and café society for out-of-town Tallulahs and suburban sheiks. Through Nathan's writing, the reader was actually engaged in a theatrical reviewing process, a drama in its own right. Because Nathan's persona is indelibly incorporated into his reviews, his readers could also recreate Nathan in their minds—the critic in his elegant apparel who casually flicks the cigarette in its holder as he saunters through the theater lobby, and out of the theater at intermission not to return. He languidly hails a cab and repairs to the Stork Club or "21" to tear at a pheasant with a bubbling ingenue. Next morning he arises without drawing the curtains of his legendary bachelor's den at the Royalton Hotel and composes with ascetic repose his week's *essai*.

Unfortunately, Nathan's influence, was two-edged. During his lifetime he forced his colleagues to raise their standards, indeed, to develop standards in the first place. He recognized superior playwrights and demanded that criticism speak for itself on its own terms. The individuality Nathan brought to dramatic criticism has degenerated into mere personality. The style that he believed was the essence of criticism has sunk to mere blurb-confecting. Nathan's impressionist approach is only as valid as the sum of those impressions. Even if, as several commentators have noted, Nathan's taste *was* a valid guide for much of the first half of the century, without his knowledge and experience, the exercise of taste alone is not enough. Today, reviewers proudly posit ignorance rather than knowledge as the basis for their assessments. They are glib journalists who presume to know no more about the theater than their readers. Many are reduced to assigning a certain number of stars or even worse, simply thumbing a production up or down. The theater community wants mindless boosters; editors, merry quipsters.

In Nathan's case, in a real sense, the critic became a playwright and a performer of an ongoing script. Each week or month, his column was a new installment of the adventures of a soul among masterpieces or, more frequently among much lesser works. Nathan, then, was the critic as a performer, acting the role of the bon vivant, the boulevardier who gives the nod now and then to this or that play or performer. However, it was not only his pronounced judgments that made his writings interesting to his readers. It was the spectacle of Nathan's persona imagined, conjured up if you will, by the reader who recreated Nathan's own experiences. Comprehending Nathan's attraction, his force as a writer, is not then simply a matter of finding out whether he disliked or liked a play. It is being able to reflect upon the tone and tint of a man wholly absorbed in his theatrical and critical milieu and recording it for the delectation of his reading public. He put his critical self *before* his readers in both senses of the word. He succeeded as a critic because he spent his life in the theater. Nathan's erudition was as real as his persona.

# Notes

## Introduction. Broadway and Its Brilliance

1. Eric Bentley, *What is Theatre?* (New York: Limelight Editions, 1984), 345.
2. George Jean Nathan, *The Theatre, the Drama, the Girls* (New York: Knopf, 1921), 290–311.
3. George Bernard Shaw to Nathan, 2 August 1950, Cornell Collection.
4. Kenneth Tynan, *Tynan Right and Left* (New York: Atheneum, 1967), viii.
5. George Jean Nathan, *The Popular Theatre* (New York: Knopf, 1918), 79.
6. Robert Forsythe, *Reading From Left to Right.* (New York: Covici, 1938), 78.
7. Robert Anderson to author, 15 May 1996.
8. Porter Anderson, "Teasers and Tormentors, The Nathan that Got Away," *Village Voice* (27 September 1994): 104.

## Chapter 1. The Critic and His World

1. History of Allen County, Indiana. "Achd'uth (sic) Veshalom Synagogue of B'Nai Israel—‹Hebrew«." Chicago: Kingman Brothers, 1880), no page number.
2. Mark Rogers, "Historical Genealogy Research Center Report on George Jean Nathan," Allen County Public Library (1997): 2.
3. Fort Wayne and Allen County directories and Fort Wayne City directories, 1877–1885.
4. Isaac Goldberg, *The Theatre of George Jean Nathan* (New York: Simon and Schuster, 1926), 45–46.
5. I am grateful to Bruce Shapiro for first noticing the similarity between "Hunsecker" and "Huneker" and bringing it to my attention.
6. H. L. Mencken, "My Life as Author and Editor," Mencken Papers, Dartmouth College Library, 542.
7. Mencken, "My Life as Author and Editor," 551.
8. Mencken to Theodore Dreiser, 7 October 1933, Mencken Papers, New York Public Library.
9. Harold Clurman, *All People Are Famous* (New York: Harcourt, Brace, Jovanovich, 1974), 71–72.
10. Mencken to Alfred Knopf, 26 October 1938, Mencken Papers. New York Public Library.
11. Lillian Gish to H. L. Mencken, 20 May 1939, Mencken Papers, New York Public Library.
12. Nathan to Isaac Goldberg, Saturday, no year, Isaac Goldberg Papers, New York Public Library.
13. Nathan to Isaac Goldberg, 22 September, no year. Isaac Goldberg Papers, New York Public Library.

14. Nathan to Isaac Goldberg, 3 June 1926, Isaac Goldberg Papers, New York Public Library.

15. Jim Tully, "The World and Mr. Nathan," *Esquire* (January 1938): 42.

16. Peter J. Lysy, (associate archivist, the University of Notre Dame), to author, 29 August 1994.

17. Herbert M. Simpson, "Mencken and Nathan" (Ph. D. diss., University of Maryland, 1965), 73.

18. Mencken, "My Life . . . ," 549.

19. Theodore Dreiser to George Jean Nathan, 7 October 1933, The Cornell Collection.

20. Robert E. Spiller et al., *Literary History of the United States*, 4th ed. (New York: *Macmillan*, 1975), 691, 1127.

21. Anna Roth, ed., *Current Biography* (New York: H. W. Wilson 1945), 420–423.

22. Peter Kriendler, interview by author, New York, 18 February 1995.

23. Arthur Gelb, interview by author, Boston, 12 May 1995.

24. Arthur Gelb, telephone interview by author, 24 July 1997.

25. Bernard Sobel, *Broadway Heartbeat: Memoirs of a Press Agent* (New York: Hermitage House, 1953), 298.

26. Richard Maney, *Fanfare: The Confessions of a Press Agent* (New York: Harper and Brothers, 1957), 214.

27. Louis Sobol, *The Longest Street* (New York: Crown, 1968), 249.

28. Alfred A. Knopf, "H. L. Mencken, George Jean Nathan and *The American Mercury* Venture," *Menckeniana* 78 (1981): 1–10.

29. Thomas Yoseloff to the author, 14 September 1994.

30. Mencken, "My Life . . . ," 837.

31. James Banks to George Jean Nathan, 11 November 1929, Cornell Collection.

32. Jim Tully, "The World and Mr. Nathan," *Esquire* (January 1938), 42, 172–73.

33. Nathan, *Monks are Monks* (New York: Knopf, 1929), 194.

34. Nathan, *The Intimate Notebooks of George Jean Nathan* (New York: Knopf, 1932), 23.

35. Simpson, "Mencken and Nathan," 75–76.

## Chapter 2. Turn-of-the-Century Critical Trends and the Making of a Drama Critic

1. T. S. Moran, "New York's Dramatic Critics," *Metropolitan* (January 1899), 105–9.

2. "A First Nighter Says . . ." *The Green Book* (May 1911), 1089–91.

3. Charles Frederic Nirdlinger, *Masques and Mummers* (New York: DeWitt, 1899), 43–44.

4. Elliot Norton, "Puffers, Pundits and Other Play Reviewers: A Short History of American Dramatic Criticism," in *The American Theatre: A Sum of Its Parts*, ed. Henry B. Williams (New York: Samuel French, 1971), 321.

5. Quoted from Arnold T. Schwab, *James Gibbons Huneker: Critic of the Seven Arts* (Stanford University Press, 1963), 234.

6. Quoted from Claire Sprague, *Edgar Saltus* (New York: Twayne, 1968), 66.

7. Tice L. Miller, *Bohemians and Critics* (Metuchen: Scarecrow Press, 1981), 16–17.

8. James Gibbons Huneker, *Iconoclasts: A Book of Dramatists* (New York: Scribner's, 1915), 14–21.

9. Schwab, 234.

10. Goldberg, *Theatre of George Jean Nathan*, 63.

11. Mencken, *Prejudices: A Selection* (New York: Vintage, 1958), 126–27)

12. Huneker, "The Seven Arts," *Puck* (3 October 1915), 8.

13. Josephine Huneker, ed., *Letters of James Gibbons Huneker* (New York: Scribner's, 1922), 203.

14. Quoted from Schwab, 290.

15. Schwab, 72.

16. Channing Pollock, *Harvest of My Years* (New York: Bobbs and Merrill, 1943), 93.

17. Ibid.

18. Montrose J. Moses, *The American Dramatist*, (Boston: Little, Brown, 1925), 354.

19. Tice L. Miller "George Jean Nathan and the 'New Criticism,'" *Theatre History Studies* 3 (1983): 100.

20. Ibid.

21. Mencken, "My Life. . . . ," 185.

22. Moran, 106–7.

23. Gene Fowler, *Good Night, Sweet Prince* (New York: Viking, 1942), 7.

24. Brooks Atkinson, *Broadway* (New York: *Macmillan,* 1970), 88.

25. Louis Sheaffer, *O'Neill: Son and Artist* (Boston: Little, Brown, 1973), 61.

26. Quoted from Jordan Y. Miller, *Eugene O'Neill and the American Critic*, 2d ed., rev. (Hampden: Archon, 1972), 241.

27. Ibid., 269.

28. Ibid., 435.

29. Ibid., 439.

30. Moses and Brown, 184.

31. Nathan, *The Theatre Book of the Year 1945–1946* (New York: Knopf, 1946), 94.

32. Nathan, *Comedians All* (New York: Knopf, 1919), 190.

33. Nathan, *The Popular Theatre* (New York: Knopf, 1918), 89–90.

34. Ibid., 91.

35. Nathan, *Art of the Night* (New York: Knopf, 1928), 3.

36. Nathan, "On the Duty of a Critic," *Puck* (October 1914), 6.

37. *The Green Book* (December 1910), 1306.

38. John Held, "The Men Who Roast the Plays," *The Theatre* (March 1917), 138.

39. Richard Lahey, Caricature of George Jean Nathan, *The Theatre* (August 1923), 21.

40. Nathan, "The Greatest NonResident Club in the World," *Harper's Weekly* (20 March 1909), 15.

41. Nathan and George M. Cohan, "The Mechanics of Emotion," *McLure's* (November 1913), 6977.

42. Nathan, *The World in Falseface* (New York: Knopf, 1923), 117.

43. Nathan, *Theatre Book of the Year 1950–1951* (New York: Knopf, 1951), 110.

44. Burton Rascoe and Groff Conklin, eds., *"The Smart Set" Anthology* (New York: Reynal and Hitchcock, 1934), xxii–xxiv.

45. Quoted from Goldberg, *Theatre of George Jean Nathan*, 253, 255, and 256.
46. Nathan, *Passing Judgments* (New York: Knopf, 1935), 147–158.
47. M. K. Singleton, *H. L. Mencken and the American Mercury Adventure* (Durham, N. C.: Duke University Press, 1962), 132–133.
48. Charles Angoff, *The World of George Jean Nathan* (New York: Knopf, 1952), xv.
49. Rascoe and Conklin, xxii–xxiv.
50. Singleton, 132.
51. Ibid., 133.
52. Gordon Rogoff, "Modern Dramatic Criticism," in *The Reader's Encyclopedia of World Drama*, ed. John Gassner and Edward Quinn, (New York: Thomas Crowell, 1969), 577–578.
53. Nathan, *Mr. George Jean Nathan Presents* (New York: Knopf, 1917), 289–290.
54. New York *Telegraph* (23 December 1933), clipping in the Billy Rose Theatre Collection's Nathan file, New York Public Library, no page number.
55. Richard H. Palmer, *The Critics' Canon* (Westport, Conn.: Greenwood Press, 1988), xi.
56. Quoted from Goldberg, *Theatre of George Jean Nathan*, 56.
57. Ibid, 61.
58. Angoff, *The World of George Jean Nathan*, 487–488.
59. Nathan, *The World in Falseface*, xvii–xviii.
60. Singleton, 117.
61. Nathan, *Theatre Book of the Year 1950–1951*, 109–110.
62. Nathan, *The Theatre, the Drama, the Girls*, 119.
63. Clarence J. Hyde, letter to George Jean Nathan, 1 March 1916. Cornell Collection.
64. Tice L. Miller, *Bohemians and Critics*, 100.
65. Morris U. Burns, *The Dramatic Criticism of Alexander Woollcott* (Metuchen, N.J.: Scarecrow Press, 1980), 8.
66. Tice L. Miller, "Alan Dale: The Hearst Critic." *Educational Theatre Journal* 27 (1974): 71.

# Chapter 3. Nathan in the Critical Arena: The Criticism of Criticism

1. Norton, 330.
2. Edmund Wilson, *The Devils and Canon Barham* (New York: Farrar, Straus and Giroux, 1973), 92.
3. Rascoe and Conklin, xxvi.
4. Mary Kolars, "Some Modern Periodicals," *Catholic World* (March 1923), 786.
5. Carl R. Dolmetsch, *"The Smart Set": A History and Anthology* (New York: Dial Press, 1966), 56.
6. Ibid., 56.
7. Angoff, *The World of George Jean Nathan*, 261.
8. Henry Hazlitt, Review of *Testament of a Critic*, The Nation, (18 February 1931), 186187.
9. *Saturday Review of Literature* (12 January 1935), 419.
10. Nathan, *Another Book on the Theatre* (New York: B. W. Huebsch, 1915), x–xi.

11. Ibid., xi.

12. Ibid., 91.

13. Nathan, *Mr. George Jean Nathan Presents* (New York: Knopf, 1917), 170–182.

14. Ibid., 171.

15. Ibid., 173.

16. Ibid., 178–179.

17. Nathan, *The Popular Theatre* (New York: Knopf, 1918), 191.

18. Ibid, 182.

19. Ibid.

20. Nathan, *Comedians All* (New York: Knopf, 1919), 14–15.

21. Ibid., 18–19.

22. Ibid., 22.

23. Ibid., 21.

24. Ibid., 26–27.

25. Ibid., 92.

26. Ibid., 93.

27. Nathan, *The Morning After the First Night* (New York: Knopf: 1938), 3–69.

28. Nathan, *The Theatre, the Drama, the Girls* (New York: Knopf: 1921), 24–25.

29. Ibid., 27.

30. Nathan, *The World in Falseface*, xi–xii.

31. Thomas Quinn Curtiss, ed. *The Magic Mirror* (New York: Alfred A. Knopf, 1960), xv.

32. Ibid., 24.

33. Angoff, *The Tone of the Twenties* (South Brunswick, N.J.: A. S. Barnes, 1966), 45.

34. O'Neill to Nathan, 15 June 1940. *Selected Letters of Eugene O'Neill*, 506.

35. Herbert Simpson, letter to the author, 19 February 1990.

36. Nathan, *World in Falseface*, xvii.

37. Walter Lippmann, "The Enormously Civilized Minority," *Vanity Fair* (March 1928), 64.

38. Edmund Wilson, *Letters on Literature and Politics*, Elena Mumm Wilson, ed. (New York: Farrar, Straus and Giroux, 1977), 145.

39. Nathan, *Materia Critica* (New York: Knopf, 1924), 3.

40. Nathan, *The Critic and the Drama* (New York: Knopf, 1922), 23.

41. Nathan, *Materia Critica*, 30.

42. Winthrop Ames to Nathan, 20 June 1919, Cornell Collection.

43. Richard Aldrich to Nathan, 16 March 1948, Cornell Collection.

44. William Saroyan to Nathan, 2 June 1939, Cornell Collection.

45. George Stevens, *Speak for Yourself, John: The Life of John Mason Brown* (New York: Viking, 1974), 106.

46. John Peter Toohey and Edna Ferber to George Jean Nathan, 25 October 1932, Cornell Collection.

47. Nathan, *Passing Judgments* (New York: Knopf, 1935), 158–161.

48. Nathan, *Theatre Book of the Year 1950–1951*, 112.

49. Nathan, *The House of Satan* (New York: Knopf, 1926), 160–161.

50. Angoff, *Tone of the Twenties*, 48.

51. Nathan, *The Theatre of the Moment* (New York: Knopf, 1936), 160–277.

52. Robert Forsythe, *Reading From Left to Right* (New York: Covici, 1938), 80.

53. Nathan, *The Theatre Book of the Year 1947–1948* (New York: Knopf, 1948), 241–245.

54. Thomas Mann to Blanche Knopf, 27 November 1948, Cornell Collection.

55. Quoted from Brooks Atkinson, *Broadway Scrapbook* (New York: Theatre Arts, 1947), 26.

56. Ibid., 25.

57. Nathan, review of *Our Town, Scribner's Magazine* (May 1938), 65.

58. Stark Young, review of *Our Town, The New Republic* (23 February 1938), 74.

59. John Mason Brown, *Dramatis Personae* (New York: Viking, 1963), 84.

60. Nathan, *The Encyclopedia of the Theatre* (New York: Knopf, 1940), 398.

61. Martin Gottfried, *The Curse of Genius* (Boston: Little, Brown, 1984), 167–168.

62. Arthur Gelb, telephone interview with author, 24 July 1997.

63. Allene Talmey, "*Vogue's* Spot-light" *Vogue* (15 March 1938), 108–109, 156.

64. Nathan, *The Theatre Book of the Year 1942–1943* (New York: Knopf, 1943), 148–150.

65. Stark Young, letters to Nathan, *Stark Young: A Life in the Arts, Letters 1900–1962, Vol. II,* ed. John Pilkington (Baton Rouge: Louisiana State University Press, 1975), 900–902.

66. Stark Young to Nathan, undated, Cornell Collection.

67. John Mason Brown, *Two on the Aisle* (New York: Norton, 1938), 299–302.

68. Mencken, "My Life as Author and Editor," 699.

69. Nathan, *Encyclopedia of the Theatre*, 344.

70. John Anderson, letter to Helen Deutsch, 2 May 1943, Helen Deutsch Papers, Boston University.

71. Review of *Materia Critica, The Bookman* (August 1924), 699–700.

72. Robert Malcolm Gray, review of *The Autobiography of an Attitude, The Bookman* (November 1925), 336.

## Chapter 4. The Limits of Impressionism

1. Nathan, manuscript, 18 June 1921, Cornell Collection.

2. Nathan, *Critic and the Drama*, 11 ff.

3. Ibid, ix.

4. Ibid., 10.

5. Mencken, *Prejudices: A Selection*, 3–11.

6. Isaac Goldberg, *The Drama of Transition* (Cincinnati: Stewart Kidd, 1922), 32–45.

7. Joel Spingarn, "The Growth of a Literary Myth," *The Freeman* (2 May 1923), 181183.

8. Nathan, *Critic and the Drama*, 11.

9. Ibid., 1516.

10. Nathan, *Another Book . . .* , 163171.

11. Nathan, *Critic and the Drama*, 22.

12. Ibid., 23.

13. Cleveland Amory and Frederic Bradlee, ed. *Vanity Fair: A Cavalcade of the 1920's and 1930's* (New York: Viking, 1960), 63.

14. Nathan *Critic and the Drama*, 29.

15. Ibid., 47.

16. Ibid., 7879.

17. Nathan, *Materia Critica*, 24–25.

18. Arthur and Barbara Gelb, *O'Neill.* Enlarged ed. (New York: Harper and Row, 1973), 732

19. *Congressional Record-House,* 1932, 5803.

20. Ibid., 5804.

21. Joseph Campbell and Henry Morton Robinson, "The Skin of Whose Teeth? The Strange Case of Mr. Wilder's New Play and *Finnegan's Wake,*" *Saturday Review of Literature* (19 December 1942), 3–4. "The Skin of Whose Teeth?" Part II, *Saturday Review of Literature* (13 February 1943), 16–19.

22. Edmund Wilson, *Classics and Commercials* (New York: Farrar, Straus and Giroux, 1950), 81–87.

23. Nathan, *Theatre Book of the Year 1942–1943,* 136. The "Peggy" to whom Nathan refers is the oft-married chorine Peggy Hopkins Joyce. She was featured in the Ziegfeld *Follies* and in Earl Carroll's *Vanities.* Famous for her ready wit, when asked "How do *Follies* girls get minks?" she replied, "The same way minks do."

24. William Saroyan, "The American Clowns of Criticism—Mencken, Nathan and Haldeman-Julius" *Overland Monthly* (March 1929), 72–79, 92–93.

24. Lawrence Lee and Barry Gifford, *Saroyan* (New York: Harper and Row, 1984), 230.

25. Nathan, *Theatre Book of the Year 1947–1948,* 111–112.

26. Tennessee Williams, *Memoirs* (New York: Doubleday, 1975), 82.

27. Nathan, *The Theatre Book of the Year 1945–1946,* 89.

28. Lyle Leverich, *Tom: The Unknown Tennessee Williams,* (New York: Crown, 1995), 552.

29. Robert Anderson to the author, 15 May 1996.

30. Williams, *Memoirs,* 90.

31. Nathan, *The Theatre Book of the Year 1945–1946,* 88–89.

32. Lyle Leverich, *Tom: The Unknown Tennessee Williams,* 371.

33. Sheaffer, *O'Neill: Son and Artist,* 575.

34. Nathan, *Theatre Book of the Year 19481949,* 279285.

35. Ibid., 281.

36. Ibid., 284.

37. Nathan, *The Theatre Book of the Year: 1945–1946,* 263.

38. Nathan, *The Theatre Book of the Year 1949–1950,* 235.

39. Ibid., 236.

40. Nathan, *The Theatre in the Fifties,* 73.

41. Ibid.

42. Joshua Logan, *Josh: My Up and Down, In and Out Life* (London: W. H. Allen, 1977), 349–357.

43. Harold Clurman, *The Collected Works* (New York: Applause Books, 1994), 856.

44. Clurman, *On Directing* (New York: Macmillan, 1972), 46.

45. Kenneth Tynan, *He that Plays the King* (New York: Longmans, 1950), 21–22.

46. Ibid., 21

47. Tynan, *Profiles* (New York: HarperCollins, 1990), 61.

48. Tice L. Miller, "George Jean Nathan," in The Cambridge Guide to American Theatre (Cambridge University Press, 1993), 335.

49. Eric Bentley, *The Playwright as Thinker* (Cleveland: World, 1955), 261.

50. Tynan, *He that Plays the King,* 21.

51. Bentley, *The Playwright as Thinker,* 261.

52. Ibid.

53. Walter Kerr, *God on the Gymnasium Floor* ( New York: Simon and Schuster, 1971), 9.

54. Nathan, "The Stage as Self-Poisoner" *Theatre Arts* (July 1958), 10–11.

## Chapter 5. Nothing If Not Critical

1. Quoted from Simpson, "Mencken and Nathan," 181.

2. Nathan, *The Critic and the Drama*, 18.

3. Oscar Wilde, "The Soul of Man Under Socialism." In *The Artist as Critic: Critical Writings of Oscar Wilde*, ed. by Richard Ellman (New York: Random House, 1969), 279.

4. Nathan, *Monks are Monks*, 222.

5. Nathan, *The Intimate Notebooks of George Jean Nathan*, 175.

6. Nathan, *The Theatre of the Moment*, 102.

7. Nathan, *The Theatre Book of the Year 1944–1945*, 183.

8. Nathan, *Materia Critica*, 20.

9. C. W. E. Bigsby, "The Absent Voice: the Critic and the Drama," *Studies in American Drama 1945-Present*, Volume 3 (1988), 21.

10. Nathan, *The Theatre, the Drama, the Girls*, 290–311.

# Select Bibliography

The bibliography includes all sources cited as well as other works that have influenced this study.

Adams, Samuel Hopkins. *Alexander Woollcott: His Life and his World.* New York: Reynal and Hitchcock, 1945.

"A First Nighter Says." *The Green Book Magazine,* May 1911, 1089.

Aldrich, Richard. Letter to George Jean Nathan, 16 March 1948. The George Jean Nathan Collection. Cornell University, Ithaca, N.Y. [henceforth referred to as the Cornell Collection].

Ames, Winthrop. Letter to George Jean Nathan, 20 June 1919. The Cornell Collection.

Amory, Cleveland, and Bradlee, Frederic, eds. *Vanity Fair: A Cavalcade of the 1920's and 1930's.* New York: Viking, 1960.

John Anderson. Letter to Helen Deutsch, 2 May 1943. The Cornell Collection.

Anderson, Porter. "Teasers and Tormentors, The Nathan that Got Away," *Village Voice,* 27 September 1994, 104.

Anderson, Robert. Letter to the author, 15 May 1996.

Angoff, Charles. *The Tone of the Twenties.* South Brunswick, N.J.: A. S. Barnes, 1966.

———. ed. *The World of George Jean Nathan.* New York: Alfred A. Knopf, 1952.

———. "George Jean Nathan." *The Atlantic Monthly,* December 1962, 46–48.

———. "George Jean Nathan: Superlative Dandy." *The New Republic,* 4 January 1964, 17–20.

"A Slapstick Satirist of the Broadway Drama." *Current Opinion,* August 1917, 95.

Atkinson, Brooks. *Broadway.* New York: Macmillan, 1970.

———. "Account Closed." The *New York Times,* 27 April 1953, sec. 2, p. 1.

Banks, James. Letter to George Jean Nathan, 11 November 1929. The Cornell Collection.

Bartlett, Randolph. "Exterminator of Humbugs." *The Saturday Review of Literature,* 12 January 1935, 419.

Bell, Archie. "The Most Hated Man in the Theatre . . ." *The Theatre,* November 1924, 20, 66.

Bentley, Eric. *In Search of Theater.* New York: Knopf, 1953.

———. *The Playwright as Thinker.* Cleveland: World, 1955.

———. *What is Theatre? Incorporating the Dramatic Event.* New York: Limelight Editions, 1984.

Biel, Steven. *Independent Intellectuals in the United States 1910–1945.* New York: New York University Press, 1992.

Bigsby, C. W. E. "The Absent Voice: The Critic and the Drama." *Studies in American Drama 1945–Present* Volume 3, 1988, 921.

Boyd, Ernest. *Portraits: Real and Imaginary.* New York: Doran, 1924.

———."George Jean Nathan." *Theatre Arts Monthly,* January 1927, 59–64.

Benchley, Robert. *Benchley at the Theatre.* Edited by Charles Getchell. Ipswich, MA: The Ipswich Press, 1985.

Bordman, Gerald. *American Theatre: A Chronicle of Comedy and Drama, 1869–1914.* New York: Oxford University Press, 1994.

———. *American Theatre: A Chronicle of Comedy and Drama, 1914–1930.* New York: Oxford University Press, 1994.

———. *American Theatre: A Chronicle of Comedy and Drama, 1930–1969.* New York: Oxford University Press, 1996.

Brenman-Gibson, Margaret. *Clifford Odets: American Playwright, The Years from 19061940.* New York: Atheneum, 1981.

Bronner, Edwin J. *The Encyclopedia of the American Theatre.* New York: Barnes, 1980.

Broun, Heywood. *Pieces of Hate.* New York: Doran, 1922.

Brown, John Mason. *As They Appear.* New York: McGrawHill, 1952.

———.*Dramatis Personae.* New York: Viking, 1965.

———."The Late George Jean Nathan: Wizard of the Verbal Cactus." *New York Times,* 13 April 1958, sec. 2, p. 1.

———. *Letters From Greenroom Ghosts.* New York: Viking, 1954.

———. *Two on the Aisle.* New York: Norton, 1938.

———. *Upstage: The American Theatre in Performance.* New York: Norton, 1930.

Burns, Morris U. *The Dramatic Criticism of Alexander Woollcott.* Metuchen, N.J.: Scarecrow Press, 1980.

Carlson, Marvin. *Theories of the Theatre.* Ithaca: Cornell University Press, 1984.

Clurman, Harold. *All People Are Famous.* New York: Harcourt, Brace, Jovanovich, 1974.

Commins, Dorothy, ed. *"Love and Admiration and Respect": The O'Neill Commins Correspondence.* Durham, N.C.: Duke University Press, 1986.

*Congressional Record.* 72nd Cong., 1st sess., 1932. Vol. 75, pt. 5.

Craig, Gordon. Letters to George Jean Nathan, 9 January 1916, The Cornell Collection.

Croce, Benedetto. *Aesthetic: A Science and General Linguistic.* Translated by by Douglas Ainslie, 1909. Reprint , Boston MA: Nonpareil Books, 1978.

*Guide to Aesthetics.* Translated by Patrick Romanell: University Press of America, Lanham, MD, 1965.

———. *European Literature in the 19th Century.* Translated by Douglas Ainslie. New York, N.Y.: Alfred A. Knopf, 1924.

Curtiss, Thomas Quinn, ed. *The Magic Mirror.* New York: Alfred A. Knopf, 1960.

Daly, Arnold. "On George Jean Nathan, and Perhaps Some Other Critics?" *Bookman,* April 1921: 163–65.

De Gennaro, Angelo. *The Philosophy of Benedetto Croce.* Westport, Ct: Greenwood Press, 1968.

Dolmetsch, Carl R. *The Smart Set: A History and Anthology.* New York: The Dial Press, 1966.

———. "HLM and GJN: The Editorial Partnership Reexamined." *Menckeniana* 77, (1980) 32–41.

Downer, Alan S., ed. *American Drama and its Critics.* Chicago: University of Chicago Press, 1965.

Dreiser, Theodore. Letter to George Jean Nathan, 7 October 1933. The Cornell Collection.

English, John. *Criticizing the Critics.* New York: Hastings House, 1976.

Ervine, St. John. "Ervine on Nathan." *The Living Age,* May 1931, 306–07.

Forsythe, Robert. *Reading From Left to Right.* New York: Covici, 1938.

Fort Wayne and Allen County [Indiana] Directories and Fort Wayne City Directories, 1877–1885.

Fowler, Gene. *Good Night, Sweet Prince* New York: Viking, 1942.

Frick, Constance. *The Dramatic Criticism of George Jean Nathan.* Ithaca, N.Y.: Cornell University Press, 1943.

Gassner, John. *Directions in Modern Theatre and Drama.* New York: Holt, Rinehart and Winston, 1966.

———. *Theatre at the Crossroads.* New York: Holt, Rinehart and Winston, 1960.

Gaver, Jack. Introduction to *Critics' Choice: New York Drama Critics' Circle Prize Plays 19351955.* Edited by Jack Gaver. New York: Hawthorn, 1955.

Gelb, Arthur. "The Atkinson Method Defined," privately printed by the New York *Times* on the occasion of the critic's retirement.

———. Interview by author, Boston, 12 May 1995.

———. Telephone interview by author, 24 July 1997.

Gelb, Arthur and Barbara. *O'Neill.* Enlarged ed. New York: Harper and Row, 1973.

Gelderman, Carol. "Critics and How they Got That Way." *American Theatre,* June 1990, 2324, 6364.

Gibbs, Wolcott. "Nathan the Indestructible." *The New Yorker,* 22 October 1949, 121–22.

Gish, Lillian. *The Movies, Mr. Griffith and Me.* Englewood Cliffs, N.J.: PrenticeHall, 1969.

———. Letter to H. L. Mencken, 20 May 1939. Papers of H. L. Mencken. New York Public Library.

Goldberg, Isaac. *The Theatre of George Jean Nathan.* New York: Simon and Schuster, 1926.

———. *The Drama of Transition.* Cincinnati: Stewart Kidd, 1922.

Goodrich, Marc. "Those Who Sit in Judgment: George Jean Nathan." *The Theatre,* August 1927, 28, 56.

Gray, Robert Malcolm. "Attitudes and Latitudes." *The Bookman,* November 1925, 336–37.

Halfmann, Ulrich, ed. *Eugene O'Neill: Comments on the Drama and the Theater: A Source Book.* Tübingen, Germany: Gunter Narr Verlag, 1987.

Harding, James. *Agate: A Biography.* London: Methuen, 1986

Harrison, Gilbert A. *The Enthusiast.* New York: Ticknor and Fields, 1983.

Hazlitt, Henry. Review of *Testament of a Critic,* by George Jean Nathan *The Nation,* 18 February 1931, 186–87.

Held, John. "The Men Who Roast the Plays." *The Theatre,* March 1917, 138–87.

Henderson, Mary. *The City and the Theatre.* Clifton, N.J.: Jarus T. White, 1973.

Highsmith, James. "The Cornell Letters: Eugene O'Neill on His Craftsmanship to George Jean Nathan." *Modern Drama* 15 (1972), 68–88.

―――. "A Description of the Cornell Collection of Eugene O'Neill's Letters to George Jean Nathan." *Modern Drama* 14 (1972), 420–25.

*History of Allen County, Indiana.* Chicago: Kingman Brothers, 1880.

Huneker, James Gibbons. *Iconoclasts: A Book of Dramatists.* New York: Scribner's, 1915.

―――. *Ivory, Apes, and Peacocks.* New York: Scribner's, 1915.

―――. *The Pathos of Distance.* New York: Scribner's, 1913.

―――. "The Seven Arts." *Puck,* 3 October 1915, 8.

―――. *Steeplejack.* New York: Scribner's, 1922.

―――. *Variations.* New York: Scribner's, 1921.

Huneker, Josephine, ed. *Letters of James Gibbons Huneker.* New York: Scribner's, 1922.

―――. *Intimate Letters of James Gibbons Huneker.* New York: Liveright, 1936.

Hyde, Clarence J. Letter to George Jean Nathan, 1 March 1916. The Cornell Collection. Isaacs, Edith J. R. "The Critical Arena I: The Theatre of George Jean Nathan." *Theatre Arts,* February 1942, 104–11.

―――. "The Critical Arena II: The Theatre of Alexander Woollcott." *Theatre Arts,* March 1942, 191–96.

―――. "The Critical Arena III: The Theatre of Stark Young." *Theatre Arts,* April 1942, 257–64.

―――. "The Critical Arena IV: The Playwright as Critic: G. B. S." *Theatre Arts,* December 1942, 755–62.

Kammen, Michael. *The Lively Arts: Gilbert Seldes and the Transformation of Cultural Criticism in the United States.* New York: Oxford University Press, 1996.

Kazin, Alfred. *On Native Grounds.* New York: Reynal and Hitchcock, 1942.

Kerr, Walter. *God on the Gymnasium Floor.* New York: Simon and Schuster, 1971.

Knopf, Alfred A. "H. L. Mencken, George Jean Nathan and *The American Mercury* Venture." *Menckeniana* 78 (1981), 110.

Peter Kriendler. Interview by author, New York, 18 February 1995.

Kolars, Mary. "Some Modern Periodicals." *Catholic World,* March 1923, 781–89.

Kozlenko, Vladimir. *The Quintessence of Nathanism.* New York: Vrest Orton, 1930.

Laemmle, Carl. Letter to George Jean Nathan, 11 January 1919. The Cornell Collection.

Lahey, Richard. Caricature of George Jean Nathan. *The Theatre.* August 1923: 21.

Lehman, Ernest. Letter to the author, 5 July 1993.

Lazarus, Arnold Leslie, ed. *A George Jean Nathan Reader.* Rutherfored, N.J.: Fairleigh Dickinson University Press, 1990.

Leverich, Lyle. *Tom: The Unknown Tennessee Williams.* New York: Crown, 1995.

Levine, Ira. *LeftWing Dramatic Theory in the American Theatre.* UMI Research Press, 1985.

"Lillian Gish and the Cynic's Heart." *The Philadelphia Inquirer Magazine,* 2 August 1925, 2.

Lippmann, Walter. "The Enormously Civilized Minority." *Vanity Fair,* March 1928, 64, 71.

Logan, Joshua. *Josh: My Up and Down, In and Out Life.* London: W. H. Allen, 1977.

Lowery, Robert G. and Angelin, Patricia, eds. *"My Very Dear Sean": George Jean Nathan to Sean O'Casey. Letters and Articles.* Rutherfored, N.J.: Fairleigh Dickinson University Press, 1985.

Lockridge, Richard. "The Nathan Phenomenon." *Saturday Review of Literature,* 24 January 1942, 12.

Lumianski, Robert M. "Stark Young and his Dramatic Criticism." Ph.D. diss. Michigan State College, 1955.

Lysy, Peter J. Letter to author, 29 August 1994.

Maney, Richard. *Fanfare: The Confessions of a Press Agent.* New York: Harper, 1957.

Mann, Thomas. Letter to Blanche Knopf, 27 November 1948. The Cornell Collection.

May, Henry F. *The End of American Innocence: A Study of the First Years of Our Own Time 1912–1917.* New York: Alfred A. Knopf, 1959.

Mayfield, Sara. *The Constant Circle: H. L. Mencken and his Friends.* New York: Delacorte, 1968.

Meister, Charles W. *Dramatic Criticism.* Jefferson, N.C.: McFarland, 1985.

Mencken, H. L. Letter to Alfred A. Knopf, 26 October 1938. H. L. Mencken Papers. New York Public Library. . "My Life as an Editor and Author." Unpublished manuscript. H. L. Mencken Papers. Dartmouth College Library.

———. *Prejudices: A Selection.* New York: Vintage, 1958.

———. *Prejudices: First Series.* New York: Knopf, 1919.

———. *Prejudices: Third Series.* New York: Knopf, 1922.

———. and Nathan, George Jean. *Heliogabalus.* New York: Knopf, 1920.

Meredith, Scott. *George S. Kaufman and His Friends.* New York: Doubleday, 1974.

Miller, Jordan Y. *Eugene O'Neill and the American Critic.* 2d ed. rev. Hampton, CT: Archon, 1972.

Miller, Tice L. "Alan Dale: The Hearst Critic." *Educational Theatre Journal* 27 (March 1974): 69–80.

———. "George Jean Nathan and the 'New Criticism.'" *Theatre History Studies* 3 (1983), 99–107.

———. *Bohemians and Critics: American Theatre Criticism in the Nineteenth Century.* Metuchen, N.J.: Scarecrow Press, 1981.

Moran, T. S. "New York's Dramatic Critics." *Metropolitan,* January 1899, 106–109.

Moses, Montrose J. *The American Dramatist.* Boston: Little, Brown, 1925.

———. and Brown, John Mason, eds. *The American Theatre as Seen by Its Critics, 1752–1934.* New York: Norton, 1934.

Moss, M. E. *Benedetto Croce Reconsidered.* Hanover, NH: University Presses of New England, 1987.

Mott, Frank Luther. *A History of American Magazines 1885–1905.* Vol. 4 of A History of American Magazines. Cambridge: Harvard University Press, 1957.

———. *Sketches of TwentyOne Magazines 1905–1930.* Vol. 5 of A History of American Magazines. Cambridge: Harvard University Press, 1968.

Murphy, Brenda. *American Realism and American Drama.* New York, NY: Cambridge Press, 1987.

Nathan, George Jean. *Another Book on the Theatre.* New York: B. W. Huebsch, 1915.

———. *Art of the Night.* New York: Knopf, 1928.

———. *The Autobiography of an Attitude.* New York: Knopf 1925.

———."Auf Wiedersehen." *Percy Hammond, A Symposium in Tribute.* New York: Doubleday, 1936.

———.*The Avon Flows.* New York: Random House, 1937.

———. *The Bachelor Life.* New York: Reynal and Hitchcock, 1941.

———. *Beware of Parents.* New York: Knopf, 1943.

———. *Bottoms Up.* New York: Knopf, 1917.

———. *Comedians All.* New York: Knopf, 1919.

———. *The Critic and the Drama.* New York: Knopf, 1922.

———. *The Entertainment of the Nation.* New York: Knopf, 1942.

———. *The Encyclopedia of the Theatre.* New York: Knopf, 1940.

———. Foreword to *Five Great Modern Irish Plays.* New York: Modern Library, 1941.

———. Foreword to *Of Thee I Sing.* By George S. Kaufman, Morrie Ryskind, and Ira Gershwin. New York: Knopf, 1933.

———. Foreword to *Chicago,* by Maurine Watkins. New York: Knopf, 1927.

———. Foreword to *Twelve Thousand,* by Bruno Frank New York: Knopf, 1928.

———. Foreword to *Lysistrata,* by Maurice Donnay. New York: Knopf, 1930.

———. Foreword to *The Critics' Prize Plays.* Cleveland: World, 1945.

———."The Greatest NonResident Club in the World." *Harper's Weekly,* 20 March 1909, 15.

———. *The House of Satan.* New York: Knopf, 1926.

———.*The Intimate Notebooks of George Jean Nathan.* New York: Knopf, 1932.

———. Introduction to *The World's Great Plays.* Cleveland: World, 1944.

———.*Land of the Pilgrim's Pride.* New York: Knopf, 1927.

———. Letter to Isaac Goldberg. Saturday, no year. Isaac Goldberg Papers. New York Public Library.

———. Letter to Isaac Goldberg. 22 September, no year. Isaac Goldberg Papers. New York Public Library.

———. Letter to Isaac Goldberg. 3 June 1926. Isaac Goldberg Papers. New York Public Library.

———.*Materia Critica.* New York: Knopf, 1924.

———. *Mr. George Jean Nathan Presents.* New York: Knopf, 1917.

———. *Monks are Monks.* New York: Knopf, 1929.

———. *The Morning After the First Night.* New York: Knopf, 1938.

———. *The New American Credo.* Rev. ed. New York: Knopf, 1927.

———. *Passing Judgments.* New York: Knopf, 1935

———. "The Physical Demands of the Stage." *Outing,* April 1909, 46–60.

———. *The Popular Theatre.* New York: Knopf, 1918.

———. *Since Ibsen.* New York: Knopf, 1933.

———. *Testament of a Critic.* New York: Knopf, 1931.

———. *The Theatre Book of the Year 1942–43 through 1950–51* New York: Knopf, 1943–51.

———. *The Theatre in the Fifties.* New York: Knopf, 1953.

———. *The Theatre of the Moment.* New York: Knopf, 1936.

———. *The Theatre, the Drama, the Girls.* New York: Knopf, 1921.

———. *The World in Falseface.* New York: Knopf, 1923.

———. and Cohan, George M. "The Mechanics of Emotion." *McLure's,* November 1913, 69–77.

Nirdlinger, Charles Frederic. *Masques and Mummers.* New York: DeWitt, 1899.

Norton, Elliot. "Puffers, Pundits, and Other Play Reviewers: A Short History of American Dramatic Criticism." *The American Theatre: A Sum of Its Parts.* Edited by Henry B. Williams. New York: Samuel French, 1971: 317–336.

O'Casey, Sean. *Autobiographies I and II.* New York: Carroll and Graf, 1984.

O'Neill, Eugene. *The Selected Letters.* Edited by Travis Bogard and Jackson Bryer. New Haven, Conn.: Yale University Press, 1988.

Palmer, Richard H. *The Critics' Canon.* Westport, CT: Greenwood Press, 1988.

Pollock, Channing. *Harvest of My Years.* Indianapolic, Ind.: Bobbs and Merrill, 1943.

Poupard, Dennis et al., eds. "George Jean Nathan." In *Twentieth-Century Literary Criticism.* Vol. 18. Detroit: Gale Research, 1985

Rascoe, Burton. "Mencken, Nathan, and Cabell." *The American Mercury* March, 1940, 364–367.

Rascoe, Burton. *The Smart Set History.* New York: Reynal and Hitchcock, 1934.

Reynolds, David. *Beneath the American Renaissance.* New York: Alfred A. Knopf, 1988.

Roberts, Nancy L., and Roberts, Arthur W. *"As Ever, Gene": The Letters of Eugene O'Neill to George Jean Nathan.* Rutherford, N.J.: Fairleigh Dickinson University Press, 1987.

Robertson, Roderick. *The Friendship of Eugene O'Neill and George Jean Nathan.* Ph.D. diss., University of Wisconsin, 1970.

Rogers, Mark. "Historical Genealogy Research Center Report on George Jean Nathan." Fort Wayne, Ind.: Allen County Public Library, 1997.

Rogoff, Gordon. "Modern Dramatic Criticism." In *The Reader's Encyclopedia of World Drama.* Edited by John Gassner and Edward Quinn: Thomas Crowell, 1969: New York, NY: 573–82.

Rosenberg, Bernard and White David Manning, eds. *Mass Culture: The Popular Arts in America.* Glencoe, IL: The Free Press, 1957.

Roth, Anna, ed. "George Jean Nathan." *Current Biography.* New York: H. W. Wilson, 1945

Rudin, Seymour. "George Jean Nathan: A Study of his Criticism." Ph.D. diss., Cornell University, 1953.

———. "Playwright to Critic: Sean O'Casey's Letters to George Jean Nathan." *The Massachusetts Review* 5 (1964), 326–34.

Ruffino, Arthur Salvatore. "A Cumulative Index to the Books of George Jean Nathan." Ph.D. diss., University of Southern Illinois, 1971.

Santayana, George. *The Philosophy of Santayana, Selections from the Works.* New York: Scribner's, 1936.

Saroyan, William. *Sons Come and Go, Mothers Hang In Forever.* New York: McGrawHill, 1976.

———. Letter to George Jean Nathan, 2 August 1939. The Cornell Collection.

Schultheiss, John. "George Jean Nathan and the Dramatist in Hollywood." *Literature/Film Quarterly* 4, no. 1 (Winter 1976), 13–23.

Schwab, Arnold, T. *James Gibbons Huneker: Critic of the Seven Arts.* Palo Alto, CA: Stanford University Press, 1963.

Shaughnessy, Edward. "Ella O'Neill and the Imprint of Faith. *The Eugene O'Neill Review* 16, no. 2, Fall 1992: 29–43.

Shaw, Charles G. *The LowDown.* New York: Holt, 1928.

Shaw, George Bernard. *Our Theatres in the Nineties.* 3 vols. London: Constable, 1932.

———. Letter to George Jean Nathan, 2 August 1950. The Cornell Collection.

Sheaffer, Louis. *O'Neill: Son and Artist.* Boston: Little, Brown, 1973.

———.*O'Neill: Son and Playwright.* Boston: Little, Brown, 1968.

SilVara, G. A. "The 'Bad Boy' of Dramatic Criticism." *The Jewish Tribune.* 23 September 1927, 15.

Simpson, Herbert M. "Mencken and Nathan." Ph.D. diss., University of Maryland, 1965.

———. Letter to the author, 19 February 1990.

———. Letter to the author, 13 April 1990.

Singleton, M. K. *H. L. Mencken and the American Mercury Adventure.* Durham, N.C.: Duke University, 1962.

Smith, S. Stephenson. *The Craft of the Critic.* New York: Thomas Y. Crowell, 1931.

Sobel, Bernard. *Broadway Heartbeat: Memoirs of a Press Agent.* New York: Hermitage House, 1953.

Sobol, Louis. *The Longest Street.* New York: Crown, 1968.

Spiller. Robert E., et al. *Literary History of the United States.* 4th ed. New York: Macmillan, 1975.

Spingarn, Joel Elias. *A History of Literary Criticism in the Renaissance.* New York: Columbia University Press, 1925.

———.*Creative Criticism And Other Essays.* Rev. ed. New York, NY: Harcourt, Brace, 1931.

———."The Growth of a Literary Myth." *The Freeman* 2 May 1923, 183–85.

Spivack, Lawrence E., and Angoff, Charles, eds. *The American Mercury Reader.* Philadelphia: Blakiston, 1944.

Sprague, Claire. *Edgar Saltus.* New York: Twayne, 1968.

Stearns, Harold E., ed. *Civilization in the United States.* New York: Harcourt, Brace, 1922.

Stevens, George. *Speak for Yourself, John: The Life of John Mason Brown.* New York: Viking, 1974.

Talmey, Allene. *"Vogue's Spot-light."* Vogue 15 March 1938, 108–09,156.

Teichmann, Howard. *Smart Aleck*. New York: Morrow, 1976.

Tompkins, Jane. *Sensational Designs: The Cultural Work of American Fiction 17901860*. New York, NY: Oxford, 1985.

Tully, Jim. "The World and Mr. Nathan." *Esquire*, January 1938, 42, 172–73.

Tynan, Kathleen. *The Life of Kenneth Tynan*. New York: Morrow, 1987.

Tynan, Kenneth. *Profiles*. New York: HarperCollins, 1990.

———.*Tynan: Right and Left*. New York: Atheneum, 1967.

Van Gelder, Robert. "An Interview With George Jean Nathan." *New York Times Book Review*, February 1, 1942, 2.

Walkley, Arthur B. "The American Stage." *Vanity Fair*, May, 1926, 69, 120.

Watts, Richard Jr. "Drama on the Carpet." *Saturday Review of Literature*, 31 December 1949, 11.

Wilde, Oscar. "The Soul of Man Under Socialism." In *The Artist as Critic: Critical Writings of Oscar Wilde*. Edited by Richard Ellman. New York: Random House, 1969.

Williams, Tennessee. *Memoirs*. New York: Doubleday, 1975.

Wilson, Edmund. *Classics and Commercials: A Literary Chronicle of the 1940s*. New York: Farrar, Straus, and Giroux, 1950.

———. *The Devils and Canon Barham*. New York: Farrar, Straus, and Giroux, 1973.

———. *Letters on Literature and Politics*. Edited by Elena Mumm Wilson. New York: Farrar, Straus and Giroux. 1977.

———*The Shores of Light: A Literary Chronicle of the 1920s and 1930s*. New York: Farrar, Straus and Giroux, 1952. . *The Twenties*. Edited by Leon Edel. New York: Farrar, Straus, and Giroux, 1975.

Woollcott, Alexander. *Enchanted Aisles*. New York: Putnam, 1924.

———. *The Portable Woollcott*. Selected by Joseph Hennessey. New York: Viking, 1944.

———. *The Letters of Alexander Woollcott*. Edited by Beatrice Kaufman and Joseph Hennessey. New York: Viking, 1944.

Young, Stark. *Immortal Shadows*. New York: Scribner's, 1948.

———. *A Life in the Arts, Letters, 1900–1962*. Vol. II. Edited by John Pilkington. Baton Rouge: Louisiana State University Press, 1975.

———. "A 'Must' Handbook." *The New Republic*, 6 November 1944, 595–96.

———. Letters to George Jean Nathan, undated, 10 August 1925, and 22 November 1932. The Cornell Collection.

Yoseloff, Thomas. Letter to the author, 14 September 1994.

# Index